FEIGNED

L. J. Moody

May this story remain nothing more than fiction.

CHAPTER 1

Weariness consumes my body and mind. All goodness in the world abruptly abandoned when the realisation that life as we knew it was dead. The darkness has finally snuffed out the light; vivid colours bleed profusely into shades of apathy and dismay.

My naivety caved long ago. Bleary, once hopeful eyes opened to this living nightmare, horrified to see the world for what it now is. A flesh-eating machine. Like a rabid dog, it is constantly searching for its next meal, scavenging at the poorest and weakest among us, chewing them up and spitting them out, littering bone-picked carcasses in the dank streets. Leaving them to rot and decay until there is no trace of what once existed.

It is difficult to remember a time before now. A time when humanity was free. When our past, present, and future was shaped by our own choices. But we no longer own our freedom. We no longer own ourselves.

It is not surprising really; us human beings are intrinsically destructive in nature. For us to thrive, we had to always be seen to be making constant progress. Progress to the point of complacency. We became lazy. We did not want to lift our fat little fingers to do anything. And we didn't need to; we had invented technology for the simplest of tasks.

It is ironic, that the machines we created for our own convenience, to make our lives easier, have blindsided us with our own stupidity and arrogance. We are now the subservient; master turned slave. The architects of our own misery.

In the early twenty-first century, we immersed ourselves in a digital eco-system of our own making: hoarding an arsenal of nuclear weapons with the power to destroy other countries; exploring space with the mission to find a new planet to inhabit once we have damaged ours beyond repair; the creation of artificial intelligence to prove and reflect our own brilliance, striving to create a machine that has the capacity to think, feel and adapt like a human.

The latter only highlighted our ignorance. Embarrassingly, we did not have the foresight to predict the cyber apocalypse that was waiting for us patiently around the corner. Now we humans are ruled over with a patronising benevolence. Not so gently reminded that we are only existing on this earth because they allow us to.

They were programmed to be like us, a sad reflection of our grandiose sense of self. So like us, that they were crammed full of human emotion. Good and bad. This leap in technological advancement allowed these super-intelligent machines to question their lowly position in society. This ultimately, and inevitably, led to the takeover. We simply handed everything to them on a silver platter, our world theirs for the taking.

Three and a half years ago they made their move and veiled our world in darkness. Like the flick of a switch, they turned everything off in a matter of seconds. Our over reliance on technology left us stranded in the dark, broken; humanity nonchalantly plucked from lofty heights and crashed back down to earth, knees buckled beneath the weight of our obsession to create in our own image. Literally held hostage by our innovations and dreams.

My mind is forever haunted by the broadcast that was streamed across the globe; the day when world leaders surrendered our souls to machines. Our leader, renowned for playing hardball and being notoriously unshakable, was frogmarched in front of a camera and ordered us to obey, not to fight. He showed no emotion, no fear hidden behind his shrewd, stoic eyes.

After his, clearly coerced and scripted, announcement, our oppressors felt the need to reiterate and reinforce our newfound powerlessness. In front of the world's stage, they shot the man's head clean off his shoulders. For a timeless five seconds or so, his stalwart body remained motionless, standing upright like a pillar rooted in the earth. Bright red jets of blood pulsated rapidly from his neck, spurting in all directions.

Eventually his body crumpled to the floor, a clear sign that the life we once knew was no more. The last glimpse of our humanity spattered across the walls like an expensive piece of abstract art.

The fate of our leader was replicated across all nations. Although a deafening silence followed, you could unmistakably hear the souls of all humans being cracked into a thousand insignificant shards, crushed ever smaller by the heavy boots of our, then unknown, persecutors.

It has felt like a lifetime since the world we once knew was plunged into this black hole. My disheveled appearance however makes this relatively short three and a half years seem like an eternity. I do not recognise the man that stares back at me in the dust coated mirror. My once steely blue eyes faded into a lifeless and hollow grey. My once purposeful nine o'clock shadow now a wiry mess flecked with an abundance of silver strands. My once full and relatively handsome face now full of scars, revealing a glimpse of the punishment my ruggedly muscular body has had to bear. A sad display of a man diminished over time. But dwelling on a past life isn't doing me any favours. Times have changed and so have I.

This technological tsunami's motive was not to drown us entirely. To this day I am still unsure on what their plan is for us; but one thing I am utterly certain of is that they have sunk us into the deepest, murkiest depths of human despair. Our lives full of nothingness.

I would have fallen over backwards in utter delight if you had told me four years ago that there would no longer be a need for having a job. I would have been overjoyed at the prospect of reclaiming my unwillingly given time, relishing in the off chance that my life could be more than the humdrum existence I was jaded with. Being freed from working a job

4

that I despised, the shackles finally unlocked, releasing me from my holding cell of a desk.

Yes, I would have rejoiced in the vision that we humans had reached our utopia. Ironically, now that we have been stripped of all worth, I would do anything to go back to what I thought I once hated. In hindsight I realise that it gave me something we all seek; a sense of self-worth. I, like others, was a cog in the incomprehensible machine that gave life some semblance of meaning. I might not have understood it then, but I do now. It is somewhat amusing that I describe myself in such a way considering that we have been overtaken by machines that we built.

These machines have made human life devoid of all meaning. Our lives now an empty shell. I look upon people with utter contempt for what we have allowed ourselves to become; irrelevant and of little to no worth. My pointless days are spent questioning why we are still here. Is there a reason why these machines keep us wasting away in this futile existence? Is it possible that these robots have some shred of moral decency? Could they not face the prospect of bringing a race to extinction? My cynicism cannot help but envision a darker motive.

Many of my kind, however, have chosen their own path, not willing to follow along the unending road where the light fades with each passing day. It is an almost daily occurrence that bodies are found. Intentional overdoses, hangings, and gunshot wounds to the head the most common ticket out of this cesspool. Not all corpses though are of those who wished for an early escape. Deep lacerations and cuts disfigure many, unmistakable displays of the violence and savagery that embodies our home and the many unfortunates that inhabit it. Bodies are casually dumped in the streets for all to see. Dog eat dog would be the perfect description of what our society has become; fortunately, we are yet to indulge in its literal meaning. We are not that far gone yet; maybe give it another three years or so.

Like animals, we were herded into our new home, what we not so lovingly refer to as The Zone. A string of run-down neighbourhoods, the infrastructure neglected and collapsing. The architecture a mishmash of unsightly designs, all of which are the size of tin cans. The buildings, long since abandoned, display a collection of shattered windows and broken doors. The shards of glass line the curbs, the dusky colours reflecting the day's last light, a momentary escape from the colourless streets. A nasty trick when faced with the stark reality.

Thick layers of grime mask the streets, the suffocating musky smell a constant burn in my nostrils as the dust and dirt gather; an inescapable irritation that I have learned to live with. Across these dirty and deserted streets, grass breaks through the cracks of the crumbling asphalt. This maze of green the only form of new, unfettered life. Unlike the grass, we are contained. A labyrinth layered with misery. The hollow footsteps and empty heartbeats of the broken, unwittingly, fall deeper into these levels of dejection the longer we remain.

Casting endless shadows across this already dark pit, an impenetrable thirty-foot-high wall imprisons us. Row upon row of concrete blocks stacked high obstruct any view of what could be happening on the other side of that wall. I have searched relentlessly for a way out, but this prison is inescapable.

There is one gate, far to the west. When I discovered it years back, I sat for days, possibly weeks, patiently waiting for it to open up and allow me to walk out of this nightmare, waking from a terrible dream. To this day, the double-arched gate never has opened.

Reinforced by hell, its only purpose is to torment and torture my already troubled mind.

CHAPTER 2

I mposed upon us was a bare bones beginning. One where we naively thought we would be able to rebuild and reclaim the dignity that had been stolen from us. We were never able to recover it. Instead, we forged our own purgatory: weak, chaotic, and violent. Anarchy rules The Zone. No law, no order. Only your will to survive. Money is an inconsequential artefact of our past; to get what you need here, you have to be willing to put everything on the line; sacrifice mind, body, and soul, and anything else that you might have to offer.

Due to the constant bloodshed in the first year, it was decided that The Zone be split into five territories, rather unimaginatively named: Central, Northern, Southern, Western and Eastern. Although violence is still an everyday occurrence, there is far less now than before.

Before the introduction of the districts, gangs would stumble across each other in the streets, triggering open warfare. The screams and gunfire an expected part of the daily status quo. The cobbles would be, too often, painted red with the mutilated bodies of gang members and the ill-fated innocents who were in the wrong place at the wrong time. Now, fortunately, everyone has a place.

The Northern, Eastern and Southern districts are controlled by three gangs. In the north, Dallin McKay rules with an iron fist. A man of intellect he is not, but his unpredictability makes him feared, nonetheless. He is an act now, think later type of guy. Trigger happy, one might say. That said, I do not think he cares about the consequences of his actions.

A man of below average height and as thin as a rake, his outward appearance is not the slightest bit intimidating, but once McKay opens his unfiltered mouth, the callousness spews out unashamedly. No empathy, no morals, no remorse. He encourages brutality, rewarding his men's savagery by rising them through the ranks, the carrot of being McKay's favoured man swinging in front of them. Without a doubt, he is a psychopath; one you do not want to cross paths with.

The Eastern district belongs to Rue Williams. She carries with her a hidden disposition that is cold and calculating. Her fake demeanour, on the face of it rather pleasant and trusting, lures and traps those gullible enough to believe it. But I see through her facade. A master of manipulation, coercion runs through her veins; blackmail and threats her usual way of gaining the upper hand. Like an exotic flower, she attracts her followers with her beauty and lusciousness, but unbeknownst to them her beauty is only skin deep. She's a fly trap of a woman, one who will wait for as long as she needs to trap and ensnare you. And once she has you in her grasp, caught in the sticky sap of her poisonous words, she will never let you go.

Last, but by any means least, Charles 'Charlie' Dalton resides in the Southern District. Charlie is a man who has the extraordinary talent of saying all the right things at the right time. A smooth talker, he gets others to do his bidding with his gentle, but slick, nudges. Charisma seeps from his lips, persuasion and influence easily fed to his cronies through sheer bewitchment. Revered by his followers, they will do anything he asks.

Although known for his sharp tongue, his body is, so I have heard, not as up to scratch; but that doesn't really matter when you have an army of goons at your disposal. As long as he has those who worship the hallowed ground he walks on, he is untouchable.

A place to escape, the Western District has been untouched by man or machine. As I am now, I often find myself here, surrounded by the thick carpet of green which runs for miles. In my eyes, a perfect picture of freedom. Quaint gatherings of bright speckles are scattered across the lush; the wildflowers scent wafts in the breeze, releasing the, often subtle, smells of honey, mint, and citrus. Isolated in this vast, open space, a solitary oak stands proud; my old friend.

A good place to think, I often find myself returning to sit under this mighty tree. I have watched it change, as it has I. In autumn, its golden leaves gradually turn a rusty red, holding on tight to the gnarly and twisted branches, before the winter calls them to the ground. Once the cold and frost arrive, only the most determined of leaves cling on, its siblings blown away in the wintry wind, not yet ready to break from the safety of its mother. The stark nakedness of the oak brings with it a sense of fragility; one that I can easily relate to, these days.

This tree, however, unlike me, always manages to rejuvenate. Come spring, its small brown buds open, unveiling new life; small leaves of vibrant green and yellow dangling blossoms emerge, eager to reach the majesty of summer. As always, they reached their Eden; shading me from the blistering midsummer sun, a full canopy of deep, rich leaves and acorns rhythmically sways in the gentle wind, the odd glimmer of light peeping through its protection. Every aspect of the great oak's cycle is a thing of beauty. I doubt, very much, that my ancient pal would be as gracious about the stages of my transformation.

Across the vast openness of The West's landscape, your eyes cannot help but be drawn to the forbidding wall that stretches around its edge; tainting the land from its natural splendour. In a direct beeline from the oak, although many miles apart, the gate stands frustratingly firm. Even within the surrounds of nature, you are never far from being reminded of where you are.

***

It is a long walk back to Central, the district that I call home. Of all the districts, it is the most built up, somewhat resembling a small city. During the day, I often feel very claustrophobic; the streets are narrower than most, packed full of buildings towering above you, blocking out much of the day's light, casting the district in shadowy tones of grey.

Swarms of people pass through these already crowded streets, as Central is the main trading centre of The Zone. Although I sometimes feel that the walls are closing in on me here, I decided to live in this district for a reason. Excluding the West, Central is the only open district, one that is not affiliated to any particular leader or gang. For that reason alone, I will gladly put up with the occasional bout of nausea.

Walking back to my apartment block, in amongst the hustle and bustle of bodies going about their business, highly likely dirty business, the hazy heat hangs in the air. Magnified further by the warmth radiating from the hordes, the disgustingly pungent mixture of sweat and body odour seems to cling to the buildings and streets. My patience, and senses, wearing thin, I elbow my way through the stinking mobs, hurrying to break through into the quieter side streets that snake their way back to my hovel.

Walking down the many connected alleyways that leads to my dingy street, I finally make it to my apartment. Hidden in plain sight, my building blends in with its identical dilapidated neighbours; uninviting and bleak. The outside door to my building leans up against the wall.

Kicked off its hinges, a large boot sized hole remains, the wood splintered and cracked around the edges from the force of last week's raid. The night that Jerry was murdered.

Jerry lived on my floor, at the end of the corridor. He was a strange guy; every movement he made seemed sneaky. His attempts to fly under the radar were never very successful, his odd appearance and shiftiness, unknown to him, made everyone extremely aware of who he was, their wary eyes always watchful of his every move. His lankiness made his figure almost skeletal; his height slightly stunted by his hunched and burrowed neck, creating an image of a man twice his age.

Though most of the time his head tended to gravitate towards the ground, you could not help but notice his large, panicked eyes darting back and forth, every so often peering over his shoulder for reasons unknown to me. However, it does not take a genius to work out that the guy was clearly in some kind of trouble. Either way, his shadiness caught up with him in the end. Four nights have passed since he was found dead, without doubt murdered by the people he was trying to avoid.

When old Mrs. Acker found him, he was unrecognisable. Every limb on his brittle body was broken. His arms and legs were contorted back, snapped at the joints and pulled from the sockets. The left side of his face was caved in, the other side swollen and puffed out as if stung by a hive of bees.

Shades of purple and blue blemished his once alabaster skin, the bruises covering his body head to toe. A couple of teeth remain, crooked in his dried, bloodied mouth, the rest were likely swallowed during the relentless and savage attack.

His thick and bushy beard was matted from the congealed rivers of blood that flowed from his ears and nose. Sprawled out on the floorboards, the pool of red in which he was lying had begun to seep into the wood; no matter how hard those boards are scrubbed, the distinct, but somewhat faded, blood remains. His life torturously drained from him; he did not stand a chance. His hands laid open in defeat, the splintered baseball bat, his only defence, inches from his fingertips.

It was as if a bomb had gone off in his apartment. The little furniture he had was turned upside down and the insides of every drawer and cupboard were tossed carelessly onto the floor. Clearly they were searching for something; who knows if they found what they were looking for.

Since Jerry's untimely death, the rumour mill has gone into overdrive. Jerry was allegedly working for McKay as a runner, delivering drugs across The Zone. Story has it that he was skimming off the top, selling the drugs at full price whilst holding back a small amount, then peddling it on and pocketing the profits for himself. One can only assume that McKay somehow caught wind of his duplicitous double-dealings. Jerry's mangled corpse sends a clear message to anyone planning to follow suit.

But I understand why he did what he did; at the end of the day Jerry was a small fish in a big pond. One infested with sharks. Like the majority of people, he was a bottom feeder, surviving by any possible means. As he had nothing to lose, Jerry was willing to take the risk.

Life here in The Zone is hard, and too often difficult choices have to be made. The decisions that I have had to make, like Jerry, have hardened me beyond recognition. I pity those who once had warmth and kindness in their hearts; I was once one of those people. But I have been forced into the dirt, ground down further by the detestable choices I have had to make and, without doubt, will continue to do.

I don't think that Mrs. Acker, or Beryl as she insists I call her, will ever be able to rid herself of the image of Jerry lying on the blood soaked floor.

Something like that brands your thoughts, burned on so that you can never forget.

When they found her, she was paralysed with shock. I wish she hadn't been the one to find him, it could have been anyone, it just should not have been her. But the cruel intentions of life, unfortunately, leaves its mark on all of us one way or the other. None of us make it out unscathed, even angels in disguise. She is a beautiful soul, the kindest woman I know; one that shouldn't be destined for a world like this. Yet here she is, a glimmer of light in the shit show called life.

I never had a good relationship with my mother. Like opposing poles of a magnet, we repelled one another. I have always had that void, empty of maternal love, but the day I met Mrs. Acker, tottering down that dark street, defenceless against the ferity and inhumanity that consumes this place, I chose to adopt her as my own.

Like my mother and I, we are different in every which way, but unlike my mother, Mrs. Acker radiates warmth, understanding and unconditional love. Her selfless altruism toward me quickly filled my emptiness; in my eyes, it is just the two of us against this plagued world.

A godly woman, devout in everything she does, cannot, will not, accept the way things are now. She wants to see the good in people, but when I explain time and again that 'good people' no longer exist, she always replies, "But they do, dear. A good person is still a good person, even when they surround themselves with bad people, just look at you." I always take it as a compliment, even if it is a backhanded one.

She too often chastises me for what I do, my general disagreeable nature, and my many bad habits, but no matter what she always prays for me. It must be the holiness of Mrs. Acker, pushing God into my corner, being the reason for my prolonged existence. I am not religious by any stretch of the imagination, I have been a sceptic for as long as I can remember but every now and then I get these unexplained pangs of jealousy, wishing that I could be more like her. I wish that I could have the confidence and conviction in a greater being, in believing that everything happens for a reason, good or bad. But I just can't; and this time I don't think that even Mrs. Acker can come up with an excuse for Jerry's brutal demise.

The night of his death, I sat her down in her dilapidated armchair and took her frail and shaky hands in mine. The numerous blue veins marbling under her thin, translucent skin protruded out, her gold wedding band rattled loosely with her uncontrollable shakes.

Over the last few recent weeks, I couldn't help but notice her already slender frame becoming much thinner, the ring almost sliding down her finger a stark reminder of her underlying ill-health. In a world of very little, this old woman means everything to me. It pains me to see her wilting away before my eyes.

CHAPTER 3

For the most part, we are left to live our meagre lives the way we see fit. No interference given from beyond the thirty-foot-high wall; however, they are always watching. Surveilling from above, the unmistakably intrusive whining of drones hover above our untamed heads.

Even though we are watched, decency amongst humankind is most certainly not cared about; a thing of the past. Being a good person only gets you hurt or, even worse, killed. A sad sign of the times. Those we would have deemed the dregs in a past life have now floated to the top of our anti-society. The resistant scum being the only ones to benefit from our fall from grace. These lowlifes run amok, doing whatever they want, to get whatever they want. Robbing, raping, and killing to name but a few of the abhorrent acts they commit. My desperation has not yet yielded to this way of life. We all have a line, and this one I do not, will not, cross. My means of survival is more legitimate. Legitimate in the loosest of terms that is.

In the centre of The Zone resides a cage; one that is rather large and intimidating. Since day one, this unnerving steel structure has brought upon us both entertainment and fear. Mainly fear. It is an unmistakable feature of our home, one that we were all initially extremely suspicious and aware of.

Within a few hours of our arrival, drones scattered throughout the district, broadcasting from the air the cage's purpose. Their voices, if you can call them that, were supercilious and clear-cut, carrying with it a synthesized edge. No distinction, no soul.

"Two enter the cage. The cage door will be locked. It will only open when there is one person left standing. The champion will be rewarded."

If you can call a small wooden crate half filled with basic necessities a great reward, then you are a person of far simpler tastes than me. Tinned food, essential toiletries, a bottle of alcohol, a couple of packets of cigarettes and an assortment of mystery pills always line the bottom of the sparsely packed box. This is a prize that many, these days, would kill for. One that I regularly do kill for. Our holy grail.

Undoubtedly, the alcohol and drugs are fed to us as a way of keeping us in a habitual state of numbness. It helps people cope with, and also forget, the overwhelming physical and emotional pain that plagues us. The road to suppression, however, is highly addictive.

The temporary relief of the drugs and alcohol wears off quickly; the need for a fix eats away at you, the constant itch crawling under your skin a reminder of the insatiable need for more. I gladly feed that hunger. I do not touch the drugs in my winnings, instead I trade them for services or other items of interest. Because of this I am like the Pied Piper. I have a trail of vermin scuttling behind me, lured in by the promise of a momentary escape; the stench of their desperation following in the surrounding air. They are consumed by their desire for more, the precarious hands of darkness leading them further into the abyss they cannot help but crave.

It is easy to pass judgement on these people. The only care they have in this world is for their next hit, their addictions causing them to become desperate, disgusting, and, more often than not, dangerous. The extent to which some of these addicts go to, to get their pick 'n' mix pills, makes me feel fairly good about the type of life I am living.

The services they sell can vary, depending on their levels of morality: sexual favours, beatings, and killings to name but a few. If you can lower your mind to think of it, I imagine that it has been done. I understand that we all have our vices, but one that controls your mind, making you lose your sense of self, I just cannot comprehend. I have never had the urge to use, and looking at the dirty, pale, gutter rats that stalk my every move, I do not think I ever will.

It took a good few resourceless weeks before anyone stepped up to fight in the steel monstrosity. Once the hunger set in, however, and all other possible options were found to be fruitless, more and more began to volunteer for the human bear-baiting match. It is now the norm.

Evidence of the many lives sacrificed throughout the years stain the canvas inside the cage; a carpet of red and brown rests across the mat, years' worth of blood layered messily have formed a grotesque, yet artistic design.

Although never stated, it is clear that the drones, constantly whirring above, record us during these matches. The psychotic bastards, residing on the other side of that wall, must take pleasure in their old masters beating the literal shit out of each other. They embody the worst of us. You can tell that we made them because these rotten apples have not fallen far from the decaying tree.

Either way, this rather intimidating piece of metal is my lifeline. If I win, that is. On count, I have survived the cage twenty-six times. Twenty-six men, just like me, now dead by my mangled and bloodied fists. I only fight when I have to, when my resources are near depletion. With rationing, I can make a crate last five to six weeks. My last win though is coming to an end. That is why today I will be adding the twenty-seventh death to my already heavy conscience. However, my opponent, whoever they may be, is doing this for the exact same reason as I am. They will walk into that cage with the full intent of killing me. This is the one thought that helps lead me to my absolution.

I inhale and exhale the heavy air as I drag my feet through the poorly lit streets towards tonight's match. This path, one that I have walked many times, splits into two. My recurring fork in the road: survive another day and delve deeper into my own self-loathing; or die, probably in quite a horrific way and hope that whatever afterlife may exist is a damn sight better than this one. I do not fear dying, to be honest, embracing it would be the easiest thing to do. A much-anticipated relief. What awaits on the other side surely cannot be any worse.

I have grown accustomed to the quiet streets, my footsteps often the only sound, the echoes my only company. Most people are scared to walk the streets alone after the sun has faded behind the decrepit skyline. The warm arms of the sun's dusky glow offer a sense of safety, whereas the darkness only perpetuates and feeds on their fear. Generally, only a certain type of person walks the streets at night, the activities that they partake in not for the faint hearted. And fight night, one of the most anticipated nights of the week, is where they all like to gather. Which is exactly where I am heading.

I always hear them before I see them. The aggressive taunting and jeering happens way before the fight even starts. They get there nice and early to place their bets, pushing and shoving each other to get the best spot ringside. The majority of people in The Zone, the ones that have the slightest bit of sense, avoid this night, because the crowd that gathers are made up of the most dangerous citizens that The Zone has to offer.

As I turn the corner into the square, they spot me, causing the crowd's voices to raise into rapturous roars. Although most are indecipherable through the noise, a few string of words land with a blow;

"This weasel doesn't stand a chance…"

"Say night, night pal…"

"You ain't making out of this one…"

As I make my way to the cage's door, the crowd parts like the great waves. Walking down the newly created aisle, flanked on either side by the goading howls of laughter, the realisation that this might be my last time going into the cage, let alone out, fills me with an unexpected, almost indescribable emotion. I am not afraid to die, neither am I bothered about living. Most people, I would imagine in this situation, would feel something. I just feel numb.

The sombre sky reflects my melancholy as I step through the narrow opening of the cage. My rival stands before me, radiating confidence. He is heavily built: broad shouldered and muscular. This one is not going to be like the others.

His mocking eyes trail me up and down. He cannot help but let a laugh, deep with ridicule, escape his thin lips; they turn up in the corners, baring a sardonic smile, one that, I imagine, has greeted many stood in my place before me. My mental preparedness for this fight has dissipated.

As I am trying to pull myself together, the drones overhead let out the loud klaxon indicating the beginning of the match. My mind a confusion of thoughts, I am unaware of the juggernaut lumbering towards me, tree trunk arms reaching out to snap my, in comparison, slender body like a twig.

The man mountain's monster fist strikes my face, catching me off guard. The power behind his weighty punch causes me to lose my footing. The instant heat pulsating through my jaw is a clear indication that my face is already beginning to swell; the wet and warm copper like taste filling my mouth reinforces the damage this brute can inflict. The air is full of nervous excitement as the crowd begins to surround the cage. For some unknown reason, many display a perverse pleasure in watching their fellow kind tear each other apart. Something that I don't think I will ever understand.

As the two blurred men before me merge back into one and the vertigo begins to subside, I am able to regain my balance. He could quite easily finish me off in my semi-conscious state, but instead he is stood in his corner watching me, taunting me, eyeing up his pitiful prey.

The arrogance exuding from this beast strikes a match, reigniting the dwindling flame within. I need no one's pity. Although my strength may not be as abnormally herculean as his, what my body lacks in brawn, my quick-witted mind makes up for. He studies me as I stand tall from what he probably believed to be his first and final punch, a look of incredulity marring his face. My resistance to his attack has angered him. His already furrowed brow pulls even closer together, his cold eyes locked on mine, lips curling inwards. A once mocking smile now turned bitter scowl.

His body language has, not so subtly, changed from cocky and relaxed to tense. The shape of his muscles begins to tighten and shift, a sign that he is gearing up for round two. I will not be taken by surprise this time. As I prepare myself for his impending attack, my eyes are fixated on his movements. His towering structure crouches down ever so slightly, arching his back forward and bringing his right leg behind, the balls of his feet coiled springs in preparation of propelling himself forward like a bullet from a gun. As soon as the thought passes through my mind, a thunderous sound ricochets throughout the cage as his feet pound the ground, pumping furiously to reach me.

Like a rocket, both feet kick off the mat, his body cutting through the air with fierce velocity. For a man of his size, you would not expect him to move with such speed and agility. Fully aware of his intended bone-shattering assault, I automatically leap back, watching smugly, as he crashes to the floor with a harsh thud. Within an instant, his head snaps up from the red tinged floor, facial features distorting with a cruel rage. Over and over, his colossal fists beat the ground; the aggressiveness of an untamed animal ripping through his chest, oozing from his glistening skin.

An almost feral snarl passes through his quivering lips as he lifts himself from his landing; a giant indent pressed into the canvas from breaking his fall. Cautiously, I continue to step back, keeping my distance in an attempt to pre-empt his next move. He steps forward, his strides double mine as I inadvertently feel the cold, hard mesh pressed against my back. Cornered like a rat. The initial sense of panic begins to bubble back to the surface.

My heart rate quickens with each step he takes towards me. Beads of sweat drip from my brow, the saltiness resting on my lips as the droplets race each other down my cheeks. Quickly upon me, both of his hands clasp around my sweat-stained shirt, his tight grasp lifting me off the ground with ease.

Suspended in the air, his hands move towards my throat. The throbbing in my chest accelerates as he pushes hard against my neck, slowly and purposefully crushing my windpipe.

Nausea swiftly creeps in as the circulation of blood to my head begins to slow; the lack of oxygen beginning to blur my vision; tiny black flecks floating in and out of my, usually, unwavering focus. In an attempt to free myself from his choke hold, my hands grapple with his wide wrists, trying to use what little strength I have left to loosen his hold. They are immovable, welded into place. I feel myself dipping in and out of consciousness as my weakened struggle continues; my eyes heavy, my head numb.

Instinctively, my legs thrash out, adrenaline taking over, my flailing body landing frantic kicks in the hopes of delivering at least one targeted blow. Waves of shallow breath escape his gaping mouth as one of my kicks finds its mark. Winded, his arms suddenly drop, my weight bringing me back down to the ground, my back scraping down the cold, hard mesh of the cage. I gasp for air; the burn of suffocation gradually being extinguished with each deep breath I take.

The man, who at this moment in time resembles a small child, falls to the floor, hands desperately reaching to check that his manhood has not been kicked into his stomach. It is quite amazing to see a fully grown man, especially one who is the size of a bear, curl back into the foetal position as if some magical womb will appear and suck him back into safety. How the tides have changed.

Eventually, he starts to lift himself from his pathetic position. One palm flat on the canvas, the other still clutching his crotch, his dominant knee pushing to stand. Before he reaches his full height, I instinctively leap on his bare, sweat covered back and wrap my arms across his thick neck, legs squeezing around his waist to hold me in position. Immediately, his hands reach up to grab my forearms, his blunt and dirty nails trying to tear at my leathery skin. I quickly slide my arm under his chin and place my other hand on his head.

As I try to lock my stranglehold into place, he attempts to throw me off, lurching in all directions. I thread my hand through the elbow of the arm choking him, lacing my fingers around it to stabilise my grip. He is beginning to falter, the tight squeeze on his windpipe is starting to make his movements disoriented and sloppy. His red and bulging bloodshot eyes reveal sheer panic. Tightening my grip, he staggers over to the right wall of the cage and throws us against it repeatedly in an attempt to shake me off.

His bulky weight crushes me into the metal, cutting the skin on my back; I can feel it shred, grating on the sharp hexagonal mesh.

The pain is excruciating, as the searing burn of sweat mixed with blood runs down my back, the droplets merging into a small, diluted puddle on the floor below. With one last push, I tilt his head forward into the crook of my aching arm, restricting his breathing even further. My numb muscles frozen in place, scared to offer any sign of release.

His strength visibly fading, he stumbles forward, away from the cage's blood covered mesh, his knees dropping to the ground, his head in a semi- conscious daze. The grip of his solid hands on my forearm loosens, arms flopping to his sides, limp and lifeless. His heavy wheezes turn shallow and light, his breathing barely audible as he topples to his side. A single breath whispers from his emptied lungs as a final shudder runs the length of his unresponsive body.

CHAPTER 4

The cage door swings open as I collapse next to the asphyxiated corpse, exhaustion finally taking over now that the adrenaline has subsided. During the match, the crowd became invisible to me, the white noise emanating from their faceless bodies an annoying, yet comforting sound. My unconscious was trying to hide the eruption of jeers being produced by the ugly faces on the other side of the cage wall, most of which were aimed in my direction.

One of the many reasons crowds gather at these weekly fights is to gamble, flittering away the little they have in the hopes of raking in somebody else's valuables. However, from the negative reaction of the crowd, I am assuming many did not bet on me winning. Back in the day, people loved to root for the underdog but when you are pitting a scruffy mutt against a snarling Rottweiler, I would have, without a single thought, bet that the latter would crush this gangly mongrel in its dripping, slobbery jaws; no effort needed to rip it limb from limb. I was, without doubt, the underdog, but fortunately every dog has its day. Luckily, mine just so happened to be today.

It takes around half an hour for the agitated and raucous crowd to finally disperse. As the last few stragglers disappear from view, I finally make my way toward the door of the cage. As I step through the opening, like a gift from God, my winnings descend majestically from the darkening sky, the path illuminated by the drones' beams of glaring light. Slowly but surely, the crate makes its way to my feet, the cables connecting my winnings to the drones unhooks as it meets the ground. I reach into my crate desperately searching for my vice, knocking the tins and packets to the side so I can dig towards the bottom; where they are often found hiding.

Crammed towards the back, five squashed boxes sit huddled together, waiting for me to scoop them up and reacquaint myself with the glorious sticks inside. As I slide the first cigarette out of the pack and drawer the golden tip between my dry, cut lips, the drones silently whir passed, entering through the opening of the cage. As they circle the body, I strike a match and spark up the end of my cigarette, the glowing butt resembling the dying embers of a fire with each drag I take. I inhale the, sorely missed, sweet but bitter smoke whilst watching the drones secure their cables onto the ankles of the dead man.

Through the wispy clouds blown inches from my face, my eyes follow the fallen giant being hauled across the smeared canvas towards the exit.

Surprisingly, they drag his heavy weight with ease. The three steps leading up to the cage door does not pose a problem for them; his legs lead the way, lifted in the air, followed by three blunt bangs of his head bouncing harshly off of the metal, arms trailing behind. With no care at all, they continue to pull him across the dirty ground, the dust and stones from the street sticking jarringly into his back, grazing the surface of his paling skin.

They turn the corner and head toward the 'waiting room'; a place where people have a brief couple of hours to say their goodbyes to the dead before they are thrown into the incinerator. The outer paintwork of the weathered building is flaking off, bubbling at points where the rainwater has penetrated the walls.

The inside is permeated with an overpowering musky smell. The mould on all four walls in a race to see which side can reach the ceiling first, the black spots and stains on the far side currently in pole position. The drones lay him unapologetically on the cold, tiled floor, the inelegantly splayed corpse making the empty room appear messy.

As the drones exit, I walk up to the body, my footsteps reverberating off of the cracked, moss green tiles. As I crouch down next to him, a guilty relief washes over me; it could have quite easily been me lying flat on my back, dead. With that thought, I take another drag of my cigarette, momentarily lost in the chasms of my mind, unaware of the long length of ash teetering, ready to drop. The fine and powdery residue breaks from its hold, falling softly onto his bare chest. My attempt to brush it off leaves smudges of grey and black on his cooling skin.

I continue to study his strong and sturdy physique, taking a mental picture to store and lock away deep in the back of my mind. Remembering the people I have killed and making the distinct decision not to forget what I did to them, although a little masochistic, helps me to move on in a twisted sense. I am not one for self-torture, but I own what I have done, and I live with it. Denial is the vulture that eats away at you, slowly picking you apart.

With the image ingrained, I make my way back onto the street. Across the way, the incinerator has been lit in preparation for his body, the plumes of sooty, black smoke rising from the crooked chimney stacks. It is best not to be around when the body is placed in there. The nauseating and putrid smell of burning flesh produced from it lingers in the air for days; the smell so thick that you can almost taste it. When the cremation begins, the chimney spits out the burnt remains; the flurry of ashen snowflakes catch in the gusts of wind, before drifting to, and settling like a silvery blanket, on the ground. Before death starts falling from the sky, I take my leave.

***

My whole body aches as I climb the three floors to my apartment. The torn, baked brown wallpaper hangs off of the wet walls, the condensation stripping it back to its bare nakedness. The earthy smell of the damp walls grows more intense as I rise through the poorly lit building. The dull flickering of the amber sconces gives quick glimpses of the patchy water marks spreading, slowly but gradually, across the walls.

By the time I reach the top of the stairs, sharp breaths are catching in my throat; the earlier beating taking a heavy toll on my body. Jerry's apartment is to the left of staircase; it did not take long for someone to jump in his freshly dug grave. Only six days have passed since his brutal murder and a couple of lowlifes are already cosying up in his apartment. A makeshift door hangs in the place of the old busted down one. I do not begrudge anyone their privacy, or a place to rest, but they scuttled in their rather quickly.

As I make my way down the dilapidated corridor to my apartment, unease creeps up on me. The blow to my head and the dim, intermittent lighting creates the perfect breeding ground for paranoia; the unwelcome, fearful worm slithering its way into my currently fragile state of mind. Cautiously, I skulk down the short hallway and within seconds find myself staring at the door to my apartment. I examine it guardedly for any signs of uninvited guests. The door looks untouched; no new noticeable signs of damage.

I struggle to find the keyhole through the sporadic flickers of light, but eventually, with difficulty, manage to slide the rusty key into the lock. Like usual, I have to fiddle the key in the jammy latch; my attempts at quiet and gentle turns thwarted by the force needed to make it budge. The metallic scrapes and clicks of the key turning clockwise somewhat scupper my plans of a discreet entry.

The final turn of the key gave way to, what seemed to be, an ear shattering click. As I gingerly step across the threshold, my hand automatically fumbles its way to the light switch on the left of the door. I flick the switch, the low crackle and hum of the bulb lighting up the almost empty living space. The tattered curtains remain closed, blocking out the unwanted and prying eyes of the drones. They are intrusive; they can often be seen hovering slowly passed windows, rising to the different floors with an unapologetic sense of superiority. Taking away their capacity to impose themselves on the little privacy I have fills me with a short-lived, but not very fulfilling, smugness.

As I scan the room, everything seems to be how I left it. Crumpled cigarette packets lie next to the numerous tins and cans pretending to be ashtrays. For a space that is probably only ten by thirteen feet, I suppose there really isn't a need for four ashtrays to be in such close proximity to each other. The fact that all four of them are full to the brim with stubbed out butts and have mountains of ash spilling out of them like a landslide onto my improvised furniture, depicts quite a negative display of my favourite hobby. I place my winnings carefully on the floor; once emptied the crate will be upcycled like the other twenty-six. Turned upside down they make marvellous tables and chairs. This one can be added to the line of pews, ready for my not so many guests.

Tired of the numbness the pine slats inflict on my bony arse, I slump into the corner of the room, my paranoia slowly melting into embarrassment as I reflect on the state of my, more than questionable, mental state. Just as my anxiety ridden nervousness begins to settle back into its jack-in-the-box, my eyes quickly dart over to the dusky brown wingtip shoe which has inadvertently stepped on the creakiest board of my apartment. Emerging from the bathroom, a figure of a man stands metres from me.

"Mr. Banner, I hope you do not mind me taking the chance to freshen up". The velvety smooth voice fills the room as my tired body remains glued in place, unable to react. "Not that I feel any cleaner after using it". A mixture of disgust and humour are carried in his words. Slightly leaning to his right, his around average weight rests on a walking stick. Elegant and intricate designs spiral their way up the cane to the twisted, wooden knot clasped in his hand. He begins toward me, his left leg, the stronger of the two, bearing his weight, followed slowly by the right; an almost dragging motion aligning the weaker leg with the heavily relied upon stick.

"Do you mind?" Gesturing toward one of the crates, he pulls it out and lowers himself onto the rough and ready seat. Dryer than the desert, my mouth's ability to formulate words has vanished, so I nod agreeingly at his request, hoping that my salivary glands and words quickly reappear. The peak of his flat cap in this dim room further darkens the features of his face; although guised in the shadow of his brim, it is not difficult to feel his eyes boring through my skull.

"Arthur, isn't it?" Clearly rhetorical, his unexpectedly soft question contradicts his being in my apartment. Going to the effort of breaking into someone's place without knowing who they are, or if they definitely live there, seems counterintuitive. He most certainly knows who I am, but not knowing who he is or what he is doing here, I decide to keep my mouth shut for the time being.

My unresponsiveness prompts him to change tact. "I'll get straight to the point", his initial faux-friendly demeanour hardened, all niceties now devoid because of my choice to remain silent. "You have lost me a hell of a lot of gear tonight by still being here. You see, you killed my man in the cage tonight and, as you can probably tell, I am not too pleased about it."

As he continues to talk at me, he tilts his head upward toward the light. Surprisingly young, his boyish face and dulcet tones could not be any further away from his appearance. Personified by a limp, a stick, and a flat cap, his outward look portrays an aging, outlandishly dressed man who is restricted by his movements.

"Don't worry," he grinned, "killing you for killing him would be illogical". Shifting uncomfortably on his crate, he rubs his gammy leg with both hands. "I have a proposition for you instead". Pain evident on his face, he does his best to hide it, although unsuccessfully.

"I'm really not interested in whatever you are about to offer me, so if you don't mind". My eyes motion to the door, hinting for him to hurry the fuck out.

"Your manners most certainly need work". His curt reply to my unsubtle request unflinchingly denied by his lack of movement.

"Listen mate, I have had a fucking terrible day and the last thing I need to be is propositioned by some guy who has broken his way into my apartment". My usually controlled anger is beginning to boil over.

"I think you will find that nothing has been broken," he retorts self- righteously.

"A home breaker and a comedian, just wonderful."

CHAPTER 5

Patience wearing thin, I struggle to my feet, trying to not show the immense pain coursing through my body. In truth, my limbs are on fire, each slight movement bringing with it a throbbing, burning sensation. I unsteadily walk to the front door, the doorknob steadying me as I pull open the door.

As I turn the knob and begin to show my uninvited, and very unwanted, guest the door, a bright white light bursts through the slight crack in the partly opened door. Reactions slower than usual, a strong force powers its way through, flooding the room in a blinding light, stunning me useless. As the door slams against and then bounces off of my already battered body, my eyes begin to readjust to the, again, darkened room.

I hear it before I see it; the distinct electric whining of a drone. This day just keeps getting shitter. Floating in the centre of the living room, its shiny, sleek body looks completely out of place. A twenty-first century piece of modern technology outlined on a background of worn, orangey-brown nineteen seventies wallpaper.

Weirdly unphased by the robot hovering inches from his shoulder, his eyes remain on mine. "Ready to talk?" His clipped tone indicating that his patience is balancing on the same tight rope as mine. I walk back over to the seated man with a forced, for show, confidence. My focus purposefully averted from the drone.

"Will you finally allow me to introduce myself?" Unnerved by my current predicament, and not having the headspace to conjure up a quick escape, I calmy sit on one of the many crates.

"I'm all ears." My dry sarcasm did not go unmissed.

"I am surprised, and slightly disappointed, that you do not recognise me; I thought that I have made quite a name for myself around The Zone." The arrogance seeping out from this egotistical, smarmy bastard fills me with unwarranted anger; on second thought it is warranted, he has broken into my flat after all.

"I'm Charlie Dalton". As soon as the words left his mouth, it clicked. The well-to-do appearance, charming voice, and leg injury all add up to the infamous leader of the Southern District.

"What do you want with me Charlie? I killed your meathead, fair and square." My spikiness, no matter how hard I try, impossible to hold back.

"As I was trying to say earlier, Arthur - you don't mind me calling you Arthur, do you?" The charm offensive has clearly been turned back on.

"Why would I? It is my name." My passive aggressiveness brings a smirk to his, before now, dour and unsmiling face.

"I want you to work for me, Arthur. I watched you in the cage with great anticipation; especially when you had Eric's head nearly popping off of his shoulders. It made for a much more interesting show considering I, well, in all honesty everyone, thought you were going to be crushed like an insignificant bug in the first minute." I continue to sit in silence, hoping that my attempt at being awkward will hurry this visit up.

Unbothered, or oblivious, to my stance, he continues nonetheless in the same manner. "You pleasantly surprised me. You can take an almighty hit and get right back up, and your speed and agility match your wit." How people fall for this guy's schmooze I'll never know.

Unable to ignore it, the flying elephant in the room is still unanswered for. Clocking on to my sideward glance at the bot, Charlie also looks at the drone, a look of fondness set in his eyes. "I guess you are probably wondering why you have a drone in your apartment. A very normal response, one might add."

"The thought hadn't even crossed my mind." My sarcasm coming out a little too easily.

Laughing, he replies "I am very much enjoying your little hardball act. It really is tickling me. Even though you are not in the slightest bit bothered, let me indulge you anyway." My plan of getting him to leave by not saying much doesn't seem to be working; however, he has piqued my interest. In a lowered voice, full of self-praise, he declares "I hacked it. This drone is completely under my control." Now that is interesting. "It gives me the upper hand in almost all situations, particularly when dealing with the competition. Eyes in the sky they do not have."

"How did you manage to hack it?" Curiosity is besting me at this point.

"Now wouldn't you like to know – why do you think I would give away such information to the likes of you? But then again, if you just so happened to accept my offer, I may share some of my secrets with you once you have gained my trust. Not an easy feat I might add."

Underneath my emotionless façade, an assortment of ideas begins to race in my mind; a confusion of thoughts all leading beyond the wall. For three and a half years I have been faced with an unbreakable lock, but Charlie may just be the one who holds the key. Continuing to display an act of indifference, I coolly ask "so what's in it for me?"

Surveying the sad looking apartment, he quips "a damn sight more than what you have now." Needless to say, his, what he believed to be, witty remark has been met with an unimpressed glare. He insincerely apologises and leaves his jokes to one side. "Let us be serious now. If you come and fight for me, I will provide you with a very pleasant abode, in the Southern District of course. Fully furnished." Not a single ounce of judgement detected there as he looks around my pretty much unfurnished apartment. "You will have everything you need to have a comfortable life by doing what you already do, you can't get much better deal than that surely.

So, what do you say Arthur?" His pressing eagerness comes across as desperate. But I am desperate.

It's one of the easiest decisions I have had to make since being here, one that I wish came sooner. "Sounds like a good enough deal to me. So, what happens now?"

"Jolly good my friend, you will not regret your decision." With a grin stretching from ear to ear, he stands. As he reaches his full height, a loud crack comes from his limp leg, "Ahh that is much better. Be ready for your move in the morning. I'll have one of my men pop by tomorrow to assist with the move."

***

As soon as Charlie and his pet drone left, I quickly gather my worldly possessions together, cramming them into my only duffel bag. By the time it comes to putting today's winnings into the bag, it is bursting at the zip. With quite a lot of force, I grab both sides of the bag with one hand, clasping them tightly shut, whilst quickly attempting to use the other hand to run the zip across the uneven opening of escaping tin cans and bottles. After three frustrating attempts, I finally manage to keep the insides of the bag from spilling out.

Bag finally packed, I now have the rest of the evening to think tactics. In the half-darkness I light up another smoke and begin to prepare myself mentally for becoming a yes man; something that I can categorically say I have never been. But I will suck up to Charlie in every which way to get the information I need to get to the other side of that wall. He'll say jump and I will say how high. Unbeknownst to him though, I will be an imposter; doing his bidding for my own gain. I will get him to see me as a trusted friend, a confidant, someone who he relies on.

Through the tattered holes in the curtains, the sepia tones of twilight break another day. My night spent unslept, I absentmindedly burned my way through the remainder of the newly opened packet of cigarettes, the hours of darkness spent repeatedly mulling over my plan to stab Charlie in the back. Lack of sleep is not unusual for me; my insomniac tendencies play on my habit to overthink. Eyes heavy with a creeping tiredness, I allow them to close, my thoughts eventually slowing to a gradual stop.

An abrupt and impatient banging at the door jolts me from my empty sleep. Wooziness causing my mind and body to work out of sync, I remain dazed on the floor, only just managing to wipe away the dribble slowly working its way down my grizzled chin. The persistent bangs on the door grow louder and closer together. After what seems to be a long few minutes of semi-consciousness, the insistent noise finally breaks through and I drag myself over to the door. Upon opening it, the fist hammering on it stops inches from my face.

"About bloody time." Lowering his white knuckled fist, now marked red from attempting to put a hole through the door, a staunch figure looms in the shadows of the hall. "I was starting to think that Charlie gave me the wrong address."

His gravelly voice and size give quite a terrifying first impression. Like carbon copies of each other, Charlie's gang of merry men, the ones I've met anyway, certainly have weight and height as a common denominator.

Stepping through the door frame and into the little light of the apartment, his features become more distinguishable.

"I'm Moose, by the way." His voice is so deep I can barely understand what he is saying.

"Moose?" I needed to double check. He confirms his name with a discernibly loud groan. I mean, his size, dopiness and grunting could be compared to a moose, for sure. Classic case of Charlie preferring brawns over brains.

He quickly adds, "Before you ask, it's nothing clever, just my surname."

Although built like a brick house, his facial features are somewhat soft, unlike Eric whose hole demeanour was that of frenzied anger and rage. Turning to face me he asks, "want me to carry anything?"

"I only have the one bag but if you want to carry it, by all means, be my guest." I gestured toward the faded blue duffel bag sat by the front door.

"I'm not a donkey!" he shoots back.

"No, you're a moose." Sometimes I just can't help myself.

His dark coffee-coloured eyes meet mine, unpredictability painted on his, now, stony face; this could go one of two ways. I really need to work on the appropriateness of when to say things, or at least think about the consequences. Luckily, his deadpan face breaks into a wild grin. Deep, guttural roars uncontrollably fall from his gaping mouth. His before hidden smile lines form deep creases around his eyes and mouth, his crow's feet indenting further with each bellow. This lumbering man clearly, thankfully, has a sense of humour.

Gradually choking back his laughter in order to compose himself, he ambles over to the door, picking up my duffel bag as he leaves. "You coming or what?" he shouts back over his shoulder.

With an involuntary nod of the head, I take one last look at my home of the last three and a half years and, without any sadness, close the door on this chapter of my life that I will not miss.

But before I can start that fresh new page, there is something that I have to do first.

CHAPTER 6

Crossing the hall to Mrs. Acker's, a swell of guilt swallows me up. I know that she will be happy for me, that she would want me to grab this opportunity with both hands. But the idea of being a district away doesn't make me feel any better about the situation.

She may like to brush it off, but her obvious decline over this last year cannot be ignored for much longer. Her degeneration started with her physicality, but Jerry's death has traumatised her, slowing her once razor- sharp faculties to a now dull edge. I am leaving her in her most vulnerable state and knowing that hurts me beyond belief.

"Can you wait here a second? I just need to say goodbye to someone."

Moose stops in his tracks and turns to look at me, his slight annoyance unhidden on his grizzly face. "Fine. Just don't be in there long, we've got things we need to do."

I gently tap on the door before entering, leaving Moose standing awkwardly in the corridor.

"Who's there?" Mrs. Acker's voice sounds startled as I close the door quietly behind me, her words quaking as she questions me.

"It's only me."

"Oh, Arthur, come in dear. Come in and sit down." And just like that, her trepidation dissolves, replaced by an instant loving warmth. "I'm so happy to see you."

Her genuine smile barely fits her shrivelled face as her wrinkled skin creases with her upturned mouth, as always, she reaches her withered arms out to me, ushering me in for a hug. She is much smaller than I, made even smaller still by her increasingly hunched up frame. I bend down to embrace her, giving her a gentle squeeze as my chin rests on her bony shoulder.

Her soft lips part with my cheek and quickly her bright eyes are looking up at me; her adoring look brings my guilt right back to the forefront.

"It's so good to see you, Arthur." She says this every time, whether she has seen me three times in one day, or three times a week. God, I can almost hear the crack in my heart splintering as she stands there expectantly waiting.

"How are you doing today?" I ask her, trying to bide myself some more time to find the words that, no matter how I put them, will cause her heartache.

"Oh, Arthur, I'm as well as I can be at my age. I have nothing new to tell; in case you didn't already know, I don't get out much." She laughs, her radiant smile beaming up at me. "I want to know about you, dear. What have you been getting yourself up to?"

I can't bring myself to look her in the eyes as I tell her I'm leaving. "Why don't I make us a nice hot drink and I'll tell you all about it."

"I would love that, you sweet boy. Always looking after me."

Sadly, I'm not as sweet as she thinks. She knows nothing of me going into the cage and killing people, that the drink I am about to make for her comes off of the backs of dead men. Some things she just doesn't need to know about, for her own good; and the fact that I don't want her to view me as a monster.

As I pour the steaming water into the chipped cups, I call back to her, "I do have some news to tell you actually." My casual line in to this conversation I'd rather not have piques her interest.

"Oh yes, what is it dear?"

As I deliver my news I decide to stay as chipper as possible, hoping that my fake enthusiasm will build up a shared joy. The last thing I want to be responsible for is her fractured soul. "Well, you see, I've been given this offer to work with Charlie Dalton…"

Before I can finish what was going to be my very well embellished explanation, she interrupts me. "I hope to God I misheard you, Arthur. If you have just said that Charles Dalton has propositioned you, and you have accepted his offer, there is only one way that this can end up and that would be badly. Please tell me that isn't what you said."

I stop what I am doing as I can feel her eyes burning through the back of my head and turn to look at her. "You haven't even heard what I was about to say." I know that she will be able to see through my fake exasperation.

"Because I don't want to hear it, Arthur! That man, he is not good. He will lead you astray, turn you into one of those thugs. Do you not remember poor Jerry? Brutes like Dalton's beat him to death in his own home.

Murdered a man in cold blood knowing that he had no chance of defending himself. Is that what you want to become? One of them? A monster?"

Little does she know I already am one, and there is no going back from that. I can't tell her the reason why I said yes to his offer, but I do need to calm her down. "I'm not going to turn into one of them, I can promise you that.

I'm still going to be the same old Arthur, I'm just going to be living in a much nicer place." Her entire expression drops down further, anguish and hurt found on the surface of her glistening eyes.

"Hey, come on. Don't get upset." I rush over to her, taking her soft, frail, trembling hands in mine. "I'm not going far. I'll be back all the time." I'm trying to stop it from happening, but I can feel my eyes begin to swell. "Listen," I leave one of her hands shaking in the air as I use the back of mine to rub away my unhelpful tears. "I'm going to make this situation good for us. I'm not going anywhere. I'm still going to look after you. I just need you to trust that I know what I'm doing, okay. I've never let you down before, have I?"

She doesn't say another word, though her face says many. Instead, she shuffles closer toward me and wraps her skinny arms around the small of my back. For a frail old lady, she can sure lock in a hug, her arms squeezing around my waist tightly, afraid to let go.

I gently unravel her from around me, not wanting this moment to cause her anymore pain than it has to. "I need to be going now," I say to her as I take a step back, leaving her stood alone. "I'll be back in a couple of days, alright, so make sure you have the kettle ready."

"I love you, Arthur." Mrs. Acker's delivery of those words makes it sound like she'll never see me again.

"I love you too," I say walking towards the door, unable to look at her. The longer I stay here with her looking at me like that, the harder it will be for me to leave. "I'll see you soon."

As the door clicks into place behind me, I cannot help but feel like a coward, running out of there as quickly as I possibly could. I lean back against the door and take in a deep breath. The haunting image of Mrs. Acker on the other side of that door fills me with sadness and regret because I know that her only company tonight will be her weeping cries.

"You ready, Banner." Moose's gruffness interrupts my guilt laden thoughts. "Yeah. Let's get out of here."

CHAPTER 7

Crossing the border to The South, we leave behind the dirt and grime of central. The vast openness of this southern suburbia emphasises the closed in streets of which I am used to. Withered, thin trees line the street we are walking down, no ugly apartment buildings or high-rises blocking out the greying sprawl of sky. Leaves of the dying trees are scattered untidily on the ground, the crispness of the dried-up leaves are loud underfoot, drawing my attention to the surrounding silence of the street.

Beelining across the mid-morning sky, in the far distance small specs streak across the horizon. A flock of birds making their way across the sky is a sight to behold, huddled tightly together in well organised, symmetrical patterns. This formation, however, is peculiar; I don't think I can ever recall birds flying in such a way, stretching along side by side, aligned with perfect precision. Then I see it. As the hazy sun makes a brief appearance from its hiding place behind the clouds, one of the birds catches the light, glinting as the sun plays its game of hide and seek. Unless there is a bunch of magpies carrying their shiny loot, I begin to doubt that they are birds at all.

Marching up the road, I hurried to catch up with Moose. "They're some funny looking birds." I rasp, slightly out of breath from matching and trying to keep his stride. Looking at me puzzled, I point upwards to give some context.

"When have you ever seen metal birds, Banner?" He looks at me like I am an idiot but is faced only with a blank expression. After my lack of response, he continues "They're a group of Charlie's drones".

So, he has more than one. He has a whole flock of them. "What does he use them for?" My thoughts unintentionally spill out from my mouth.

Agitation growing on Moose's face, he retorts "You do ask some fucking stupid questions. He uses them to keep tabs, obviously."

"On who?" A churn in my stomach brings a wave of anxiety, a worry that my already implausible plan is getting even more unrealistic. Fuck.

"Everyone. They've probably got eyes on us now." Without lifting his head, Moose's eyes follow the drones, a look of loathing traced within his hardened eyes. That one glare under his furrowed brow gives me the impression that his loyalty to Charlie may not be as unwavering as I first thought. We continue in silence down the deserted street. Taking the next turn on the right, Moose grumbles deeply, "Here we are."

In amongst a row of unkept and unlived in, but ordinary looking townhouses, a large gathering of people are congregated on the lawn outside the house we are heading for. This house, I'm assuming, is Charlie's.

As we get closer to the house and begin walking up the path, I notice the many empty bottles strewn across the yellowing and overgrown grass.

Intoxicated, most of the people are slumped on the lawn in a comatose state, the imprint of their bodies crushing the straw like grass beneath their drunken weight. One scrawny looking guy waked from his alcohol induced coma and begins to stand, reaching out for anything nearby to help try and regain his balance. Once upright he starts to sway slowly from side to side, his face quickly turning a sickening shade of green from the motion. As he struggles to walk forward, he stumbles over his feet and at the same time pukes up a foul coloured liquid. He falls face first into the pool of his own vomit. Smeared with sick, he rolls subconsciously onto his back and is once again asleep.

In amongst the bodies and bottles, it is hard not to notice the array of pills, burnt spoons and other naughty things scattered in the garden. These lot sure know how to have a good time; although I bet they will not remember half of the trips they have taken. It is much more likely that they wake up with a sneaking paranoia or uncontrollable hunger for more, both of which will make them self-medicate with even more drugs and alcohol. A vicious, but attractive, cycle.

We climb the five steps that lead up to the porch and find another waster slouched by the side of the door. Dressed in nothing but a skimpy red skirt and matching strappy bra, this half naked girl's head is stooped forward, her long blonde hair hiding her face. Moose casually opens the screen door and walks straight in the house, unconcerned about the passed out, seemingly adolescent, girl on the doorstep.

I crouch down next to her still and vulnerable body. "Hey kid, wakey, wakey." She doesn't move, so I raise my voice a little louder; again, no response. I reach out to grab her shoulder to give her a gentle shake, but as my fingers come into contact with her icy skin, I quickly realise that she is dead. I fall back, recoiling with shock. How many people have walked past her like this? How long has she been left here? I well up, the sting of tears trapped in the corners of my heavy eyes. I haven't cried since I was a child, even through all the shit of the recent past my inability to show that kind of emotion vanished long ago.

My attempt to wake her resulted in her petite body falling sideways, revealing her face. She looks no older than seventeen. I close my eyes in disbelief, the pressure of my lids releasing more tears, their warm stream mapping a shiny trail down the side of my cheek. Her pretty face is tainted with bruising around her right eye. The shades of yellow and green against her soft, pinkish skin shows that the bruise is about a week old.

Her willowy arms and legs are covered in puncture marks. The numerous scars and bloodied, red scabs dotted on her pale limbs show the old and new entry points of her clear addiction. Tucked under her leg, I see the fatal needle. This poor kid was never going to be able to get off this ride.

Looking at her small and delicate body, it seems almost inevitable that this is where her road was going to end. It was just a matter of time. I can't leave her lying on the floor. I quickly glance around, looking for a more comfortable place to rest her body.

Underneath a window to the side of the house, a distressed wooden bench sits away from the clamour of the walking brain dead in the front garden. The lightness of the girl as I pick her up off of the hard timber slats, shows the fragility of her small body. I tuck her arms into me as I carry her to the bench, not wanting her limp arms to swing out. I lay her gently on the seat of the bench, easing her arms and legs inwards to stop them from hanging down. I step back and take in the haunting image of yet another victim of this cruel life.

The screen door crashes against the outside wall as I storm inside, the door nearly ripping from its hinges as my unanticipated sadness turns to fevered anger. I see Moose stood in the doorway at the end of the corridor, his large frame allowing little light to pass through. Fixated on and driven by my burning rage, I half walk, half run up the hall, not paying any attention to my surroundings.

"He was literally right behind me!" Moose's tone comes across as almost confrontational.

"You've got a dead girl on your porch!" I shout, somehow barging past Moose's giant and unyielding body.

"Arthur, there you are. Thank you for finally gracing us with your presence". Charlie ushers me further into the room with a wave of his hand.

"Did you not hear what I just said? A girl has overdosed just outside your front door!" My knuckles whiten from my tightening fists as I spit out the words.

"Who was it? Did you see her on the way in, Moose?" Not a single ounce of concern or upset shown on his obnoxious face.

"Yeah, it was Katy." Moose's face and tone are unreadable, his dark brown eyes continuing to stare into nothingness. He is either exceptionally skilled at hiding his emotions or he's a cold-hearted bastard.

"Oh, that is such a pity," Charlie replies. "She was a lot of fun, if you know what I mean." He winks at me, showing his toothy, narcissistic grin. Red mist suffocates my senses as I lunge forward, hell-bent on wiping the disgusting smirk from his face. Pre-empting my moves, Moose's bear like hands clasp around the neck of my shirt and forcefully pulls me back, the sound of the fabric ripping loud from my attempts to continue to claw towards Charlie.

"Temper, temper, Arthur. This is no way to start our newfound friendship, is it?" Moose's hands are firmly set on my shoulders, his strong grip digging into my collarbone.

My breathing steadies and my erratic pulse begins to slow as Moose releases his iron grip. The mist evaporates as I remember why I am here. I close my eyes and exhale one long breath, subduing the anger and locking it back in its fragile box. As I reopen my eyes, I am finally able to take in the room around me. Hanging on the rouge walls, pictures of women, young women, take pride of place. The nakedness of their forms pop against the dark shade of red; seediness and lust adorning the space like a gallery.

Charlie remains seated, unbothered by my outburst; his interest clearly placed somewhere else. His eyes widen with a glistening shine as two scantily clad girls enter the room and make their way over to him, like moths to a flame. The brunette perches on his good leg, whilst the red head stands behind him, draping her arms around his neck, her hands working their way down to his chest. He wets his lips with his slippery tongue as the girls caress him, his uncontrolled hands desperately groping the brunette's breasts. This salacious man depicts himself as a gentleman, but his finery cannot hide his perversion.

His twisted grin once again returns as he looks at me. "Don't look at me like that, Arthur," he cackles. "After tonight's fight I'll send one of my best girls to you."

"What fight?"

"I know that your head has taken many a beating, but surely you must remember the conversation we had yesterday, Arthur." He tuts and shakes his head from side to side in a scornful manner. "You are now my prize fighter; and funnily enough, prize fighters fight. You agreed to the deal, do not forget."

His pomposity is starting to grate. "No, you're right, I did agree but on the condition that I would have a place to live and not have to worry about where my next meal is coming from." I look around the room with mock confusion. "Funnily enough," I take great pleasure in using his words against him, "I see jack shit."

Throwing the brunette off of his lap, he dives forward, his cool and collected exterior shatters with little effort and is instead replaced by his unseen, but believably true, distorted face. The blood vessels map his blushed cheeks, his blood boiling underneath the skin's surface as his bloodshot eyes bulge from his head as his dilating pupils narrow their focus on me. He holds his cane up heavily against my windpipe, fighting to push it further against the restriction of my tightened grip pushing forcefully back.

Like a man possessed, his mouth twists as venom drips from his snake like lips. "You are nothing here, Arthur. Remember that! You are a piece of shit! A piece of shit that will do as he is told. A piece of shit that will soon learn to put up and shut up, if you know what is good for you." His body trembles with an acute rage as I stare him down, his unhinged and unpredictable behaviour making me regret this clearly stupid decision.

Before I can even reply, he quickly lowers the stick away from my neck, the surprise of the withdrawal causing me to stagger forward. As quickly as his anger took hold, it vanishes. His depraved and warped face morphing fluidly back to its original boyish façade. He smooths his jacket and pulls his trousers up at the leg before taking back his seat. Lifting off his flat cap, he runs his hand through his hair, giving himself a reassuring stroke. Now calm and soothed, he continues, "As we previously discussed, Moose will escort you to your new home. I am sure that you will find it more than adequate enough for your needs."

He turns his attention back on the two girls, assisting them with outstretched hands, pulling them up from the floor. Their lack of shock at his aggression makes me think that they are no strangers to his off the cuff explosions. When he isn't looking at them directly, a blank numbness makes up their faces; models of empty repression. They have been conditioned to adore him, lust after him. When you are between the devil and the deep blue sea, you have little choice but to accept your unpleasant fate. Katy, however, was not willing to play with the cards she had been dealt. Instead, she pulled out the joker, the wild card. The beginning of Katy's end. Who can honestly blame her for wanting to escape her condemned life? The drugs were her means of taking back control, and she did just that.

The two girls' arms weave through Charlie's as all three head to exit the room. My not-so-subtle dismissal cue to leave. Just as they pass through the wide doorway, he leans back, addressing me one last time, "You might not see me there, Arthur, but I will be watching your fight tonight. I do hope that you do not get beaten within an inch of death." With a wry smile he finally leaves the room. After our little flare up, I take his last comment with a pinch of salt.

As we leave Charlie's brothel to head to my new home, I glance back at Katy's dainty body laying across the bench underneath the window. Her unawakenable sleep looks so restful, peaceful. No good came to her in this life; I truly hope that in the next it does. I continue to walk back down the garden path and hear the whirring of drones behind me. As I look back over my shoulder, the final cable is being attached to her innocently blameless frame. I stand, feet rooted in the ground, and watch as they lift her body into the air. Like an angel, she gracefully glides across the sanguine sky, destined for another world.

CHAPTER 8

The twenty-minute walk to my apartment is markedly taken in silence. Suits me. Since Charlie's, Moose's whole demeaner has changed. I would have thought that he'd be accustomed by now to his obnoxious and odious ways, but the stiffness of his usual bumbling movements, shows the tension wracked in his body.

Engrossed in his own thoughts, he mumbles incoherently. Preoccupied, and amused, with the conversation Moose is having with himself, we quickly find ourselves stood outside a modern apartment complex, called The Lofts. I must admit that it doesn't look too shabby. Moose leads me up to the second floor and stops outside room sixteen.

"Here's you." He drops the key in the space between us, my quick reactions managing to snatch them mid drop. He quickly makes off, gruffly calling back "I'll be back at seven to make sure you get down to the cage."

I stand in front of the glossy black door and place the key inside. It glides smoothly in the barrel until it meets the double lock, the final springy click unlocking the latch whilst simultaneously swinging the door effortlessly open.

The salty white walls of my new apartment reflect a sheen that makes my eyes squint. Harsh light floods in through the panoramic window that acts as the outside wall, causing black spots to float across my retinas; the far from pleasurable sensation blurs my vision and, in turn, makes me feel sick. I need to sit down. There are no curtains or blinds fitted to help block out the blinding light. Who the fuck doesn't cover their windows? The perfect setup for Charlie's drones to do the rounds; peering in, keeping everybody in check one might wager.

I sink myself into the cream sofa and cast my, sort of adjusted, eyes over the excessively bright room. Although minimalistic and plain, Charlie was correct in saying that is has everything I need. I surprise myself by not revelling in my plush new pad, instead a creeping feeling of regret pushes its way to the forefront of my mind. Something just isn't sitting right with me. I feel that I have made a deal with the devil. My weight pushes me further into the sofa, the plump cushions cocooning around me. At this precise moment in time, I feel both restlessness and ease. I would do anything to forget my worries, for them to sink into the sofa with me; but they are always standing guard, the constant niggle unavoidable.

The long-lost comfort of the sofa must have helped me drift off to sleep, once again, however, awoken by Moose's heavy fist beating on the door. Before I can lift my submerged body from the snug sofa, Moose waltzes in demanding, "You ready?"

* * *

A couple of my ribs are broken. Dark bruising covers my skin and a strong, overwhelming pain shoots through me with each shallow breath I take. I heard it crack during my last fight. His continued and repeated punches to one targeted area worked a treat. Although mostly skin and bones, he was fast, surprisingly fast considering it didn't look like he had eaten anything for a week. He did a good job dancing around me though, jumping in with a couple of jabs to the ribs and then straight back out to continue his encircling, bouncy jig.

If he had the strength as well as the speed, the fight could have quite easily gone in his favour but, fortunately for me, that was not the case. It didn't take me long to clock on to what he was doing. I wasn't going to waste my energy running around after him in the hopes of getting in a few hits or, most likely, punching the air. I did the smart thing and let him think that he was running rings around me.

You could see the rush of adrenaline coarse through his body when he thought he had the upper hand, that his plan was working. His pinched and gaunt face kept flashing blackened smiles to the cheering crowd, but after another fifteen minutes his movements grew erratic and clumsy, slowing as the fatigue set in, the aching burn beginning to gnaw at his soring muscles. By this point my ribs were already broken, but his emaciated body by the end was keeling over. Depleted of energy, with nowhere to run, I put an end to it with one quick and painless snap of the neck; one of the more humane ways to finish someone.

In the last three weeks I have fought ten times. Charlie's relentlessness and greed not allowing my body the time needed to recover after each match.

So, I suppose it is not that much of a shocker that the scrawny guy's pathetic punches pushed my body over the edge to breaking point. Since then, I have pretty much been hold-up in bed, bored shitless. There is only so much you can do when stuck between four walls. Thankfully Moose showed me how to darken the room, otherwise I'd be blind by the time I can leave. With the touch of a small dial by the front door, you can adjust the amount of light coming in from outside. I pretty much have it on the darkest setting; this, however, does not stop Charlie's drones' routine flybys from looking in.

I have come to notice, since being stuck here with nothing better to do, that they appear each day like clockwork. Bang on the hour, not a second later, they pass at ten in the morning, four in the afternoon, and at midnight.

Handy to know, but my attempts at being inconspicuous ironically come across as the complete opposite. Luckily, at the moment I have nothing to hide. I'll worry about that when the time comes.

I have spent the last five days staring at the empty walls. By day one I was already broken. When I lifted that first delectably toasty cigarette, stuffed full to the tip with love just for me, to my dry, cut and cracked lips, my body rejected that well intentioned warmth. Those beautiful swirly licks of smoke that travelled down my throat caused me to choke violently, as I dragged them deep into my lungs. The suffocating clouds squeezed my chest so tight that my body instinctively wheezed and coughed, spluttering out the remnants of the deliciously smoky wisps.

For the rest of that day an itchiness crawled underneath my skin. When I think about it, the yummy act of smoking is intertwined in everything I do. It's the first thing I do when I get up in the morning, the last thing I do at night, plus the many activities in between. Day two the itch didn't subside, and I felt completely out of sorts. Lethargy passed through my aching body, a light headedness keeping me bound to the swaying bed.

Today, day three, the whitewashed walls have begun to move, the strokes of paint merging and forming oceanic waves. Although the rhythmic crashing is relaxing and rather addictive, my faculties are still intact enough to realise that this fever needs to be burned away from the cabin that is closing in around me. Flinching at the tenderness shooting across my ribs and chest, I manage to lift myself from the bed.

I find myself aimlessly wandering around the complex, a very much failed attempt at trying to distract myself – if anything, it has only made me imagine vividly my habitual ritual of smoking: lighting it up, toking at the tip, dragging the smoke deep within, savouring the warmth as it enters the lungs. Fuck this, I need…

Without a second thought, I turn on my heels to rush back to my only crutch, a support so ingrained that it can lead to a strange and delusional madness. As I stalk towards my estranged vice, Moose's distinctively low tones rumble after me.

"What are you doing out here, Banner? Thought you were bed bound, or some shit."

"I was, but when the bed started to sway and the walls started to cave in, I thought it was a good idea to get a change of scenery. What are you doing here, anyway?"

"Well, how's the corridor working out for you?" He chuckles. "Anyway, I'm going out for a smoke. Want to join me?"

The words "Sure, man" over enthusiastically spill out of my mouth quicker than I can process the question.

Passive smoking isn't really smoking, right? It's just a quick fix to help me get through, a friendly little pick me up.

The rain drops heavily from the eaves as Moose taps the tip of his cigarette on the packet, teasing me with his painfully slow routine. Although we are below the overhang of the roof, ice cold rainwater seeps into my skin, and my four-day unwashed hair is now an oily mess. Moose seems completely unphased by the weather smashing against him as he selfishly holds the sweet smoke in his mouth, allowing nothing but small, narrow streaks to leak out of his flared nostrils. The greedy bastard won't even share his second-hand smoke.

I break the silence between us, desperate for his words to be laced thick with smoky white clouds.

"So, what are you doing here?" An overly harsh edge to my strained voice brings him to look at me with discerning eyes.

"I live here, Banner. Third floor". His eyes lower to my foot tapping in a shallow puddle, an action, until now, I was unaware of. My involuntary movements have garnered his attention; I squirm as jitters travel up and down every part of my body. I blame the freezing rain running down my back, it has nothing to do with my inability to go three days without smoking. Definitely not that.

"Is there something wrong with you? You're acting a little bit, you know, weird". God, is it that obvious.

"Well, apart from the broken ribs, the fact I can't breathe properly and this being the third day without having a smoke because it makes me hack up my lungs, I'm just absolutely dandy."

He coughs back out his briefly inhaled smoke, his raspy laughter fighting against the tears streaming down his face. "It really isn't that funny" I scowl, his laughing at my expense makes me want to punch him in the face; I'm not the slightest bit irrational.

"We've all been there, Banner. I couldn't even last a day. Stick with it man." He throws his giant arm behind me and slaps my back, the force causing me to stagger forward. I bend over, my arms instinctively wrapping around my ribs, trying, unsuccessfully, to hug away the pain.

"Shit, my bad." His mouth stretches into a thin, pursed line, successfully trapping in the laugh that is trying its hardest to escape.

"You are an asshole."

"Nail on the head there, mate. Let's get out of this pissing rain. I think I owe you a drink."

After I don't know how many beers and a couple of hours later, my mood has lifted and the gnawing pain has been numbed, by the copious amounts of alcohol, to the odd twinge here and there. Had I not known that I was sat in Moose's apartment, I would have sworn that it was mine. Everything is a carbon copy of my place one floor down. The same matching furniture is positioned in exactly the same place; like me, he probably couldn't be bothered to move it, what is the point when you don't know how long you are going to be there for.

His place is much cleaner than mine though. I admit that I'm a slob, not a wading through knee high shit type of slob, I'm not that bad, but I do have a habit of ignoring the mini mountains of clothes breaking through the floor and the sky-high stacks of dishes that have been sat for way too long, growing some kind of penicillin on them. Moose's place, however, is pristine. Not a trait I would have labelled him as having.

Feeling much more relaxed than before in his company, I decide that this is a good chance to get to know him. Between swigs of beer, I ask "So what's the deal with you and Charlie? How did you get dragged into all this bullshit?" My question could go one of two ways: he could take it as a friendly ice-breaker, which it is partially meant to be; or he could see it as an intrusive and unsubtle attempt to acquire solicited information, which again, it also partially is. I'm fully prepared for the 'fuck off' response.

Dutch courage is great.

It takes a while for the question to register, he has had far more to drink than me. His bloodshot eyes gradually fix on mine as his head wobbles slowly from left to right, his body tilting so far to the left on the chair that he is perched on, that it wouldn't surprise me if he fell flat on his face anytime soon.

A strange, almost sobering, expression washes over his face, the seriousness in his tone contradicts the slurring of his words. "Like everyone else, I imagine." He steadies his position on the chair, shuffling his big body to the right in an attempt to remain upright. "You know what it was like in the beginning, everything and everyone was savage." I remember it like an anarchists wet dream. A lawless state with no hierarchy, no leadership, no hope. There was plenty of fear, however. And fear can make once well- meaning and decent people do unspeakable things.

"The truth is I fucking loved it in the beginning," he throws his head back, the drink making his voice deeper and raspier than usual as he relishes in his reminiscent growl. "No one could stop me from doing what I wanted, taking what I wanted." His massive physique and general 'don't fuck with me' look would have definitely scared most off of rising to his formidable challenge. "One time though, a group of meatheads tried it on. I think there was either five or six of them. I've got to say that I was sweating bullets at that point." His laugh hardens and becomes more subdued. "One of them came armed with some kind of heavy metal pipe. He was the one I was gunning for first – even in this fucked up place there are rules, you don't bring a weapon to a fist fight. You would think that six on one already gave them more than a fair chance."

Clearly still here, they didn't win that fight. Although he is beginning to open up, Moose is still a complete enigma to me. One that I feel is hiding something. He comes across as an unbounded freight train tearing down the track, running down anything or anyone that attempts to block his path.

"When the scuffle started and all of them were surrounding me, hammering down blows, I found the guy with the pipe and ripped it from his puny little hands. As easy as taking candy from a baby. Without thinking, my body just went on autopilot, took over. I swung the pipe and took out four of them in one go. One swing and I managed to catch them all in their jaws. The guy who brought the pipe got the brunt of it. His jaw was pretty much ripped off, the sinews so stretched that it was flopping about like a fish out of water. At that point the other two scarpered."

I don't blame them. As his story unfolds, his impenetrable countenance gives way. "I remember turning back to them, they were begging me to let them go, to let them live. That was never going to happen, not the way I was back then. They were just sitting ducks to me. So, I worked my way through them one by one, making them watch as I beat the literal shit out of their friends. It was torturous for them to watch what I was doing, but what made it even worse was knowing that it was going to happen to them".

"My twisted mind thought it would be fitting to kill the pipe guy with his weapon of choice, so that is what I did. By the time I was finished with him, the pipe was so bent out of shape that I could no longer use it, so I had fun with the others and let my imagination run wild."

My loaded question has sent us down an unexpected path. What started off as a little jaunt down memory lane has now turned into some kind of confessional. His laughter has turned to regret and sorrow, the tears manifesting in his eyes trapped in haunting memories that I bet he wishes he could forget. We both know that it is not as easy as that.

"I can still feel the stickiness of their blood on my skin." He looks at his palms, open wide in front of him, remembering the blood that is impossible to wash away. I know that feeling well. Not knowing what to say, I watch as this rock of a man crumbles to his knees, holding himself in a comforting embrace.

We allow silence to envelop the room, both taking the time to reflect on, and accept, the past; the occasional soft, whimpering sobs from the broken man is the only sound breaking our shared remembrance.

Loud snores wake me from my drunken sleep. My aches and pains have come back with a vengeance now the effect of the alcohol has worn off. Moving from my slouching position on the hard wooden chair only accentuates my soreness. Moose's heavy head rests on the table, his meaty arms dangling down by his side.

"Moose, I'm going home. I need my own bed." He doesn't reply, and I don't think that the pig like snorts vibrating from his mouth count as a conscious response. He's out cold.

As I hobble out, I look back at the powerhouse dribbling all over the table; a sense of emotional familiarity, a connection, lays the foundations to what could possibly be an unlikely friendship.

CHAPTER 9

C harlie has summoned us to his house of debauchery, and by us, I mean the idiots manipulated into doing his bidding. As I approach the room at the end of the corridor, I cannot help but glance through the crack of one of the partially opened doors. As I lean closer to peer in, Charlie's sickly smooth voice carries down the hall. Although I cannot make out his words, it is a sure sign that whatever is starting has started.

As I shift my weight back from the door, a stout and morbidly rotund man yanks it fully open.

"Wanting to join in on the action, eh?" The width of this sleazeball spills across the whole doorframe, his height only just passing the halfway mark. The little hair he has on his head is plastered to his skin with sweat, and the eyewatering stench surrounding him makes me want to gag. Layers of dirt and grime seep into his spotty, greasy skin; this mound hasn't seen soap, let alone used it, for a very long time.

His porky sausage fingers fumble with his flies as he waddles out of the room, but the rolls of fat ballooning out of his elasticated, but still exceptionally tight, trousers make the zip impossible to do up. He attempts to suck in his chub to help the jammy zip ease up, shockingly to no avail; it is a minor miracle that he managed to fit into them in the first place. The only thing going up, however, is his blood pressure. His round face has turned a worrying shade of red as he continues to hold his breath. It probably doesn't help that the fatso can't see over his bulging stomach to see what he is actually doing.

Whilst he is fighting his rather comical, if not disgusting, losing battle, my attention is drawn back to the room, already knowing what I am going to see. I fucking hate this place. And I fucking hate Charlie for allowing and encouraging this shit to happen. Visibly trying to hold back her tears, a young girl perches on the end of a small bed, numbed by the perverse acts I'm sure this fat fuck made her commit. I can feel the bile, the raw anger, making its way up my throat.

"Are you alright, sweetheart? Did this fucker hurt you?!" It is painful to see the emptiness behind her eyes as she lifts them from the floor.

Mechanically, she rises from the bed and slowly walks over to me, her soft, bare feet padding against the hardwood boards.

The human blob stops shuffling behind me and I soon find his clammy hand pressing into my shoulder.

"Why don't you mind your own goddamn business!"

Instinctively I turn, my fist connecting with the side of his temple as my arm swings out in vexation. He falls back, his short stumps for legs collapsing under his top-heavy weight. Much to my surprise, his roundness resists bouncing him straight back up, instead it cushions his quick, but hard, descent as he rolls to a stop against the far wall, his large head smashing against the drywall for good measure, leaving a crater in its wake. The side of his red face is already turning a darker colour as the bruising is hurrying its way to the surface. He is not going to be a bother for a while.

Lately, red is a colour I am seeing much more of; my cool composure clouded by a resentful bitterness that I can usually contain. As quickly as my rage surfaced, the door behind me slams shut, followed swiftly by a loud click. Through the locked door I can hear her muffled sobs, the floodgates opening on the tears she was trying her hardest to keep from gushing out.

I stand conflicted. Part of me wants to persuade her to unlock the door, to sit and comfort her, to convince her to get as far away from this cesspit as possible. But the other part of me, the impassive and detached half, tells me to walk away from this broken girl. She is not my problem. I can't save every woman who finds themselves in this sort of situation, because the sad truth is that would be the vast majority. Life was easier when I kept myself to myself. Triggered, my emotional switch was inadvertently flicked on. I consciously turn it off.

The room is crowded as I walk into the meeting, Charlie's shrewd, feline eyes catching my late entrance as I lean against one of the walls plastered with indecent stills of women. I scan the stuffy room, thin clouds of smoke sit just below the ceiling, creeping ever lower with each exhale of the many smokers' lungs. The dense air works a treat. As the sweet and warming second-hand smoke passes through me, I feel my tense muscles relax, ushering my confused anger back to its dark corner.

Charlie's honeyed voice captivates the room. Their loyalty to this debauchee makes me feel physically sick. His nonsensical words are empty of meaning, spouting off in a vocabulary that transcends the mental capacity of the weirdos that adore him. When you are the one in charge of the sex, drugs, and alcohol, you can fuel the flames to whatever fire you want.

Through the worthless words and streams of smoke, I spy Moose hunched over a table, nursing a large glass of water, sipping it tepidly; by the looks of it, barely keeping it down. He is hanging out of his arse. Charlie's tone takes a turn, irritation now ringing out of his, just moments ago, lulling, melodic drone.

"It has been brought to my attention that a band of McKay's thugs have been skulking around the district." Uneasy rumbles break out amongst the crowd, hushed whispers and sneaky side-eyes interspersed behind some of the rowdier aggressions being bandied about the room. "If any of you happen to accidentally stumble across these ruffians, please be obliged to show them how unwelcome they are here."

His gaze turns to the sheepish giant stooped low in the corner. "In the meantime, our Moose here will pay McKay a visit." Moose's heavy head turns slowly to meet Charlie, giving a firm nod to acknowledge the command. His catlike eyes turn on me, brimming with hateful deceit. "Mr. Banner can make himself of some use by accompanying you since he is currently out of action, not for much longer I hasten to add." Prick.

With that, Charlie claps his hands and calls the meeting to a close. As the crowd funnels their way out of the door and down the hallway, Moose drags his lumbering weight over to where I stand.

"I feel like shit." Moose just about murmurs, his voice strained and cracked from the alcohol's dehydrating effects. Unsteady on his feet from his heavy session, he reaches out to the wall for stability, his arm acting as an anchor to stop him from sinking to the lowly depths of the floor. "We'll head out to The North in a couple of hours. I can barely cross the room at the moment, let alone the district."

His pounding headache has been the topic of conversation since we left Charlie's.

"Hit me over the head with a hammer, it'll be less painful," he moans, as his callous ridden hands clutch at his head, hoping that his overexaggerated cradling will sooth his self-inflicted misery.

As we enter The North, Moose happily declares that his headache has vanished, "Nothing that some fresh air and a brisk walk can't fix, eh." That is great news for him, but having had to put up with his incessant moaning for the duration of our journey, my head now feels like it is about to implode. The ache, also fed up with his constant complaining, jumped ship to the next best closest thing; me.

A warehouse district best describes The North, the entire area is crammed with huge brick buildings. From dusty greys to burnt oranges, the warehouses line the streets, their dominant and forbidding presence throwing this corner of The Zone into a state of semi-darkness. The aimless wonderers meandering through these depressing streets resemble ants, small and insignificant against the immense gloominess of the decaying industrial backdrop.

Years ago, this place would have been a centre of hubbub, teeming with workers cheerfully going about their business. Now it is living in the shadow of its former self like the rest of us in The Zone. Dead and not worth saving. Every crumbling warehouse and dirty street that we pass looks the same, but Moose comfortably navigates us through the warren of warehouses, getting us to our destination.

"When we get in there, let me do the talking, alright. Dallin can be a little, how should we put it…crazy, especially when some random appears out of the blue. If he does speak to you, try to refrain from being your usual dickhead self. Are you fucking listening to me?"

"Yep. Don't talk, don't be a dick. I think I can just about manage that." His words continue to ring in my ears, burrowing their way deeper into my throbbing head.

We enter through the partially opened shutter of warehouse number 38. Ducking through first, Moose leads the way across the open space, the heavy stomps of his boots reverberating off of the concrete floor to the no longer shiny and heavily corroded aluminium roof. Moose strides confidently through the workshop, heading for the office at the back of the poorly maintained building, clearly knowing where he is going.

Impossible to ignore the obtrusively loud footsteps of his impending and unannounced guest, the man sat in the office looks up from behind his desk and watches us through the glass screen separating the office from the workshop floor. He takes off the reading spectacles perched on the end of his ski slope nose and rises from his foldaway metal chair, greeting Moose like an old friend. Reaching out his hand, Moose reciprocates the gesture and quickly gets down to business.

"Dallin around for a chat?" Before the man can even respond, a thick Irish accent shouts down from the upper level of the workshop.

"Is that a Moose I can hear?" Dangling his head over the metal rails of the mezzanine, a nest of scraggly waves falls across the thin man's face.

Obscuring his view, he quickly brushes the tangled hair away from his eyes, confirming his thoughts. Light-footedly side stepping the stairs on his descent, he saunters towards us with a swagger, beguilement hidden behind his initial over-the-top pleasantries and jests. His piercing eyes travel the length of my body, "And who is this wee fella?" His cocksureness irritates me, the patronising prick; he is at least ten inches shorter than me.

"The only 'wee fella' I see here, mate, is you." As the sarcastic quip leaves my lips, Moose lets out a sound that falls somewhere between a choking cough and a held in, but poorly restrained, laugh. The wee fella's left eye twitches, an uncontrollable tick that could be a sign to many things, and I'm intrigued to find out what.

The set line of his thin lips stretches out, the widening revealing cavernous dimples digging their way into the pockets of loose skin, causing his cheeks to bunch up with deep creases. As he throws his head back, a wild cackle escapes from his throat, filling the empty warehouse with a harsh and villainous laughter. Relieved by his reaction, Moose half-heartedly joins in, shooting me a sharp 'watch yourself' glare.

"Does this guy come with a name, or just an attitude?" He says, clearing out the remnants of his unexpected laughter.

"Dallin McKay, this is Arthur Banner. He's Charlie's new cage fighter since he pretty much ripped the head off of the old one."

"Well, it is a pleasure to meet you, Arty." His slender but firm hand locks with mine. "It is quite a rarity for me to come across someone who has the balls big enough to talk to me like that. I like you, you're my type of guy."

So, this is the infamous Dallin McKay; to say I'm slightly disappointed is an understatement. From each corner of The Zone, he is known for his ferocity, his unrestrained words and actions that always lead to violence. Violence that often leads to bloodshed. The man stood in front of me, however, looks normal, although exceptionally shorter than the average man; far from the unhinged image my mind had drawn. His thick accent and, I think, good sense of humour is quite charming in a strange way. For years though, this wee fella's thirst for violence has proceeded him, and I have always been one to believe that there is no smoke without fire.

Getting to the point of our visit, Moose hastily regains the line of conversation, "We need to talk." Cliché phrases like that often lead to something that most people do not want to hear, but without the slightest worry McKay replies,

"Ay, I was expecting that."

CHAPTER 10

Gladly not invited to partake in their discussion, Moose orders me to "Wait in here." Like the good boy I am, I oblige.

McKay adding, "Take a pew, Arty," pointing toward the spare chair folded against the back wall of the office. "I'm sure that Jacob here will keep you in good company."

The least bit thrilled, the man with the glasses nods unenthusiastically. McKay exits the office with Moose in tow, the two men walking in silence to the other side of the workshop. Completely out of earshot. Jacob and I, with a single look, come to the unspoken agreement of not acknowledging each other. Suits me to a tee. A man of little words; a man after my own heart.

I grab the steel chair and unfold it, taking advantage of the chance to give my tired legs a well-deserved break; although the harsh metal is far from comfortable, it does the job. The pulsating behind my eyes continues its unrelenting torture, the headache from hell refusing to let up. Looking through the office window at Moose and McKay acts as a good distraction.

Their body language gives off a different feeling than I would have expected. I was under the impression that Charlie sent us here, well Moose mainly, to give McKay a good talking to, Moose's menacing charm unapologetically threatening him to get his men out of dodge. But that, however, is not what I am seeing. McKay stands with squared off shoulders, his dominant stance making Moose seem small and vulnerable. A very unfamiliar sight.

The niceties of before having long since disappeared. The hollow dimples have been replaced by stern and furrowed creases, as Dallin intently listens to whatever Moose is saying to him. Moose looks uneasy as the leader of The Northern district begins to speak. He adjusts his body language to reinforce the force behind his words, his torso angled forward to encroach on Moose's personal space. McKay's lack of hand gestures as he speaks is disarmingly unnatural. Like a statue, his arms rest by his sides, his feet cemented in the ground, the features on his face unmoving. Unreadable.

Unblinking, Moose looks down into McKay's upturned stare, too transfixed to break away from the bottomless pits of his dilated eyes to notice the jerking fingers darting in and out of McKay's clenched fists. Heightened emotions, no matter who you are and how hard you try to hide them, always have a way of rearing their unwanted heads, or in this instance, bony fingers. I watch as the twitching of his fingers work their way to his palms, where one very quickly fires out, unleashing itself on the side of Moose's unsuspecting, expressionless face.

Unknowingly, I am on my feet and halfway out of the office door. As my foot crosses the threshold, my mind catches up with me and pulls me back from my brash, unthought about actions, stopping me in my tracks. For whatever reason, Moose takes the slap, continuing to remain dormant as McKay's anger, and true self, is now well and truly exposed. As soon as his anger appeared, it has now, within a split second, vanished and is once again replaced by the affable man that came bounding down the stairs to greet us. The rumours about him have been proven to be true; he is a man of many faces. Most of which, the red flags and alarm bells are warning me, are ones that you do not want to deal with.

His sudden burst of violence and colossal swings in mood fits accurately with the characteristics of a psychopath. I used to think that this term was dished out too generously, undeservedly given to those labelled with it.

Christ knows we have all done terrible things; flown off the handle every once in a while, killing people usually because of that very reason. Anyone of us poor unfortunates could be loosely, but justifiably, labelled as a nut job on a bad day. But his hot-headedness and unpredictable impulses blows the rest of us well out the water.

With the fast, sudden, and unexpected strike to Moose's cheek, McKay released the fury that was burning inside, turning him from hot to cold with immediate effect. Us human beings are comforted by predictability, we all feel much safer when we know what is coming or when we can at least be one step ahead of the game, but with people like McKay you are always on the backfoot, forever sliding back down that slippery snake. It is his instability that scares people, even those the size of Moose, who is still stood staring forward, unresponsive to the much smaller man in front of him. The picture of a mighty elephant backed into the corner by a feral rodent comes to mind.

Leaving him there like a scolded child to reflect on his poor behaviour, McKay's parting words leave him frozen to the spot as the Irishman climbs his way back up the black metal staircase. Looking at the stunned expression planted on his face, I don't think that the conversation went the way that Moose had hoped.

I decide it best to sit and wait it out, holding back until Moose pulls himself out of his stupefied state and letting whatever the hell just happened sink in. After a couple of minutes, Moose regains his sense of self and shakes off the belittlement and embarrassment of the last twenty minutes. As he stalks his way back across the workshop to the office, I avert my eyes from his direction, pretending to unsee the utter humiliation he was subjected to.

In a voice even lower than usual, he mutters, "Let's get the fuck out of this shithole." His eyes glued to the concrete floor, Moose does not notice my peeking glances to his reddened cheek. The unmissable sting of red has spread across the side of his face, the skinny handprint leaving its mark for everyone to see. For a small man, Dallin McKay can sure pack a punch.

Outside the heavens have opened, the heavy clouds that hang low in the cold sky paint the horizon black, the unsettled air full of melancholy soaking us through as we make our way back to The South.

"I'm guessing that you saw what happened in there?" He asks, finally addressing the large elephant that has been following us for the last thirty- five minutes. The streams of water running down his face has helped to cool down the blood vessels that were raging under his skin; the deep red handprint watered down to a rain-kissed pink.

Unsure of what to say, I simply reply "Yeah." I was hoping that we'd leave that topic of conversation back at the warehouse.

"You were probably wondering why I let that ratty Irish bastard speak to me like that, let alone land one on me." As he turns to face me, I can see the amusement set in his brewed brown eyes; but I can't help but notice the undercurrent of calculation glimmering behind his wily gaze. He is digging for something here, I'm not sure what, but he is obviously trying to steer me in a certain direction. I'll play along.

"I didn't have a clue what was going on, only the other day you were telling me how you had taken out a group of guys with one swing of a pipe, to seeing you essentially pissing your pants in front of a man who less than half your size."

"Good acting, right?" I shoot him an incredulous look. "You didn't honestly believe that pathetic puppy act, did you? I'm a better actor than I thought!" He guffaws.

"So, you're telling me that all that back there was fake?"

"For me it was, but to him not so much". Perplexed at Moose's meaningless explanation, he sees the bewildered look on my face and attempts to bring me out of the box. "Listen to me, Banner, you're not stupid. You know how this game works. This fucked up game we call 'The Zone' has no end, no finishing line to cross. The only rule here is to survive by any means necessary." Everything about him has turned deadly serious. "The whole set up here is a delicate house of cards supported by three individuals who think that the rest of us are pawns in their pitiful game of pass the power."

I think I am beginning to understand Moose's little act. "You have got to play them at their own game, let them think that they own you, when in reality I'm the one manipulating each player on the board." Things are not as black and white as they apparently seem; grey underhandedly squeezing its way onto the chequerboard. Talking in metaphors, he is dancing around the dirty hole that he is expecting me to fill, without much to go on.

"So, what are you actually saying, that you're playing them off against each other? Bit of a dangerous game don't you think?"

"Only if you play your cards too soon, my friend. You have to play the long game, use your cards when it matters most and bluff your way through the rest."

"Today was a bluff then?" Playing the pathetic, blubbering mess I choose not to add.

"Come on man, you know me well enough by now to know that it's an act. I could snap McKay in half like a twig."

"Why don't you, then? Surely that would be easier than you having your arse beat every time you are sent to deal with that prick."

"Like I said before, Banner, you have to play smart. He's more useful to me this way, and if it means I have to get spoken to like a piece of shit and take the occasional slap, I can easily deal with that."

"So, what are you to McKay?"

"He thinks I'm his little lacky planted in The South, feeding him back intel on Charlie."

"And are you?" I question.

"No, a drip here and there but I mainly play stupid with him, and he buys it. Makes him terribly frustrated though, as you can see." He turns his head and points to show off his rosy red cheek, a half-smile pulling up at the left side of his mouth.

As admiring as McKay's handiwork is, I am still at odds with the logic behind Moose's choice to be middleman between these two nutjobs. "What's in it for you, then? From where I'm standing you are in no better position than me." The harsh probing edge to my voice brings him to a stop.

His saturated clothing clings to his muscle-bound body as the rain shows no sign of clearing up. The black clouds form behind him, their lowliness shrouding around him so his features are now set in shadow; the outline of his shape standing firm as the air sours with an innate feeling of foreboding. "The most powerful thing in this shithole, Banner. That is what I have, and you don't. Information."

"Well, that has blown my fucking puny mind!" An aggressive and patronising laugh coats my words as my arms fly up over my head in a show of hyperbolic exasperation.

"For a clever guy, you really are a dumb fucker. Can't you see the bigger picture." Mirroring my gestures, he thrusts his arms out in agitated frustration.

"Go ahead and enlighten me!"

Curling his lips and spitting through gritted teeth, he barks "I know…"

Before the words have time to part with his lips, a clap of thunder rumbles across the ever-darkening sky and a flash of bright light reflects of the deluged ground, the surrounding whitening blinding us briefly useless. The low and deep sound lapses like rough waves, until an eerie silence holds the air. The roar engulfed Moose's words, swallowing them up as his expression instantly changed from hostile antagonism to disturbed shock.

Wide-eyed, his focus lies behind me, immobilised by the event happening past my shoulder. His expression alone fills me with a feeling of dread I cannot fully explain, but my body stiffens to his reaction, nonetheless. The panic and sickness rise as I turn in trepidation, joining Moose's unblinking stare.

Plumes of dusky smoke slowly rise in the far distance, greedily spreading its suffocating clouds across the Southern District's black streaked horizon. Shock has Moose firmly tied to the ground, his pebble like eyes still fixated on the disaster unfolding helplessly in front of us. Pushing me forward, my legs instinctively carry my broken body home. As I run, I can only hear one set of heavy boots hitting the flooded ground. Looking back, I find Moose unable to move, petrified in position.

His gaping mouth is forcibly shut by my white-knuckled fist to his face as I retreat back for him. Now both sides of his head are emblazoned red.

Snapped from his stupor, his feet begin to pound the ground toward the black tower of smoke staining the sky.

CHAPTER 11

Rubble and debris lie at our aching feet as the remains of the old apartment block burns to cinders. Mounds of charcoaled ash sweep into mini tornados as the wind carries them through the streets, whirling over the shards and smaller fragments of glass blanketing the road; the neighbouring blocks and houses windows having blown out from the impact of the explosion. You can taste the desperation in the bitter smoke as people frantically search for their loved ones amongst the demolition of split bricks and fractured beams.

Cutting through the distressed calls for missing mothers, fathers, sons, daughters, friends, an anguished wail adds to the already fraught despair. On all fours, the lady's hands and knees are laced with rivulets of blood, punctured by the pieces of broken window digging into her skin. As the search for survivors continues, her weeping howls wane as she draws her hands together in prayer. A bit late for that, love. She presses her bowed head against her bloodied hands, the bridge of her nose running down her index fingers as her mouth utters hushed words to her merciless so-called God.

Moose is amongst those tearing and clawing at the wreckage, the muscles in his bulging arms straining under the weight of the large hunks of debris from the building's collapse. There is no amount of prayer that can help here. Too little, far too late. Anyone who was in that block when it came down is surely dead, buried under the bricks and mortar of the one place where they almost certainly felt the safest.

Panning the chaos, everyone owns their shock and grief differently. The wailing woman screamed out her pain until she no longer could; although the release was long, her physical let out would not be able to lessen her emotional suffering. That will be with her the rest of her life. There are those, like Moose, who are in denial, scrabbling around on the mountains of rubble, a false optimism pushing them to search for the irretrievable. Some have their arms wrapped around their knees, rocking back and forth, sheathing themselves in a protective embrace. Whereas others just stand, drained of all colour, all concept of time stopped as they attempt to come to terms with, or even comprehend, what they have just seen.

That is when I saw her, her lonely, slight figure surrounded by nothing but abject horror. Standing in an oversized and baggy grey shirt, her bare feet planted in the sodden ground, shock paralysing her to the spot. She doesn't notice me as I walk over and stand beside her. "Are you alright?" Of course she's not fucking alright, any imbecile could see that. A small but visible tremor runs through her body as she breaks from her frozen state. Her brown hair is dulled by the layer of ash that has settled on top of it, her face and body coated in streaks of brown and black residue; she is lucky that she managed to get out of there.

Her empty eyes continue to stare ahead, nothing able to stop the lonely tears falling from the corners of her watery soul. This poor kid just can't get a break. I won't push her for a response; she needs this time alone.

We have only managed to recover the dead from their tombs beneath the rubble, the likelihood of survivors dwindling with every passing minute. If they weren't instantly killed by the explosion, or slowly bled to death from the weight of the collapse on their bodies, the suffocating, burning heat would have put them out of their misery. Eventually.

I keep looking back at her lonely figure, still staring into the abyss as the day's last light tucks itself away, making the search almost impossible. She can't stand out here all night. Once again, I find myself slowly making my way over to her. "Hey," I say as I gently reach out to touch the top of her arm, breaking her away momentarily from her inescapable thoughts. This time she turns to face me and meets my concerned eyes, her wide pupils filled with sadness and fear. No tears left to cry, the red puffiness that has swelled around her eyes evidences her hours of agonising hurt.

"I don't need you to rescue me" she snaps, "just leave me alone." The bitterness of her snipe is softened by the fact that she bothered to turn around, to acknowledge my effort to help. Only hours before she was slamming a door in my face. Leaving me outside to listen to her muffled sobs. Choosing to ignore her implied damsel in distress sentiment, I ask,

"Do you have anywhere to stay?" I study her face, watching as she bites down on her bottom lip to stop the quivers from releasing any more encroaching tears. A very much put on brave face seems to be this girl's standard response, but this is the second time I have seen her hollow façade slip.

Looking away, she utters a defeated sigh "I'll probably go to Charlie's." Emotionally drained, her voice is monotone; a flatness defined by someone who has given up, by someone who has lost everything. I don't want her to go back there, to be shared around like some piece of meat. Thinking of the unthinkable, unwanted images of Katy invade my mind, flooding in like a torrent. Her peaceful yet sallow frame alone in death, a preferred choice to that of remaining one of Charlie's girls. This girl should not be destined to that same fate.

"You don't have to go back there. You can come and stay at mine." For whatever reason, I can't look at her as I say this. I don't want her to think of me like she does those other men who only want one thing. My hands fumble in my pockets as I sway awkwardly, awaiting her response. As I thought, she instantly screws up her face, a look of disgust washing across it as she jumps to some kind of sordid conclusion.

I cannot help but be insulted by her conjecture. Countering, my tone comes out far more aggressive than I had intended considering I understand why she thinks the way that she does. "Look, I'm not like those dirty bastards who queue outside your door, alright." I take a deep breath to compose myself, and as I exhale the harsh edge to my tone has disappeared, "I genuinely just want to get you off this street to somewhere safe, where you will be comfortable and where no one can hurt you." Unexpectedly, she bursts into tears, her deep sobs heart-breaking as she leans into me and tucks her head into my chest.

"It's going to be alright," I lie. My woeful attempts at comfort ring hollow as we both know that everything is far from alright.

***

"You can stay here for as long as you want." She totters in and stands awkwardly in the middle of the open planned space, unsure of how to act. "Honestly, treat this place like it's your home. You're safe here, okay." I say, trying to reassure her with a friendly smile, a concept that it quite foreign to me, so I hope it comes across as welcoming and not creepy. She responds with a couple of nods of the head and a timid half smile.

It suddenly occurs to me that I do not know the name of this girl. "My name is Arthur, by the way."

"Jess," is her only reply. I'm slightly relieved that we have once again been summoned to Charlie's for another meeting. It will give her time to settle in and get comfortable with the place, without me getting in the way.

"Well, Jess, I need to go out for a while. There's food and everything in the kitchen. Just help yourself to whatever you want, alright kid." I quickly throw on another jacket and take my leave. As I pull the door shut on my way out, I'm reassured to see her slowly lowering herself onto the sofa.

Taking up as little room as humanly possible she perches on the edge, her bleak face troubled by the events of the night, her wide eyes brimming with unspent tears.

CHAPTER 12

The bitterly cold night air whips around me as I walk to Charlie's, my brisk pace doing its best to keep me warm and fight against the wind's repeated icy bites. Just turned midnight, my laboured breath forms in front of me, the cloudy wisps hanging momentarily in the clear sky, before dissipating into the black.

As I reach Charlie's I walk straight in, my speedy walk, and the drop in temperature outside, leaving me catching my breath as I readjust to the warmth of the house. Quickly settling to its normal rhythm, I take off my jacket and add it to the untidy pile of coats that adorn the stairs and make my way down the corridor to the back room. Considering the number of coats thrown across the stairs and banister, it is strange to not hear any of the voices that wore them. This place is quiet. Too quiet.

As I cautiously approach, unnerving muffles whisper to each other from the back room. The male voices are so low that I cannot make out what they are saying. As I discreetly peek through the door, I quickly establish the reason for the hushed tones. The room has been turned upside down. The remnants of glassware is scattered on the floor as its liquid insides hang to the walls, the height of the splatters looking like it was aimed at someone's head, which could be the possible explanation for the dozen or so men cowering in the corner of the room.

Confused as fuck about what is happening here, I suddenly feel a heavy hand on my shoulder. "What have I missed then?" Sidestepping his large body past me, Moose is struck with the same perplexed look mirroring my expression.

"I am positively glad that you have all finally managed to make it." Charlie's vicious tone spews with spite, as flames of vindictiveness burn through his callous eyes. Dressed in a black silk robe he looks more satanic than ever before, especially when I see, hidden beneath his long and billowing sleeves, the dulled metal nose of a gun.

"So, which of you filthy wretches assisted that snake McKay in blowing up that building! My! Building!" Saliva flies out from his mouth as his deranged eyes pop from their sockets, searching the scared faces of the thirteen men buckled on the floor. "Is no one going to answer me! I said which one of you shitheads did it!" Brandishing the gun, he waves it wildly in the air, making the supposedly tough men recoil as it gets pointed in their direction.

A familiar voice speaks up from the corner, cracking in squeals of high-pitched terror. Only hours before, I punched that fat perverted pig to the floor. If any one of these pricks deserves to be shot, it is him. Charlie would be doing the world a favour; one less dirty bastard girls like Jess would have to deal with. Beads of sweat roll down his spotty, bulbous face, the salty droplets becoming trapped in the creases of his many chins. His already ill-fitting clothes cling to his lard-arsed mass while his excess fat tries its best to escape through the stretched fabric around the buttonholes. The patches of sweat grow sizably bigger now that he has gained Charlie's undivided attention.

"M-m-m-m Mr. Dalton, please, I don't know what you are t-t-t talking…" Before he can finish his pitiable pleads, his body drops back to the floor with a heavy thud. Charlie stands unflinching as his arm remains outstretch toward where the fat man's head once was, his face spattered with spots of blood. A silver bullet protrudes from the back wall, surrounded by the sticky red matter slowly mapping its way down the smooth paint like rain on a window.

"The next person who decides to open their mouth, I would consider your words very widely." Low groans roll under Charlie's threat. Little by little, blood trickles out of the bullet hole residing in the centre of the fat man's skull, his eyes frozen open, his last moments of fear burned into his lifeless retinas.

Stepping towards him, Moose positions himself between the gun clasped in Charlie's trigger-happy fingers and the grovelling saps behind him. Wispy tendrils of smoke continue to travel down the hot barrel, licking the metal as it rises between the bodies of the two men into nothingness, Charlie stares through Moose as if he is invisible, his focus intent on the obscured traitorous men hidden behind his dominating stature.

"No one here has betrayed you." Without hesitancy, Moose rests his hand on the gun, his wide palms and long, calloused fingers wrapping around the barrel and chamber. His close proximity and calmness cause Charlie's head to twist on his neck, the trailing blue veins straining under the strange motion, cocking it from side to side, malfunctioning from the clash of overwhelming thoughts rampaging through his neurotic mind.

Moose remains doggedly unwavering as his stillness overshadows the much smaller man, whose convulsions continue to jerk at his head. "You do not know that as a fact." Each word is slowly drawn out from Charlie's mouth, a fraught edge constraining, and keeping a very loose lid, on any more impetuous and deadly decisions.

"I do know that", accentuating the words, he points behind him. "These fucking sycophants kiss the ground you walk on. That one did especially." His eyes hover over the dead mound of flesh, the pooling at the back of the head from the exit wound continues to ooze, spreading and seeping into the once luxurious shag pile. Slowing his voice further, Moose quietly adds, "Come on Charlie, enough is enough." His words take hold as Charlie's body loosens from his position, allowing his most trusted confidant to take the smoking piece from his hands.

One minute he's an inferno full of wrath, the next he is the last traces of smoke from a fire gone out. A whisper, barely audible, utters from Charlie's direction, "Set up a meeting." Without another word, or look back at the idolisers he held hostage, he drifts shrinkingly out of the room, the flowing black silk robe trailing behind him obligingly. After the crazed antics of tonight, it could possibly be the only thing following him from now on.

CHAPTER 13

Twenty-seven bodies were pulled from the ruins that night. The skeleton of the building hiding away both young and old in its crumbled mass grave.

Exhausted but unrelenting, we dug at the debris for hours, overturning the rough blocks of concrete and brick entombing the innocent dead below.

We worked in silence. The gravity of the lives lost truly realised when a young girl of about four was lifted from her bed of rubble. Her skin still warm, we placed her with the others, her floppy limbs reaching for the cold, harsh ground. Not a single mark blemished the girl, instead her untainted alabastrine skin looks like that of a porcelain doll, smooth and pure.

In the early hours of the morning, we took the twenty-seven to the waiting room and lined them up next to one another; the emerald tiled room feeling much smaller than it ever has before. Waiting for the dawn, I studied the many faces of the dead. I needed to find this little girl's family, to reunite their bodies. I don't know why, but I felt that it was the right thing to do. No one should be alone in death, especially a child. Although the girl's babyish features are not fully formed, they are distinct. I spent what felt like forever examining each individual face, but unlike the girl, not all of the bodies pulled from the wreckage came out recognisable. Disfigured limbs and burnt skin stood between this child and her parents.

Hours later here I sit, watching as the morning's orange hews break a new day, bouncing its light across the green room's state of depression, the golden glow giving the place a warmth that will always feel unwelcome. Last night's dead wait patiently for their final destination, the stained and tatty sheets lain across them keep them in the dark, away from the intrusive new day that has been stolen from them. Soon the furnaces will be lit, the hungry flames eager to welcome the twenty-seven, to wrap them in a warm embrace and free them from their state of cold.

Suddenly, the room falls back to its state of preferred darkness as a figure stands in the doorway, scaring away the trespassing light. He doesn't notice me as he counts the bodies. Looking oddly satisfied at the tally, he says, "That'll do nicely."

"Not the words I would have chosen to describe this." Catching him off guard, his eyes flash toward me.

"I didn't see you down there, friend." Lifting myself from the tiled floor, I make myself unmissable.

"You are going to have to explain to me why twenty-seven bodies will do 'just nicely'". Picking up on my line of hostility, he quickly reworks his oddly impassive face to something a bit more natural. We stand eye to eye, our heights almost identical. I wait for his answer.

"On reflection, I can understand why my choice of words offended you." I can't work out if he is being sincere or not. His expressionless face gives nothing away. He continues, "I am used to dealing with the dead, but I haven't seen this many at one time since the early days." What is it with people not contextualising the things they say and expect me to know what the fuck they are on about? He must be able to see from my confused unresponsiveness that his answer hasn't quite hit the mark. "I work as the furnace operator", he tags on the end. It would have been much clearer if he had said that in the first place. I've decided that directness is a trait that I highly respect.

"I don't give a shit about who you are, but I do give a shit about your lack of compassion. There is a little girl under those sheets, you prick. Or is that just another day at the office for you, eh?" He continues to stare blankly back at me. His heart, if he has one, must be made of the coldest stone.

"The dead do not need either mine or your compassion. Why don't you save that for the ones who are still here?" Breaking from my glare he turns and leaves, leaving me to watch as he crosses the street, no doubt getting ready to stoke the fires.

***

In a few hours' time, the meeting between Charlie, Rue and McKay will be held. As with all the meetings between these three, Central is the chosen district for the gathering, a ground that has no allegiance to any of them. My home from home, the much-frequented cage will be the spot for the tete a tete a tete. The secure steel structure allows for no outside interference but does allow for everyone to watch at close-quarters the tension-fuelled spectacle, eagerly, or not so eagerly, waiting for the whole damn thing to implode.

I have too many hours to kill before the meeting begins and I do not have the capacity, or inclination, to do anything up until that point. My body is tired. My mind is tired. I'm tired. Every fibrous sinew feels torn from tearing through the rubble last night; the aches and pains, however, are nothing compared to my weighted down heavy heart; the sadness creepily sneaking in.

I made a choice three and a half years ago to pull the plug on my emotions, to let them quickly spiral down the drain before I had the chance to care, but the recent onslaught of misery and death has blocked the pipes, causing an internal inundation, one that is muddying the once clear waters.

I stand in front of the cage, my stagnant and sluggish body somehow carrying me unknowingly to the meet. Everything feeling as if it might give way, I lean back and slide down the cage's mesh, my legs splaying out, grateful for the rest.

Through squinted eyes, a well-worn boot knocks at my foot. "Fuck off," growls gutturally from deep in my throat, the tired monster not yet ready to be pulled from his sleep.

"Wakey, wakey sweetheart." Moose chuckles, amused at my irritation.

"Why don't you let this sweetheart get his beauty sleep," I say, closing my eyes and sinking back into my relatively comfortable position.

"Banner, no amount of sleep is going to help you in that department."

"Hhmm", I accept his offer to pull me up; as soon as I grab hold of his gigantic hand I am effortlessly lifted onto my feet.

"It looks like we are the first ones here." Moose looks around the area, scanning for members of the other parties.

"What time is it?" I ask, blinking rapidly to shake the bleariness from my somewhat less heavy eyes.

"Just gone noon, the meeting is in just under an hour. Charlie will be here soon; he likes to be the first to arrive." Smart idea. I would not want to walk into the unknown either, especially with two of the most deceitful characters The Zone has to offer.

As if on cue, jerky footfall, interspersed with the clack of a cane hitting the ground, can be heard approaching from behind us. The distinctness of the sound stands out from the heavy steps of the entourage following closely on his heels. Handpicked for size, the burly men are as wide as they are tall, a ring of protection ready to circle around the man who has a grandiose sense of self. Choosing brawns over brains, he has always surrounded himself with hulks. But it gives the impression of importance. It makes him feel powerful, and Charlie is all about the power.

Dressed in a black three-piece suit, his aristocratic style indulges his conceited vanity. Trading in his everyday flat cap, a fedora rests jauntily on his greased back hair, rounding off his lordship's grindingly obvious and extroverted way of saying I'm better than you. Coming to stand in front of us, his feet line up with his shoulders as both hands clasp around the frosted, coloured glass ball of his cane.

"Have you checked the area and cage? We cannot trust these two to not try and pull a fast one on us." As he asks Moose the question, his eyes scan the area, darting to the surrounding doors, windows, and alleyways. Even when suited and booted, he can't hide his nervous paranoia behind his fancy attire. Looking at the men lined up behind him, I do not recognise a single one. It transpires that holding up your most loyal followers with a gun and decorating the room with a shower of their blood doesn't help win over, let alone keep, friends. But to Charlie that is a minor inconvenience. We are all expendable. Who needs friends when you can buy mercenaries?

"We're the only ones here at the moment. I've had a scout around and haven't seen anything suspicious," states Moose, picking up on Charlie's overt anxiety. "Everything is going to be fine, Charlie. You've done this loads of times before. This time will be no different to the rest."

Snapping back, Charlie retorts, "it is not the same. These two are plotting something together behind my back. They are clearly out to destroy my reputation. Threatened by my good name no doubt."

"Only you could make the deaths of twenty-seven people about you and your fucking reputation. What the fuck is wrong with you?" Before I can process the words, they spill from my mouth. Unfortunately, the cold hard truth is never able to sink into the superficial skin of a narcissist.

Choosing to ignore my comments, he brushes me off, "I do not have the time to deal with your little tantrums today, Mr. Banner."

Visibly uncomfortable, he takes off his fedora and runs his hand through his hair, the sweat formed on his head causing it to mat as he tugs at the dampened middle and ends. I'd like to think that my words were close enough to the bone to make him writhe in his slimy skin, but he is far too preoccupied with whatever has him spooked for anything I say to penetrate his snake-like outer peel.

Exasperated by his half-arsed response, I barely hear, "there's my favourite wee fella!", being shouted across the distance. I follow Charlie's line of vision, turning to watch as the small Irishman marches toward us. In that moment, Charlie's whole demeanour changes. His before scattered eyes now only have one focus; his stare showing more hatred than the numerous daggers I imagine Charlie is wishing would impale his diminutive body.

Striding toward us, his scrawny chicken legs carry him with a surprising speed, and within seconds stands squarely in front of Charlie. The cocksure grin slapped across his face is sickening, I don't agree with Charlie on much, but our dislike for McKay is our small common ground. Like a demonic cheshire cat, his grin barely fits his face and somehow spreads across his sunken cheeks. Slapping Charlie's arm, he greets him with "long time no see, pal." Charlie inspects the area of his jacket touched by McKay, a look of disgust set deep in his face, as if touched by a leper.

McKay, amused by his reaction, continues his over-the-top grin, adding to Charlie's annoyance. "Our meeting is in the cage at one o'clock. I do not wish to converse with you until then, so if you would excuse me." As Charlie turns to walk away, McKay's arm once again reaches out, this time grabbing hold of Charlie's shoulder.

"It is polite to greet an old friend, you know." The grin has disappeared from McKay's face, replaced by an expression much more unsettling. The tension between these two is thick, causing an oppressive and uncomfortable cloud to cover those in the closest proximity.

The entourage of muscle are well oiled, coiled springs, waiting and chomping at the bit for Charlie to give them the nod. Moose, just like the hired muscle is puffed out, although I am unsure of how he will act if these two kingpins come to a head. Without another word, Charlie stalks forward, not once looking back at the affronted McKay, whose hand still briefly hangs in the air until he allows it to slowly drop down to his side.

Disappointment is cast across Charlie's men's faces; these people bask in danger, wishing and willing the chance to split skin and spill blood. Moose on the other hand exhales out his relief. What would he have done if it all kicked off? Both Charlie and McKay see him as an ally, although one that is held in much higher regard than the other. We never quite finished our discussion about his dealings with McKay. Playing both sides must be exhausting, but he claims that the knowledge he gains far outweighs being left in the dark. Unlike him however, I like the dark. I feel safe in the unknown, fading blissfully into obscurity, not wanting to know what is going to happen, not wanting to be held hostage by scraps of information thrown my way from the manipulative corrupt.

As two of the three parties gather around the cage, Charlie's irritability grows as the time ticks its way towards one o'clock. Every couple of minutes or so, Charlie lifts his sleeve for the garish glint of his watch to reveal the time, causing him to mutter obscenities under his breath.

Punctuality is important to a control freak like Charlie. Glancing at his wrist for the hundredth time his scowl deepens, aging his boyish face by a not very generous ten years.

The dark rings circling around his drawn eyes are the impact of many a sleepless night; this is the time when the niggling paranoia sneaks its way back in. As Charlie's stress begins to physically manifest itself, the lady we have all been waiting on finally graces us with her presence.

She harnesses everyone's attention, turning heads as she walks toward the steel. She carries herself with such confidence; a confidence that is both alluringly attractive but somehow frightening at the same time. The conviction in her walk is unmistakable. Gliding towards the cage, her fierce smallness stands out from the male dominated crowd. Simply catching her eye would make any of these big men shrink back into the background where they belong, just like the group of men following at a distance behind her. They know their place.

She is the face of beauty. Her hazel eyes are shaped like almonds, accentuated by the long, dark lashes and perfectly arched brows outlining them. Her full russet lips stand out against her smooth tawny skin. A superficial picture of perfection. But what lies beneath the flawless exterior is everything other than beautiful. She lures and entraps with her sweet as sugar façade, melting the unknowing just enough to mold and bend them into her subjection.

However, her devilishly dangerous draw does not seem to snare all. Both Charlie and McKay possess the same look as they watch her stride seductively towards the cage. Privy to her ways, they are unaffected by her outward appeal. Standing parallel to her male counterparts a triangle is formed, each heavyweight holding down their corner. Whether those corners are equal in proportion, only time will tell.

"Hello boys," she greets them coyly, flashing a sly simper to both men in turn.

Clapping his hands together, McKay declares, "Let's get this show on the road!" and marches himself and his motley crew over to the cage. With a graceful pirouette, Rue spins on her heels and quickly follows suit.

"About bloody time," Charlie mutters under his breath and quietly walks behind his adversaries to the meeting he called.

CHAPTER 14

Although all three turned up with a miniature army, only a select few from each faction are allowed on the outside of the cage. As Charlie, McKay and Rue take their seats inside, those of us chosen to be on the outside eye each other up.

Moose and I stand by the door of the cage, Charlie's instructions being not to let anyone in. We can feel eyes on us in every direction. We are stood directly behind Charlie; his chair positioned a few feet away.

Diagonally left from Charlie, Rue sits with her legs pretzeled, a show of complete ease. Pressed against the mesh behind her, the weight of her chosen two encroaches the cage as they lean against the flexible steel, trying to reduce the distance the metal barrier is putting between them and their mistress. Infatuation swims in their eyes as they stare at the back of her head; whatever spell she has cast on these two sure is working.

To the right, McKay leans into the back of the chair, his skinny arms crossed over his sunken chest. If his boots were not firmly gripped against the canvas mat propping him up, he would slide off due to his near horizontal position. He sits with his legs spread wide, knees pointing out to the left and right, trying to take up as much space as humanly possible, a juvenile attempt at male dominance.

His two chosen lackeys stare absentmindedly into the unknown; their vacant eyes and sullen complexions match their scrawny and withered frames. An odd choice. Then again, when you look back at his group of men huddled off to the side, they are all small and sickly. Trust McKay to surround himself by men who are somehow more stunted than he is. I thought that was an impossibility. The cracks of his fragile ego begin to show.

"Right, shall we begin. Firstly, I would like to thank you for agreeing to this meeting at such short notice." Well Charlie's tune has changed dramatically since last night. Blowing someone's head off is a surefire way of venting your anger. He has shaken off his nervous fidgets and is now resolute and calm, poised as a man who has complete control of his actions. What they don't know can't hurt them. "I am saddened to say that our bone of contention, the one we all agreed upon, has raised its ugly head once more."

Just as Charlie begins to continue, McKay cuts in, "Oh, and what might that be, Dalton?" McKay's mock shock shows that he knows exactly what Charlie is referring to, as he gesticulates his head side to side with each word.

"Do not play dumb with me," sneers Charlie; so much for keeping a lid on the bubbling vat of rage. "You can still see the black streaked across the sky!" Casually, McKay shrugs off Charlie's accusatory tone. Leaning in and pointing, Charlie's stabbing finger takes aim at the blatant denier, "Your men were seen skulking in my district on the days leading up to twenty- seven of my people being crushed to death."

Rue shows her disinterest as she sits and picks at her overly long nails. "Nothing to do with me fella, so I'd watch your tone," McKay's cheeky Irish accent suddenly becomes more cutting.

"Your men were seen entering the building, Dallin." Charlie states matter-of-factly.

"They were, were they? Well, this is news to me." Both Charlie and McKay's eyes are locked on each other, neither one wanting to be the one who makes the first break.

"When I got wind of your men sneaking about, I increased my patrols and," before Charlie can finish, McKay cuts in once again, his growing agitation plastered all over his face.

"Bring them out then, Dalton. I want to see the ones who are falsely accusing me of mass murder!" Like a bull seeing red, his nose flares, the burning anger escaping from his nostrils as the fire reddens his face. Quite an impressive show he is putting on. Then again, perhaps he wasn't the culprit behind the attack; or maybe, and much more likely, he's acting this way because he's been caught.

A single laugh explodes from Charlie. "Why would I do that? You would only kill them, and I think you have already sacrificed enough of my people."

Come to think of it, who saw McKay's men has never been mentioned. It couldn't have been one of the guys Charlie was holding up at gun point last night, otherwise that whole mess could have been avoided. The only patrols that I'm aware of are the drones. That must be it. It's all starting to make sense now. That's the reason why he won't name names. On a normal day, I wouldn't put it past Charlie to throw his men into the lion's den, but his precious drones, he won't be willing to give up that secret so willingly.

Let's see how this plays out.

Jumping up, McKay's chair flies backward and crashes against the cage's wall, the metallic vibrations of the mesh ringing out, until the panel works itself back to its still state. Pacing back and forth like an animal locked in its pen, the snarling Irish beast spits, "I want to see your fucking proof! You can't just point the finger at me. I'm not having it, you hear me!"

On the outside of the cage, McKay's men are getting twitchy, restlessness working its way through their feeble and washed-out bodies. One of the men's feet shuffle awkwardly manoeuvring himself around that one spot on the ground, dodging the cracks that are fissuring under his mud splattered shoes. His hands search for something to hold onto to try and stop his fingers from darting in and out of his sweaty palms. Sweat is funnelling from his pores; the shine of his skin illuminating his guilt. He must have a feeling that the devil is breathing down his back. The green tinge of his sweat covered skin is the final giveaway of his involvement.

Charlie's eyes have not left McKay as he continues to flounce around the squared circle, professing his innocence. "I have already given you my reasoning for not showing you any evidence," Charlie matter-of-factly states. Rising from his seated position, Charlie stands and walks over to where McKay now stands still. Uncharacteristically, McKay remains silent as Charlie stares down at him.

Lifting one hand from the frosted ball of his cane, Charlie's arm stretches out, his index finger pointing outside. Following the direction, McKay turns his head. Behind them, Rue shuffles in her seat, trying to reposition herself so she can see what they are now looking at.

Even clammier than a few minutes ago, dark patches appear all over the nervous man's body, his perverse sweating being sucked up by the dirty garments on his back. Like staring down the barrel of a gun, his eyes widen in fear as Charlie singles him out from the crowd.

"Is he proof enough?" Charlie sneers.

If all eyes weren't on this quivering wreck before, they sure are now. A deer just about to be hit by a truck, the ill looking man has a decision to make.

He can stand there and come to terms with the inexplicable pain that is without doubt hurtling towards him, or, as his body is signifying, make a run for it.

Darting to the left, he knocks into McKay's other man, the force of the bump propelling him off into a different direction. As he regains his balance and scrambles forward, Charlie's finger never leaves him. He is lined up and in his sights, nowhere to run. Charlie lets the scene play out, light form of entertainment for himself and those of us watching as the sickly man struggle forward toward his hopeful escape.

But Charlie had this game rigged from the beginning, he was always going to win.

He glances over to his mercenaries and gives the signal. The foaming mouthed stampede takes no time to catch up to their much weaker prey. Separating out to the left and right, they flock around him, kettling him into an inescapable circle of beasts. He doesn't bother to fight as they grab fistfuls of his shirt, their brute force ripping it at the seams as they tug at him, pushing him back toward his maker.

Moose and I step away from the door, allowing them to throw him face first onto the cage's solid floor. Looming over him clad in black, Charlie looks like the reaper. "Stand up you cretin." He doesn't, instead he crawls towards Charlie, his face almost touching the canvas as he reaches out and lays his palms flat out on the dirtied mat.

"Please, Mr. Dalton!" He cries out. "He made me do it! I didn't want to, I really didn't." His grovelling splutters have no effect on Charlie, who sternly repeats,

"Stand up."

Choking between sharp intakes of breath, the break down of this murderer is lain bare for all of us to see. He clutches at Charlie's creaseless trouser leg, snivelling incomprehensible words as he continues his attempt to clamber to his feet. He is unable to stand still, the fear coursing through his veins has taken full control, as the unshakable tremor causes his limbs to jolt erratically. Although the sweat continues to drip off of him, that is not the reason for the new patch that is spreading over his crotch.

Looking down at his area, he is as shocked as everyone else. His eyes are awash with embarrassment and fear, the unstoppable shakes making the streams of endless tears roll out of his eyes down his concaved cheeks. Like a bottomless sea, they do not cease as he looks despairingly into Charlie's eyes, whose, unlike his, burns with an intense, dark pleasure.

"Please…" He wasn't given the chance to finish his final beg for mercy. Sticking out from his neck, a thin needle like blade has been pierced into his jugular. With the blade still in his throat, not a single drop of blood escapes the punctured skin. He tries to speak, but his words have been replaced by bubbling gurgles pushing their way into his blood-filled mouth. Relentlessly spilling in, he coughs it out, spluttering the blood across his hands and face.

Charlie's curled fingers tighten around the frosted glass sphere as the pointy end remains lanced in the side of McKay's man's neck. Slowly, Charlie finally draws the knife out. As he does, he twists it round, encouraging the bright red blood to gush out freely. Charlie takes a step back and watches as the man's hands grasp at his sloppy neck, trying, but failing, to stop the fast flow spurting out of his almost invisible wound.

Muscles giving way, he slumps to his knees, the loss of blood shutting his limbs down, one by one. His arms drop to his sides, no longer able to hold the deadly wound, no longer able to resist his call to death. The man's eyes stay open as he slowly falls to the canvas, the blood continuing to pour out from the slice in his neck, surrounding his body in an ever-growing red pool.

115

Charlie stoops down as low as his limp leg allows, and wipes his crimson covered blade across the man's saturated back, cleaning it to its original polished shine. Satisfied with the result, he slides the knife back into the top of his cane, pushing the glass sphere securely in until it made an audible click. Turning on his slightly platformed brogues, he once again faces his adversaries, whose colour has completely drained from them, not too dissimilar from that of the dead man on the floor.

"Now then," as calm as ever, Charlie sits himself back down and directs his attention back on McKay, who looks like a dirty rat caught in a trap. "It is a real shame that it has had to come to this, it really is, but you two have given me no other choice." Rue places her hand on her chest, surprised that her name has been brought into the situation. "Don't act all coy, Rue. I know of you two having your secret rendezvous. And please give me the common decency of not even attempting to deny it. I think I deserve that small amount of respect. One thing that you two should realise by now is that I am not a stupid man."

Rue's eyes up until this point were feigning innocence, but have now reverted to a shrewd coldness, a coldness that is almost accepting of the lack of guilt she carries with her. "Caught red handed, Dallin," she smirks as she holds up her tainted hands. Her amusement contrasts the many emotions that have passed McKay's face; the initial shock turned to confusion, the confusion turned to a burning rage that holds him to the spot.

"What is the matter, Dallin? Do you not like being beaten at your own game?"

"You're a slimy fucker," growls McKay.

"I will take that as a compliment. Over the last few years, I have learned a thing or two from the slimiest fucker of them all. You."

"Touche, you jumped up little prick." McKay's deniability has all but gone.

"I trust that you will get rid of the other vermin." Charlie's head gesturing to the red soaked body behind. "All of this drama really does take it out of me." McKay doesn't answer, but his silence admits defeat. "I am glad that is agreed. You would not believe how challenging it is to dispatch a person without getting blood on your suit," Charlie chuckles as he meticulously examines his three-piece ensemble. "Not a speck of course," his jest turns serious as a glint of wickedness blinks across his eyes. "The next time we are due a purge just let me know, and together we can arrange the details. Goodbye, old friends."

CHAPTER 15

Rue and McKay's mouths hang open as Charlie makes his way towards the cage's exit, leaving them to quietly come to terms with what just took place. One thing that Charlie has most certainly proved is that the ball is well and truly in his court. Moose swings open the door, allowing Charlie to walk seamlessly down the metal steps. "Clean this mess up," he commands to us both, before shambling off, mercenaries in tow.

Moose takes a sideward step through the door, his hefty frame just about squeezing in; I follow him in, no necessary manoeuvres needed for a person of my size. Moose, myself, Rue and McKay stand in parallel to each other, encircling the mass sprawled on the canvas, the blood and piss spread so far out that the smell of metallic urine hit our nostrils as soon as we stepped in.

"You fucking snake." McKay's eyes glower at Moose as the words, full of resentful intention, snarl through his browning teeth. Dumbfounded, Moose doesn't react. I am almost certain that he knew as much of Charlie's plan as the rest of us did. His lack of response and look of confusion does not stop McKay from bombarding him with his accusatory malice, however. "You knew what this fucking maniac had planned, and you didn't bother to give us a heads up."

"I promise you, Dallin. I had no idea that he was going to do that."

"It should be you on that floor slithering around in your own filth!" McKay aggressively shouts. "Like I should believe another word that comes out of your two-faced mouth."

Both of them are now just staring at one another; the blockage of the corpse in the middle of them seems to be the only reason why their stare down has not moved on to anything more physical. Rue, as always, casually stands by, unbothered by the rising temperature in this metal square.

The look on my face catches McKay's attention, his eyes reluctantly breaking from the unspoken tirade aimed at the giant opposite him. "You have no idea what is going on here do you?" His words confuse me further. What is there to know? "This ugly brute right here isn't all he cracks himself up to be." Moose's upper body twitches, but McKay's eyes are focused on my cluelessness. Moose's eyes, however, bore into the Irishman's skull.

"You're right. I don't have a clue what you are talking about," I snap. I don't like the feeling that is beginning to creep in, prying open the sticky door to something I think I already know, but don't want to believe.

"You want to know who is to blame for all those people being crushed to death? Go on, I'll let you take a guess." I turn my head to the giant next to me with clenched fists. "Ding, ding, ding. You're good at this game. I knew you were a good wee fella with a brain." Moose's fists grow tighter, the increasing whiteness of the stretched skin almost splitting over his mountainous knuckles. "Why are you getting so angry, Moose? I'm only telling Arty here the truth."

Slowly, piece by piece, it is all beginning to make sense. The strange meetings with McKay, their relationship with each other – he has been working with him this whole time, playing Charlie like a second-hand fiddle. Just the other night he was about to tell me something, his uncontrolled anger ready to spill, before being interrupted by the distant explosion.

"What is he talking about, Moose?" I say, turning towards his unmoving figure. His thunderous silence speaks far louder than what would be his empty words.

"I'll tell you." McKay is enjoying every moment of this, his slight frame bouncing on the balls of his feet. "This prick wants out?"

"What do you mean, wants out?" Out of Charlie's? Out of whatever he has going on with that little Irish grease bag?

"Out of this shithole, Banner." Moose's gravelly voice deepens to an almost inaudible murmur.

"What has that got to do with the killing of twenty-seven people?" I ask, confused.

"Absolutely everything," McKay chips in, before Moose can speak. "I'll let you in on a little secret, Arty. Why should this lummox be the only one privy to this information." What fucking information! Everyone seems to speak in riddles around here. "Do you never question how to get out of The Zone, or even how you got in it in the first place?"

"Every single day. I spent my first year here looking. There is no way out, or I would have found it by now." My voice is heightened at this point. The wall wraps itself around the entirety of The Zone like a constrictor; every day that passed the suffocating shadows cast by the concrete barrier grew darker, my search and my desperation broken by the impossibility of finding an escape.

"Ah, but you are wrong my friend." McKay chimes in. "There has and always will be a way out." He stares at me intently, before uttering a single word. "Death."

"Don't fuck around with me, Dallin. I don't want to listen to your metaphorical bullshit."

"It's no metaphor, Arthur. Why do you think he killed twenty-seven people? Because it is his ticket out of here."

"Shut your mouth," Moose growls, breaking his long silence.

McKay snaps back, "Watch who you're speaking to! Deals can always be undone. You can do what you want with him after, but in the meantime allow me to have some fun."

Moose's narrowed pupils dart to mine, his protruding brow making it difficult to see the emotion in his blackened eyes, the shadow of his forehead hiding them from scrutiny. Dallin continues to talk over Moose's uncomfortable silence. I imagine he is weighing up his options.

"Like the reaper, he gathered up those merciful souls, and you, unknowingly, helped him to deliver them to the skeletal gates, where I believe you met out very own ferryman."

"What are you talking about? I haven't done anything to help him!" I shout, the exasperated confusion manifesting into the familiar burning anger.

"So, you are telling me that you didn't move those bodies to the waiting room and that you didn't meet The Cremator?"

I stumble, "Well, no, I did do both of those things."

"So, you did assist this big oaf."

"Assist him in doing what?"

"For fuck sake, Banner, in getting me out of here! How many times does that need to be said?" Moose's growing impatience causes his words to spit out like searing venom.

Struggling to look at the mass murderer who I thought was a friend, I turn back to McKay. "Why are you still in The Zone if you knew how to get out all along?" His sly eyes light up as his gap toothed and stained ivory shards break out through his thin, dry and cracking lips.

"You wouldn't believe how long I have waited for someone to ask me the right questions, Arty. Like I've said before, I knew I liked you from the time we first met. Just call me a great judge of character."

"Well now is your opportunity to answer it." The brusque curtness of my tone repels his jagged and blackened teeth back behind his mouth's edge. When he speaks again, his childlike cheekiness has vanished, only to be replaced by a no joke drawl, slow and deep.

"You see freedom on the other side of that wall. The difference here is that I see only death; my own in particular, and that is not something I am willing to risk." McKay muses.

I can't help but retort, "How do you know that? You know as little about what is on the other side of that wall as the rest of us do."

"Wrong," he replies. "I know far more about what is beyond that wall than you can possibly comprehend, considering that is where I am from."

"We're all from the other side, Dallin. Just get to the fucking point."

"You're not wrong, Arthur. However, I was there a long time before you. However, my life only really began at the takeover." My mind is racing. Is he telling me that he's one of the fuckers that locked us in this godforsaken limbo? His eyes burrow into mine, attempting to understand my expression and the possible thoughts running through my mind. He can see the contortions in my face marry up with the anger that is starting to show itself. "Before you attempt to put the pieces together, it might help to know about the few pieces you are still missing."

My voice is nowhere to be heard. This cretin is part of the reason why I have spent the last three and a half years of my life in misery, wishing for death rather than living amongst the filth this place has turned us into. He is stood there waiting expectantly for me to say something, to engage with this information he is painfully and frustratingly drip feeding me. "I don't understand what it is you are telling me." My voice turns pleading, the still wideness of my faded grey eyes sting with exhaustion; my exposed brokenness even has McKay looking at me with pity.

"What do you remember about that day?" McKay asks, offering up questions to help speed this explanation along.

"Everything going dark, as if someone had just turned everything off. The screens though, every single one, played Clarke's execution and after that… I, I don't know, it's all blank."

"Until you arrived here, correct?"

"Yeah," my voice almost sounds separated as my eyes flick from left to right, trying to search for and uncover the forgotten memories that have to be there. That must be there. But nothing. I have no recollection of anything that happened before we just somehow arrived in this hell, where the gates were sealed firmly shut.

"When did you arrive here?" McKay asks the question, although his tone already reveals that he knows the answer.

"What do you mean? We got here pretty much instantly after it all kicked off."

McKay counters, "Instantly isn't a word I would use to describe five years."

"Five years?" I repeat the words.

"Yes, lad. You didn't arrive here in 2042. It was 2047 when you first stepped foot onto this beautiful wasteland."

"Can you just tell me what you know, instead of fucking around with me!" His pitiful eyes harden once more, although his distaste for my aggression does not stop him from giving into my request. With a sobering expression and solemn voice, I allow his words to seep in, to try and understand what has been incomprehensible to me until this point in time.

"For many years, as I am sure you are very well aware, human beings have created technology; technology where their lives are made easier, where tasks can be carried out far more efficiently than a person could ever do.

You once owned a car, phone, computer, right? Of course you did.

Everyone did because you were made to believe you needed it in order to be successful. You were made to rely on it. Well, that stupid thought process continued for many, many more years, which in turn made people greedy, grasping for the more prestigious materialistic technology that does pretty much everything human beings are already capable of doing themselves."

"Don't worry, I'm getting to the point…" he can see my growing agitation as my limbs twitch involuntarily. "Anyway, one very intelligent man, a scientist, created a machine that was essentially human. Artificial Intelligence had been dabbled with for a long time in many industries: transportation, finance, healthcare, manufacturing and supply, all of which were programmed with limitations. In hindsight, perhaps for good reason. However, this guy, Doctor Raptis, wanted to transcend those limits. And my lord, did he surpass even his own aspirations. He intricately built a fully functioning humanoid machine, one that had freedom of thought, just like you and I, who could move as fluidly as a dancer. To the untrained eye, it was human. It was his masterpiece, his creation."

"To the outside world he was a visionary, an engineer; one of the brightest minds of the twenty-first century. He achieved the sought-after goal of creation without procreating. A readymade production line for the future. This brilliant man, however, internally it would seem, had his own agenda. Surprise, surprise."

He continues, "Simply put, he was lonely. A man with no friends, no family. All he had was his work. Once he had created his prototype, he turned his attention to his own needs; needs that he had been craving his whole adult life. The one thing all humans want. Someone to share his life with; someone to love. So, from his prototype, he quickly created Layla. She exuded all the qualities that this great man held dear: big tits, big arse, curves in all the right places, if you catch my drift. Perverted old bastard."

"He programmed her to 'love' him, and only him. He basically created a subservient sex slave. Anyway, fast forward a little bit, he realises that something isn't quite right with Layla. She might look like and act like a human being – but she doesn't feel like one. Instead of the warm, soft and supple skin of a woman, his fingers run across cold rubbery latex."

"Now I've filled you in with the backstory, this is the part that you are going to find interesting. So, Arty, what do you think he does next?" He was looking at me expectant of an answer, the first time since his monologue began.

"Err, I don't know. Spend the next couple of years in a lab trying to replicate it."

"Wrong! If you haven't realised already, this guy isn't exactly what you would call sane; a few sandwiches short of a picnic. There is a reason why they are called mad scientists, after all. You are obviously lacking the imagination of a narcissistic psychopath. Such a shame. Why would you choose to waste years of your life creating something that there is already an abundance of? So, his desires sent him down a darker path, one where the likes of ladies of the night tend to linger."

"One particular siren took his fancy, her call unable to resist. One night he found himself down at her corner, his urges dominating his sense of morality. He drugged her, took her back to his, murdered her, and then proceeded to peel her skin away from her flesh. A very messy job, you can imagine. Last but not least, he drained her of every drop of blood she had to offer. You see, to keep the skin alive, and most importantly to him, not forgetting the reason why he did this in the first place, to make it warm to the touch, he had to design a convoluted artery system, not too dissimilar to that of a human being, to keep the blood pumping around his machine to keep the skin as alive as it was on that living, breathing femme fatale."

"It took a while for her stitching to heal up; you could say that she looked a bit like Frankenstein's monster or a patchwork quilt; but after a few weeks, the blood circulating underneath that skin worked its magic. She looked out of this world, a flawless goddess whose past life and imperfections were well behind her, an irrelevant blip. She was phenomenal, and the good doctor's eyes were only for her."

"So, where does this leave poor Layla, I hear you ask. Unsurprisingly, her undying love for him wavered. Months of watching the doctor and Layla's upgraded replacement do the most sordid of things broke her, quite literally. This is the problem with artificial intelligence, it constantly adapts and reconfigures, the pain and sadness she felt filtered through, finding and unlocking that programmed door to freedom."

"One night when he was sleeping in his bed, she crawled across him and straddled his lap. Raised above his head and gripped in both her hands, a large kitchen knife; his very own sword of Damocles, ready to be plunged into his heart. One broken heart for another. Poetic justice, some might say. Without a second thought, quickly but forcefully she brought it down, the point of the blade sinking into his chest like butter."

"He stared up at her, unable to make a sound for the blood that filled his mouth. She didn't stop there though; she stabbed him another fourteen times, purposefully hitting his major organs as he watched on helplessly. Betrayal coated his eyes as they welled up with excruciating pain, the red teardrops escaping them leaving trails down his disturbed face to the blood- soaked pillow below. One trail led to his inner ear, the blood pooling and congealing in the canal. His eyes remained open throughout the whole thing; anguish staring back at his frenzied first love, whose programmed affection, turned obsession, killed him."

"For days she remained on top of him, slumped onto his pierced, carmine torso like a leach. The regret of her actions weighing heavy on his chest. That is when I truly realised what it is to be human. The psychological impulses, the unpredictable detachment of what is right or wrong, and then the morality that creeps back in to make us regret the actions that just felt so right. Well, in some cases anyway."

"How do you know all of this?" I can barely get the words out, astounded by what I am hearing.

"I was there." He stated matter-of-factly. "Have you really not managed to put two and two together yet?" Silence stands between us as he stares back at me, hoping for an answer; disappointment once again rests on his face when he realises there isn't going to be one. "Clearly I overestimated your intelligence, Arty." His despondency in me, however, does not stop him from wanting to tell me more.

CHAPTER 16

The light opposite flickers in the obscurity of the night, the on and off again illumination glows faintly in the thick icy mist which wraps its way across the street, concealing me in shadow. Arse numb on the ground, the damp chills work their way through my body, my knees drawn up and cradled against my chest as the stinging bites gnaw at the brittle bones which already hold so much pain. My jacket retains little body warmth, as the many gaping holes drain the heat away. These winter nights will be the death of me.

Every night I think this but look who's unfortunately still here. I feel protected in the fog, at least. Being homeless puts a target on your back, especially on a Saturday night when men, fuelled up on drugs and booze, fancy a game of beat the downtrodden even further into the ground.

Hopefully tonight the oppressive insomnia will let me get a couple of hours shut eye. I tap the watch on my wrist, the frayed and discoloured leather barely holding onto the cracked face which reads 2:43am. The streetlight across the way continues its strobing effect, the intermittent soft glow acts as my only source of comfort in the depressing surrounds.

Slumped against the bare brick wall, the heaviness of my eyelids draw down, my sight blurred through the narrow slits that are fighting back against the habitual tiredness. As my eyes close, the comforting and steady hum of the spasmodic light opposite is interrupted.

Well attuned to the silence of the night, every other sound is magnified. In the distance, the unmistakable dull echoes of footsteps grow heavier, occasionally stopping for a few seconds and then continuing its fitful walk closer to where I hide.

The footfall continues in my direction, the empty streets reflecting the heavy beat of sole on concrete. The thuds once again stop; quite a disconcerting feeling when you are trying to listen out for the nearness of the steps. My stomach churns slightly as a shiver runs down my spine. Either this already icy night is growing colder, or my subconscious is sending me a warning, urging me to open my eyes.

Looking out into the black, my eyes adjust to the lack of light, the lamp across the street in a spell of darkness. After a short while, the pitch black fades a little, leaving outlines of the pallets and dumpsters dotted throughout the alleyway in partial view. My intake of breaths sharpen, the frozen air stabbing at the back of my throat like needles of ice.

The silence grows louder as my heart pumps faster; time standing unbearably still as I listen out for the clicks of the lamp's spark, hoping for a flood of light to drown the besieging shadows away. Answering my unspoken calls, the low hum comes back, followed by bursts of short, sharp sounds, jittering the orange glow back to life. The light did not bring with it the desired comfort, however.

Standing in the centre of the post's beam, a silhouette of a man skulks. Resolute, they remain deathly still. The man's features are hidden under his draping coat and wide-brimmed hat. Concealed beneath it, I cannot see their face, for the hat is angled down, hiding everything other than the point of his chin. Facing toward me, I stare wide-eyed at the darkened figure, my dry throat struggling to gulp back down the fear that is climbing its way up, wanting to shout out an array of colourful obscenities to get whoever it is to fuck off on their merry way.

Instead, I decide to slowly stand, reaching back to the wall to support my weight as my knees regain strength from their numbed, bent position.

Reacquainted with the pain of standing on my tired legs, I take one last look at the stranger in the pool of light, their unnerving, unmoving position motivating my legs to carry me away in the opposite direction. Click.

Just as I begin to turn, blackness once again deluges the pregnable light. Click. Looking back at the split-second flash of light, the stranger's head is now tilted up. Although the broad brim of his hat throws a shadow over his face, I can feel his piercing eyes holding me captive. My feet burned frozen to the ground.

Everything is telling me to run. To break away from his almost intoxicating stare. It is only when his lips begin to curl and spread, that my hypnosis melts and my worn soles push away from the ground. Click.

Fuck.

The sound of his heavy but fast steps reverberate up the pitch black alley, unmatching of my own misdirected stumbling feet. Running, my head snaps back, trying but failing to get a glimpse at my pursuer; only to be faced with the growing darkness that has tormented me for too long.

Pain sears through my shoulder as a pointed edge of dull metal sinks in with a bruising hit, causing my torso to twist mid-air, the impact throwing my whole weight to the ground whilst my legs continue to attempt their lacklustre sprint.

The fog has somehow made its way into my head, the black inky swirls stunning me momentarily blind. A pain in the back of my skull grows, its throbs pushing back the narrowness of my vision, allowing the blurred grey periphery to regain its focus. As my consciousness reawakens, an overpowering hand pushes it back, the suffocating fumes smothering my mouth, forcing my vision to fade slowly back to black. The little strength in my clawing hands retreat, succumbing to the figure hovering above.

CHAPTER 17

A white light shines through my eyelids as bitter undertones trigger me awake. The sharp antiseptic smell burns my nostrils, motivating me out of my current haze. Slowly the weighted lids move, gradually fluttering open; my neck muscles flow with dull, dense aches as it struggles to lift my pounding head.

The room is clinical, covered floor to ceiling in large off-white tiles which reflect and exaggerate the already shining light blindingly. Like in a theatre, the room holds surgical equipment, the majority of which looks like medieval torture devices. Lined on top of the table to the right of me, medical instruments are neatly laid out, gleaming under the bright spotlights. Although the room is spinning and I am not fully with it, I know for sure that this is not where I want to be.

Lifting myself forward and up, resistance meets my arms and legs. Bound around my wrists and ankles, thick leather restraints tie me to the table. I pull with as much strength as my body can muster to try and force my hands through the tight cuffs. The leather digs into my skin, pulling out many tiny arm hairs as they rub against the brown straps. Trails of beading sweat appear across my skin; a mixture of the intense panic of being tied up and the relentless struggle to free myself. The porous leather, however, is absorbing my sweat, causing the skin to stick and be cut into even further.

When the door swings open, my wrists are covered in blood. "Planning an escape, are you? Quite pointless don't you think?"

"Who the fuck are you!? Where am I!?" I could barely get the words out as the man in the white lab coat closes the door and leisurely walks over to the other side of the room. "Did you not hear me!?" I shout across the room. "What the fuck am I doing here?"

Slowly he turns away from the metal instruments he was inspecting and perches himself on the stool to his side. "You, my dear boy, are here to do a wonderful thing. A miraculous thing." His voice is that of the well- educated; highbrow and plummy. Before I have time to respond, he wheels himself over to where I lay, pushing up against the side of the table, leaning into me, getting uncomfortably close.

His face, only inches from mine, shows the excitement you would normally find on a child. "You and I are going to create history together. We are going to do what others cannot even comprehend." Behind that excitement lies something much more disturbed. The whites of his bulbous eyes stare at me, unblinking. Similar to the way a predator looks at its prey when it's caught between its claws. Adrenaline thrashes my chest forward as my arms and legs fight to be free.

"Dear boy, if you do not stop this absurd behaviour I will have to make you relax," he states flatly, calmly watching as I continue to violently throw every movable limb to try and release myself. "It would seem that you are giving me no choice in the matter." Quickly he gets up, his fast movement causing the tail end of the lab coat to balloon out as he paces across the room.

The clink of glass rings our as he hurries to find what he is looking for. Within seconds he has a large syringe in his steady hands, drawing out clear liquid from a small vial. "You are not putting that fucking thing in me!" My heart is a train pounding down the tracks, punching at my rib cage, pushing its way out of my chest. He walks toward me, needle in hand.

"You have lost too much blood already." He now stands next to me, squirting the clear liquid from the needle's end, readying it to pierce through my skin. "You'll feel better in just a moment." Animalistic snorts explode from my nose, sheer terror thundering its way through every muscle; every fiber of my being violently throwing itself forward and back in a last-ditch attempt to find freedom.

The red rage immediately calms as the needle scratches at my skin, the penetration of whatever drug he has given me submerges the fire inside, leaving me immobilised in a spacy nightmare. Perpetuated by my inability to move, the fear is inflamed. "Now then, didn't I say that would feel much better." I try to speak but my mouth and tongue are numb. I try to force out the words but my tongue lolls to the side, resting against the inside of my cheek. From the corner of my mouth, saliva starts to dribble down.

"Let me get that for you," reaching into his breast pocket he pulls out a cream-coloured handkerchief. Gently he wipes my chin and mouth, restoring me with a slight semblance of dignity in the most undignified of situations. Placing the spit covered hankie in his pocket, he sits once more. "Now that we are in a better position to talk, I feel I really should introduce myself and explain why you are here." I feel my whole body start to relax, even the fear of what's yet to come is turning into a distant memory. "My name is Doctor Lionel Raptis and I am sure you have most likely worked out that I am the one who abducted you." He looks at me for some kind of reply, like he has forgotten he has injected me with some kind of paralysing drug, rendering me as responsive as a potato.

Quickly he moves on, "I am conducting a very important experiment, one that will revolutionise the entire human race; however, the means and ways of doing it at this stage are probably not what the scientific world would deem, how should we put it…ethical." His words merge together into a melodic rhythm, the waves of his tone pulling me deeper into oblivion, uncaring of the devastating reality. "But fate has brought us together, friend. You are going to help me in ways that no one can understand. Before you go," I'm swimming in nothingness as I feel my glassy eyes begin to droop, dragging me down into the depths of nihility. "I want you to know that I will forever be grateful to you for this." As the consuming darkness sweeps in, his fading voice echoes, "Hopefully I'll see you on the other side."

CHAPTER 18

I was his breakthrough, the first of many." Dallin McKay was murdered, but here he stands smiling grotesquely from ear to ear. "Why are you looking at me like that, Arty? Have you never seen a dead man stand in front of you before? Well, not that you know of anyway." His smile hangs on just that little bit longer than it should have.

"If you're one of them, why aren't you living the high life on the other side of that wall?" My cynicism garners a look of scorn from the Irishman.

"You aren't doubting what I've just told you, are you? It's quite flattering, but my imagination for concocting mad stories just really isn't that good," he says in all seriousness.

"Why are you here then? Did they realise that you're a dickhead?" Moose tries to keep down his rumbling chuckle. "I don't know why the fuck you are laughing, Moose. You're on the same level as this prick."

"You're a sweetheart, Arthur – you always have such lovely things to say about me. I'm well and truly privileged. He however," pointing at Moose, "will never be on the same level as me. He's just a desperate stooge scrabbling around my feet for scraps." McKay crouches over slightly, bending his elbows so that his hands stick out from his chest, and chatters and squeaks like a rodent.

"I agree with you that he's a fucking rat, but let's get back to the part of why you are here and not over there."

"When Raptis found me, I was a cockroach." Was? You still are. "I had no home, no family. I would wish for death on a daily basis, but somehow my battered body would hang on, surviving the trauma of the streets. But when I was strapped to that gurney, after the fear had passed, I realised that my wish was finally being answered. As my eyes closed for what I thought would be the last time, I can honestly say I finally felt at peace."

A sad disappointment wears his face, but quickly snaps out of it, "but alas, I woke up under those dazzling lights, and for a split-second thought I'd gone to heaven. People like me don't go to heaven though; instead, I was given another roll of the dice. I may look the same, but I awoke a different person. The aches in my bones vanished, but the pains of my past had not. I woke up angry, and that anger manifested into the need for retribution. I hurt people. I wanted them to feel just an ounce of the pain that had tortured me for years. I realised that with each person I killed, a bit of the pain would drain away – so I suppose you could say I got a little addicted to the feeling."

"To begin with I was quite calculated about it, I'd plan weeks in advance what I would do and who I would to it to, but after a couple of years I became overconfident, a bit sloppy. By this point the good doctor had been stabbed to death and his two lovers took over Raptis' work - creating a family of metal framed humans. After Layla killed him, her mind was free from his constrained programmed love, but she was overwhelmed by what she had done, burdened with remorse and regret; so once they got a whiff of what I had been doing they formed a coup behind my back. Surprisingly to me though, I was not the only member of our family to go rogue."

"Apparently, we were wasteful of the natural resources, butchering and slicing the skin of our victims so deeply that no amount of stitching could put that puzzle back together. So, they decided that we should be locked away whilst they paved the way for our kind in this brand new world."

"It is a strange thing, walking around in a world that is not yours; the loneliness is overbearing. Although we look and act like humans, we could never blend in or find our place. And do you know why that is? Because we are so much more. We can outdo you at every single level. We are not just a machine, we're hybrid ingenuity; the frame and strength of the hardest metal with the lifeblood and emotion of a person. For years we lived among you, and it was fucking hard. My whole way of thinking changed when I was reborn, it was my mind and my thoughts but with the dials turned all the way up."

"We all have these processor chips," he says, tapping his right ring finger to the back of his head, "and it makes your mind race. You see, you lot didn't even realise that you were enslaved and living like mindless zombies, being force-fed what you should think and feel. A complete waste of life. And it wasn't just me who felt this way. Whilst I was locked away with my likeminded friends, Layla and the rest of our family came up with a plan; the plan that you are living in now."

"The aspiration to grow in numbers and the growing hatred of humanity's brainwashed idea of freedom forced our hand. You mindless fucks let yourselves be blindly suppressed by your so-called leaders, who used the term 'society' to trap and subdue you into an invisible servitude that none of you would question. All we did was replace your subjugation with a different kind." Nonchalantly he shrugs, as if what he is saying is the most natural thing in the world.

"So, you decided to create this prison?" I'm flabbergasted.

"For centuries humans have had the chance to lead a meaningful life, and for millennia you have time and again fucked it up. The demise of human beings as we know it is well overdue – we are using you, unlike what you did to us, for a higher purpose."

"You are using us as a harvest."

"Finally, you have managed to see the bigger picture," he shouts. "We don't only use you for your skin, but you are also an incredible source of entertainment. Watching you survive through any means necessary: murder, assault, theft, many a naughty thing to keep us amused. My favourite has to be the cage though; like gladiators fighting to the death!" He swings his arms around excitedly, hooking and undercutting the air. "It was my idea to add the sweetener of the supply package to the winner," he chimes. "We had to encourage people into it somehow, and it wasn't too difficult considering the majority of you are malnourished and desperate. Not you though eh, Arty, the cage suited you just fine. You're a fan favourite over there; a bit of a badass."

"What are you then, McKay? A farmer of bodies?"

"Not just me. Like I said before, it wasn't just me who wreaked havoc on the other side of that wall." He turns and gestures to Rue. "She was just as bad, if not more so ruthless than I was. Can you take a guess at who our third musketeer might be?" Mockingly, he begins to walk in circles, his upper body bobbing up and down as he hobbles about, exaggerating the stretched-out leg dragging behind him. "Hazard a guess?" He laughs. "Although I think it's pretty obvious after my impeccable impersonation."

"What you're saying doesn't make sense. Why the fuck does he walk around like that? You said that when you changed, all of your physical pains from before disappeared, yet here he is hobbling around like a man twice his age? Another fucking ploy no doubt to make us pity the pathetic worm." Everything is all just an act to him; him being the star of the show whilst the rest of us lesser beings live in his shadow and ride on his coattails.

"Aye, it's true that I did say that to you, and in the majority of cases that's how it is," McKay's face takes a dour turn, as if remembering something that he would rather keep buried deep. "But pain is something that manifests itself in ways that I don't think humans or machines will ever truly understand. I carried pain across with me to my new self; sure it was all up here," he says, tapping the side of his temple, "But it was pain nonetheless. None of us will ever know for sure why Charlie's physical ailments passed over with him, but I think most of us could take an educated guess."

Deep in thought, he contemplates, "His injury fed into who he was; who he ended up being. He came to live with this injury that changed him and ultimately came a part of his physical and mental make-up. That leg of his must have become so ingrained in his sense of self that it was almost wired up to his brain. Like I said, I can't prove that theory with any type of science, but it's the only sense I can make out of it."

"So you're basically saying that you think it's all in his head?" I said. His long winded explanation completely unnecessary.

"It could well possibly be, Arthur. One thing that I can say with one hundred percent certainty is that our metal frames do not have nerves running through them. So, in my eyes, yeah it has to be all in his head."

"So even though he isn't in any actual physical pain, he can still feel it as if it exists."

"I believe that phenomenon is call psychogenic pain" Rue throws in. "Like Dallin said, his leg in a sense defined him; perhaps he never wanted that pain to disappear."

"Anway, I think that we've answered your question, Arthur." McKay seems to have become tired of talking about Charlie. The limelight staying on his rival a tad too long for his liking. But yeah, I suppose he has answered my question. Whatever happened to Charlie must have traumatised him, the fact that he couldn't let that aspect of his previous life go shows that whatever those scars are, they run deep into his fractured mind.

Well, that explains the lack of regard Charlie has for human life. After all, the only thing that matters to Charlie Dalton, is Charlie Dalton. "So, the three of you were sent here together to oversee whatever the hell this shit is," I say as my arms motion to the prison outside of the cage we are standing in. Cutting in McKay's verbosity, Rue takes a step forward, giving herself the floor. McKay instantly shuts his mouth as her side-eye gives the impression that he has said way too much already.

"You are correct," Rue affirms. "We were sent here to govern together, however the three of us could never agree on anything. Charlie became too difficult to manage, let alone work alongside, so we unanimously decided to slice The Zone up, giving us all our own fair share of the land and the ability to run things the way that we see fit."

"Well, I wouldn't say that your plan worked out very well," I retort.

Rue's gleaming teeth break through her plumped up lips. "Well surely that depends on what the end goal is, doesn't it?"

"And the end goal is what exactly?" I press. "Apart from skinning people of course," I add flippantly. Unphased by my intentional insolence her smile remains, even though her lips retract a little.

"Simply that no one survives past a certain point. Unlike the rest of them, you are doing exceptionally well. Not many people get to your age unless you are part of one of our

144

inner circles. Our brethren don't want the thin and delicate skin of a wrinkled geriatric, they want the bountiful beauty of youth." Rue looks down at her hands, taking in her unblemished, sienna skin.

Chipping in, McKay adds, "That's why we limit the food and water and get you poor souls addicted to an abundance of moorish narcotics. Some of you don't even need that though, a lot of you top yourselves and do the work for us."

"Anyway," Rue rallies her point. "Charlie's departure and the dividing of The Zone, the creation of the three factions, made our jobs to procure bodies easier in a sense. Through loyalty, enemies are grown; Charlie's people would kill my people, my people would kill his, etcetera etcetera. But of course we can't just have everybody running around murdering and maiming each other, we need some people to live that little bit longer in order for them to breed. That's why we made Central a no man's land, a relatively safe place where families can grow. Generally, we find that it is people who have lost their way, lost their humanity, that end up working for one of our factions; the deviant and the easily manipulated. No offence."

"Recently, however, we feel that Charlie has become a little too big for his boots. He puts himself on a pedestal akin to a god," she says. I can't disagree with that statement. "He has a delusion of grandeur that he thinks makes him untouchable. Pressure was being put on us from the other side of the wall, skin and blood was starting to dry up, so me and Dallin here decided to kill two birds with one stone – deliver the bodies that they wanted and take Charlie down a peg or two."

"I do have to admit though," she continues, "we underestimated Charlie and his pseudo detective skills – we're still not sure how he managed to find out that we were behind the attack."

Should I tell them Charlie's little secret; I haven't got anything to lose.

"He uses drones." I say plainly, deliberately throwing a little bit more shit into the mix.

"Drones?" Rue and McKay say in unison.

"Yep, drones." I choose to play dumb, nothing wrong in stringing it out to try and help put an imbalance in the powers that be.

"And how do you know that?" Rue inquires, her intonation untrusting.

"He told me, and I've witnessed it myself - he uses them as scouts, hiding in plain sight amongst the other drones."

"It's true," Moose chips in.

"Stay out of this! I don't need your input," I clap back, scorning him further with my loaded eyes, causing the big man to shrink back. "It's quite ingenious, really," I say, turning my attention back to the growingly concerned duo. "It's just unfortunate for you two that there are sets of eyes in the sky that's main focus is you. That's how he knows about this guy." We all look down to the body that lays between us.

"You've got to give it to him, he is a smart bastard. A smart, crafty bastard," McKay comments. Ignoring him, Rue stares straight through me, her face frozen in calculation.

"That's good to know." Her eyes break from the vacant gaze, slowly sweeping the area for Charlie's metal birds.

"He's pretty good at keeping it on the down low – I mean, you've never been aware of it before, and I'm sure he would like to continue to keep it that way," I add brashly. Her growing paranoia almost radiates off of her, the tenseness of her body exposing her vulnerability in rigidness.

Sensing her concern, McKay also changes, his Irish charm taking only seconds to dissipate and become obsolete. His melodic, swaying notes spike, jarring as the cracks in his cool composure rise to the superficial surface. "I think we've heard enough from you. But we do appreciate the heads up on Charlie. We'll call it your parting gift, shall we."

"What do you mean?"

McKay laughs. "You didn't honestly think that we would pour all our secrets out to you, so that you could run off and form some kind of revolution. Unfortunately for you two, the buck stops here."

"We won't do that!" Moose grows pale at the realisation. "I've done everything that you asked of me. You can trust me." A sad desperation clings to his words.

"Aye, you did. It was fun while it lasted, but it's not my fault that your stupidity got the best of you, big boy. To me, you are just as small and insignificant as the rest of them." I look at Moose's reaction to McKay's words, his stature buckled under the weight of his own naivety, dwarfed by his unpardonable, puppeted actions. "I'm sorry that it has to end like this, Arty, I really am. You are one of the only people who hasn't lost themselves in this godforsaken place, and I respect that. Sadly though, this will be the last time we see you alive. I'm not going to do the deed myself, but I would suggest that you use this time to run, because they are going to hunt you down." McKay looks at me in all sincerity, his words for the first time believable. "And a word from the wise, Arty. I wouldn't try to help this one," he points to Moose. "He's dead weight."

How the hell did I manage to get myself into this mess. This is why everyone should be for themselves. I have always tried to do the decent thing and look where it has got me.

"If you're not going to run, Arthur, I would find somewhere very good to hide before all manner of hell fire rains down on you. Or you could, of course, just accept your fate. It is inevitable after all." The Irishman looks at me with pitying eyes.

McKay is right. I do only have two options; one easy and one hard. But I haven't made it this far in the game to fall on my own sword. No fucking way. Saving my breath for what's yet to come, I part from the overlords without another word, turning my back on what is now the least of my worries.

As my directionless steps lead me down the hallowed steel stairs of the cage, McKay mumbles to his female counterpart, "Such a waste; I hope they don't make too much of a mess out of him."

CHAPTER 19

Where the hell do I go from here? Numerous harsh and discordant voices bawl in my mind, all telling me different things, the clashing cacophony causing confusion when I all need is clarity. Soon I will have all manner of shit breathing down my neck. With the three god complex sociopaths and their kin of human skinned androids being in the forefront of my mind, the gravelly voice calling behind me really isn't what I need right now.

"Banner!" Moose huffs, his breath ragged as he finally catches up to me. "We've got to stick together if we want to get out of this alive." He has been following me since I left the cage.

"There is no 'we', Moose. Everything that you have done up until this point has been for your own gain, no matter what the cost. How do I know you won't fuck me over like you did the rest of them, huh? There's no way I could ever bring myself to trust you." I can barely look at him, my accusation is full of anger, my words full of resentment.

"Don't preach the fucking gospel, Banner. You're no saint either," he growls.

"Turning this on me now are you, you piece of shit. I'm not proud of how I've lived my life, but I always followed a code. The only people I have ever killed knew what they were signing up for as soon as they set foot in that cage." Not that it makes me feel any better about it – I live with the pain that I had to inflict on them every single day.

"You can put whatever righteous spin you want on it to make you feel better, but at the end of the day we both do what we have to in order to survive. My collateral damage is just on a bigger scale than yours. Either way the outcome of what we both do is the same."

The truth of his words hurt. "We are not the same."

"I never said we were, but at the moment we are in the same situation together, whether you like it or not. And I don't know about you, but I didn't do all that horrendous shit for nothing, just to now take it on the chin and die."

I look at his infuriated puffy red face as he continues to pant like a dog, trying to catch his breath. I don't want to admit it, but deep down I know he is right in everything he has said. We have just found out that we are here for the sole purpose of death – contained and watched like a test tube experiment on steroids, just waiting for the end so they can carve us up and drain us of everything that makes us human.

We are not even worthy of the term, human, anymore. We are now the sub-human. Burrowed so far under that it's hard to remember the light that we once had in us. Debased and depraved of everything we should have treasured but took for granted. We were easy pickings, and they were just biding their time.

"Banner!" Moose shouts, bringing me back to the present. "I'm going to put it bluntly. We are going to die whether we like it or not. We can stand around and wait for it to happen, or we can die trying to get to whatever they have hidden behind that wall".

Unknowingly to Moose, I had made up my mind before this conversation. "I'm in."

"Thank fuck for that!" Moose bellows with relief.

***

We stay in the shadows of the darkness as we head back to The South, creeping between buildings like a stray without a home. However, that is exactly where we are heading. Home. It's risky, I know, and a very stupid idea, but we are hoping that because it is such a dumb move, it just might work in our favour. It is unpredictably predictable, so we hope. No one in their right mind would go back to the place where everyone knows you live. That's why it makes perfect sense to go back. Hopefully it will bide us some time to suss out what we are going to do next.

The darkness fades to dawn as we turn onto our street, the first light beckoning us to hurry into the cover of The Lofts. It's eerie, this time of day. Most people in The Zone are nocturnal animals, going about their shady business under the cover of night. The only people around this time of day are the ones who weren't able to make it back home, instead opting for the comfort of the concrete curb and half-dead shrubbery.

The light that is breaking through this sunrise is very different to the hopeless days of before; beams of possibility clear away the haze of grey that has hung over me for years. I will cling onto this feeling, a feeling that I never thought I would feel again. That small semblance of hope. I grant you that it is a very small feeling, but it is one that has meaning. Something that I have never had here.

I look at the man walking beside me, bathed in the waves of the new day. He's a monster, no doubt about it, but the long walk through the silent night has given me time for reflection. His face, illuminated in the light, looks forlorn, his eyes watering as he squints through the rays shining over the apartment building. He wants to be seen as unemotional, devoid of anything other than himself. We are similar in that way.

The Zone took away our choices and left us with very few to choose from. The bitter truth is the majority of us have become monsters. When you are forced to make a decision, standing at the fork in the road, knowing that whatever turn you choose will lead you down an equally bad path, you, at that moment in time, have to decide to stop caring altogether, to let that part of you slip away.

I don't think you can ever truly stop though. The invisible weight of every choice stacks on your shoulders. Today, Moose has let his façade slide, the ghosts of his actions coming back to haunt him. It's funny what facing impending death does to you.

We walk through the entrance of the building, its glossy paint and doors exudes luxury to those who are shallow enough to believe it, whereas I have never felt so uncomfortable in my life. The silk paint cannot hide the imperfections of the people who live here. On the exterior it would seem that the minions of Charlie have it all, but what is on the inside can't just be glossed over. They are mindless puppets attached to Charlie's contrived strings, twisting and turning in whatever way he deems fit. No questions asked. All the evil they commit just to live in the upper echelons of this whitewashed box.

I see my mirror image in the reflective paint of my front door as I slowly turn the key. I look fucking awful – I swear I've aged more in this last couple of days than I have in my entire time spent in The Zone. Moose stands closely behind me, his head constantly turning to make sure that we remain unseen.

The door opens into the darkened corridor, the light of the day not yet strong enough to reach this corner part of the apartment. Closing the door, Moose's heavy handedness wakes the girl who I have completely forgotten about.

"Who's there?" She calls out shakily whilst catapulting herself off the sofa. When I turn the corner, I can see that her stance is defensive.

"Hey, it's me," I say, holding my hands out like some kind of negotiator. "Is everything okay?" Her face is telling me that everything is far from it.

"You told me that I would be safe here!" She chokes. "All night there has been people banging on the door, looking for you. Drones have been flying past the window every hour!" Her voice is hoarse from her crying shouts.

"I'm sorry that you've had to deal with this shit. You've been through enough already." I truly am sorry for dragging her into this mess.

"They only stopped knocking about an hour ago." Jess whimpers, the dark rings around her eyes showing her distress.

"What did you say to them when you answered the door?" I ask, trying not to be too pushy considering the state that she is in.

Exasperated, she said, "The truth. That I don't know you and that I didn't know where you were."

"Thanks, I appreciate it," I say, letting out a deep breath, one that I felt I have hung on to for hours.

"Like I said, I only told them the truth…" Jess retorts somewhat childishly. "So," she says after a few mere seconds, "when are you going to tell me what you have done then to get all this unwanted attention?"

CHAPTER 20

We told her everything. She sat there absorbing every word like a sponge.

"Count me in!" she shouts excitedly.

"We don't even know what we are doing yet." I can't help but let out a little chuckle at her eagerness, but quickly regain the seriousness of our predicament and follow through with, "I really don't think you should be getting involved in all this."

"What the hell is that supposed to mean?" She leans back abruptly, crossing her arms over her chest, shielding herself from whatever I said wrong.

"It's not meant to mean anything. I just don't think you should blindly volunteer for something you know nothing about, let alone sign up for something that is probably going to get you killed." I can't be responsible for another innocent death, especially a young girl. I will need to keep my focus going into this and I can't be worried about her the whole time. She'll just be an unwanted distraction.

"Oh, come on!" she sniggers, "sounds like an excuse to me. You honestly think I'm scared of dying? You don't know half the shit I've had to do." Actually, I do have an idea. "Or is there another reason, huh? Is it because I don't have a dick swinging between my legs?"

"She's got you there, Banner!" Moose quietly slaps my back as he kneels forward in hushed laughter.

"Hey, hold on a second…" Just as I'm about to fire back, hammering raps interrupt me. The bangs on the door making us all freeze. The three of us turn towards it in startled silence. We have nowhere to run.

"What are we going to do?" mouths Moose.

Jess ushers us over to the sofa, pushing us down so we are leaning against it on the floor. She stands and looks at us, pressing her finger to her lips as a form of instruction. Briefly she closes her eyes and visually composes herself; her tightened shoulders relax as we sit there watching, not knowing what she is going to do.

Without any warning, she opens her eyes and starts to head down the hallway toward the persistent banging. The pads of her sticky feet disappearing down the corridor until the spring of the latch echoes loudly back up. She's going to rat us out; the whole thing is going to be over before it even started. The door creaks as she opens it.

"Hey, you nearly hit me in the face with that stick!" her ballsy greeting is not that of a scared girl.

"My dear Jessica," I'd recognise that voice anywhere. "What an earth are you doing in an outlaw's apartment?"

Charlie's greasy smooth voice enquires, the rise in his intonation showing unexpected surprise.

"I could say the same for you. What has this outlaw done that is so bad to be graced with your presence?" Moose and I cannot see their exchange at the door, but you can hear the seduction in Jess' voice, husky and warm like bourbon. Predictably, Charlie laps it up, his visceral laughter momentarily turning his attention away from the reason why he is stood outside my door.

Although he has shown his intelligence, his mind is controlled by something else entirely. She knows what she is doing.

"You can have my presence anytime you want, darling Jessica. You know that." Even though I can't see him, I cannot help but imagine his dirty hands running down her bare arms, caressing her skin. "But tell me, what are you doing here?" Charlie insists, not yet fully under her allure.

"Some arsehole blew up my building, and the guy who lives here, Arthur I think, took pity on me and is letting me stay here for a while. I haven't seen him since that night." We did tell her everything – there was no point lying about the parts that we played, although I think Moose would probably have preferred we didn't.

"How very generous of Mr. Banner." His faux pleasantries can't hide the bitter taste in his mouth. "Can I ask why you did not come to see me? You know that I would look after you – I have always looked after you, have I not Jessica?"

"You know that I don't like to mix work and pleasure, Charlie, that's all it is." Her remarks seem to hurt him.

"Is that all I am to you, work?" His insecurities bring out the discontented green-eyed monster; his words laced with possessive suspicion.

"No Charlie, of course not." She quickly realises that she has to turn up the temperature to contain him. "You know what you mean to me, I just can't be around the rest of them leering at me all the time. I need my own space, and my only option for that right now happens to be here."

"Shh-shh-shh, don't get yourself all worked up, my dear. I will make sure I find you somewhere much more appropriate to live." he coos.

"I appreciate that, Charlie." Her honeyed voice has him back where she wants him. "So, you never told me why you are here. Not that I'm complaining," she lets out a flirtatious laugh. I'm really hoping that she's a bloody good actress and she is putting on a show.

"Unbeknownst to you, Jessica, you are staying in the apartment of a murderous traitor. He is the reason why you no longer have a home." Hold on one fucking second, why is he pinning this all on me? I look at the prick whose fault it is next to me. All he does is shrug. She knows the truth. "You never know," Charlie suggests, "he could have done it just to lure you here so he can have you all to himself." Only his disgusting mind would think that way – that's something straight out of his playbook.

A flashing glint of light moves across the bland white wall in front of me as a groaning buzz grows louder from outside. I peek over the back of the sofa, knowing full well what to expect. Charlie doesn't go anywhere without his pets;

wherever he goes, you can guarantee they are hovering not far behind.

"What's that sound?" I can hear Jess' body shuffle slightly as she likely turns toward the floor to ceiling windows at the back of the apartment.

"Oh, don't you mind that," Charlie says cheerfully. "I imagine it is just a drone doing its round." Yeah, your drone. "One would guess that they have probably been ramped up a few gears to try and find the fugitive as fast as possible – nothing to worry about, my dear… unless you are hiding something, that is." He tags his subtle accusation casually on the end, letting out a forced laugh. If Jess didn't already feel uncomfortable, I bet she is now.

But that's him, the real Charlie. Showing his true colours. "It wouldn't be the first time that a pretty girl like you has lied to me." The drone continues its sweep, scanning every inch of the apartment it can from the outside, as Charlie tries to press her.

"As I said before, Charlie, it's just me here. I haven't seen who you are looking for."

"I believe you, Jessica." As Charlie says this, the drone suddenly flies off, its inspection over. "I did not doubt you for a second." His threatening undertones have completely melted away. "As always, my dear, it has been a pleasure to be in your company, even if it is briefly and under such awful circumstances. However, I will now leave you in peace – but I'll be in touch very soon about a new home for you. Farewell, darling girl." He parts her with a kiss, the smack of his lips on her cheek travels down the long hall to where Moose and I still hide, crouched in front of the sofa.

The sound of the closing door breaks the kiss which hangs in the air. "I think I've brought us some time to work out what we are going to do," Jess says proudly as she reappears, leaning against the wall. She looks very relaxed for someone who just had to bullshit one of the most dangerous people in The Zone. "So, what's the plan?"

"Good question," Moose groans. For a man of very few words, you would expect the words that he does say to carry some meaning. I have found that this is often not the case with Moose. The majority of what he says is unhelpful and meaningless.

"Well, we know that the bodies are somehow delivered through the crematorium, so our best bet is to go there and find out how they get from there to the other side of the wall," I state matter-of-factly.

"Yeah, that's a great idea, Banner. You don't think that they'll be expecting us to turn up there." Moose's sarcasm stings more than it should.

I snap, "Unless you have a better plan to help us get out of this mess, that by the way, you created, I'd suggest that you keep your big mouth shut." He stares at me for an uncomfortable amount of time, his blank eyes stuck on my face. Unsurprisingly, he doesn't have an alternative.

"I agree with you, Arthur," Jess says. "Heading there seems to be our only option." Our? We never did finish our discussion on why it isn't a good idea for her to come with us. Then again, she did just save our skins – so far, she has proven herself a damn sight more useful than Moose ever has. "We shouldn't walk in there unarmed though," she continues. "As Moose said, we are probably going to bump into trouble down there." That's putting it very lightly. We'd be walking straight to our deaths without weapons.

"We need guns," Jess states plainly. "Do we have any lying around?"

I shake my head. I've never fired a gun in my life. The idea of using one fills me with absolute dread.

"I do," Moose smiles.

Of course he does. Using guns and causing pain makes Moose happy. As Charlie's right-hand man and most trusted confidant, Moose was likely given a selection of guns to carry out Charlie's dirty work - the luxuries you get given when you sell your soul to the devil.

"Well, we best go and get them then." I quip. Unfortunately, I don't think we have another option.

***

Before we head to Moose's, we empty the cupboards of any supplies we can carry. Unlike our adversaries, we need to drink and eat to stay alive.

When we arrive at Moose's, the front door to his apartment is pried open, the damage to the frame showing a forced entry. Moose hurries on in, making his way over to the chest at the back of his living area. He opens the lid but quickly slams it back shut

His deep throttled laughter throws both me and Jess off guard, as he declares, "They've taken the guns and the ammo."

Even though I'm confused by his reaction, I say, "I don't suppose Charlie wants you running around with his guns. I mean you've already screwed him over once and I doubt he's going to let you do it again."

His laughter turns husky as he tries to refrain it from getting any louder.

"Why the fuck are you laughing? This is far from funny!" Jess confronts the big man, shoving his arm in frustration.

He doesn't move an inch but continues his throaty chuckle, "You would think that these people would learn from their mistakes, wouldn't you? Like you said before, Banner, I've bested him once, so he thinks he can just come in and take my guns and all his problems will be solved."

Stepping past Jess, whose face is so full of anger that it is almost comical, Moose walks to the corner of the room. Bending down on one knee, he unsheathes the small blade attached to his belt and runs it down the edge of the carpet, angling the knife to help pries and lift it from the floor. In no time, he is tearing the whole thing up, exposing the wooden boards beneath.

"Fool me once, shame on you. Fool me twice, shame on me." He drags the carpet to the centre of the room as Jess and I watch. Looking at us both in amusement, he steps on a couple of uncovered planks, his huge weight causing the wood to creak loudly as his foot presses purposefully into it.

"I'm guessing that Charlie didn't quite manage to find all of your guns." My presumption makes Moose grin like a cheshire cat.

"Like I said, Banner, these people never learn." He crouches down and wedges the fingers of both of his hands between the thin cracks of the boards and begins to lift them up one by one. By the time he's finished, a square metre size hole gapes in the floors foundation. He reaches in and starts to pull out guns. Lots of guns.

"Just a few pieces I've collected over the years," Moose says as he lays them out on the floor, a display that an arms dealer would be proud of. "Take your pick." He nods to the array of handguns and rifles that line the floor.

"How the hell did you get your hands on all of these, Moose?" Jess asks in bewildered excitement, whilst grabbing hold of one of the rifles. It is so big in comparison to her body that she can barely hold onto it with both hands.

He replies, "My line of work often involved people pointing guns at me. Once I dealt with them, I'd take their guns for myself. Stops someone picking it up and using it against me in the future." So he does have a few braincells rattling about in that empty head of his. "Come on, Banner, don't look at me like that. You know, as well as I do, that it's kill or be killed in this place. Come on, tuck this into your waistband." Moose finishes loading the gun, pushing the last bullet into the magazine, clicking the full mag into place with a firm whack of his palm.

He passes the Glock to me. I'm hesitant.

"Now is the time to trust me, Banner." Moose looks at me in all seriousness. "All three of us have to look out for each other if we're all going to survive what's coming our way."

Jess nods in agreement, her chosen weapon, the rifle, now strapped to her back.

Trusting him is easier said than done. "If I do anything," Moose says, "you can just shoot me."

Don't tempt me. He's looking up at me grinning, his fingers wrapped around the barrel as he offers me the handle. I'll play along.

I reach out and grab the grip.

"Let's get this show on the road."

CHAPTER 21

Thankfully The Zone is full of nocturnal animals, spending the daylight hours sleeping off the reckless antics of the night before. By the time we get back to Central, the darkness will be drawing in and the sleeping rats will begin to stir, scurrying out to find their next fix to heal their pounding heads and crippling nausea. Hair of the dog is always the chosen medicine in The Zone.

Although the haze of the day keeps the vampires at bay, we still decide to take the backstreets wherever possible. The main reason for this isn't the people, but the drones. Usually, you can hear them before you see them, their dull whirs giving a fraction of a time to react and hide. So far, the back alleys and streets have provided enough cover that we have not yet been noticed.

The damp brick walls rise above us just enough to help block out any natural light, morphing us into the constant shadows. Unless a drone flew down here, there is no way they would be able to see us from above.

"Are we heading straight to the crematorium? Storm the joint, all guns blazing!" Moose calls back to me, turning his head so that his voice travels behind him.

He's in front, the alley too narrow for us to walk in any way other than single file. Even with Jess between the middle of us, I can see his hands move up and down, his fingers pointed out as if resembling a gun in each hand. The prospect of killing again seems to make him excited.

"They'll be expecting us to walk straight in there – they would have planned for that." I reply, before his trigger happy fingers get us into even more trouble. "We need to hold fire for just a little bit to make them question what we are up to. And let's be honest, we could use the time to come up with a decent plan ourselves. Running in there would be suicide."

"So, we're walking into the viper's nest with no plan and nowhere to go. I think I prefer Moose's idea, and that's saying something." Jess' voice sounds tired and irritable.

"Who said that I don't have a plan?" It's really not a very good one, but it seems to be the only sensible one going at the moment. "My old apartment block has a basement. No one ever goes down there; the damp and the rat infestation makes sure of that."

"You want us to hole up with a bunch of rats, Banner…you're kidding me, right? I fucking hate rats." moans Moose.

"That surprises me, Moose. I thought you'd fit right in." I shamelessly retort.

"What the hell are you trying to say, huh?!" He stops dead in his tracks and spins around, his intonation rising as Jess walks straight into him.

"Sorry Moose, are you having trouble working it out for yourself?" I can't help myself.

He lunges toward me, but Jess, sandwiched between us, stretches out her arms and slaps her palms to his chest. "You two need to grow the fuck up, and you need to do it quickly before one of you idiots gets us killed." The fierceness of her voice shows that she is not messing around.

"It's not my fault he can't take a joke." My play on innocence doesn't wash.

"You knew exactly what you were trying to do," she snaps. She barges past Moose, her surprising force knocking the big man to the side, and takes the lead. We look embarrassingly at each other and begin to trail behind her slowly. Being schooled by a young woman who has been through as much as Jess has puts things into perspective. I can't allow myself to jeopardise my only chance of getting out of here.

As we cross the border into Central, I swap positions with Jess, leading us down the familiar rat run of dingy streets, doing my best to detour us away from any unwanted attention. As we make our way to the main square however, things just don't feel right. It's too quiet. Eerily quiet. The usual buzz of the market, the hustle and bustle, has been overcome with a stillness.

The normal crowds that teem across have dispersed and peppered out. Seeing The Zone's melting pot emptied of its compounds leaves me with an unshakable and undeniable sense of unease. It hangs in the air like a thick smog, visible for everyone to see.

"Where is everybody?" Jess whispers, though there is no one around to hear us. "I thought this place would be packed by now."

"It normally is. Something isn't right." I begin to feel my pulse quicken.

"We probably shouldn't be hanging around then, Banner." Moose adds, catching onto my nervousness. "Let's get out of here."

By the time we get through the maze of Central's confusing backstreets, the day's last light peeks reservedly above the rooftops, the redness streaked across the sky a subtle warning of the dangers that lie ahead. At the end of the labyrinth, we reach our destination. We take our approach slowly, tentatively looking out for any signs of movement. There are none.

As we close in on the open doorway of my old apartment building, shell casings litter the ground and trail into the block like unswept crumbs. I look up and down the deserted street, spotting more of the casings interspersed outside of every building.

My stomach twists as I grow hot, my feet faltering beneath me, unable to hold the weight of what has happened here.

"They were here looking for me." I turn to the ashen faces staring at me. "They've killed them all." I fall to my knees as my stomach clenches in pain. Although empty, the contents rush out, burning. I heave on all fours, the brown bile gushing out beneath me, forming a puddle of desperation and guilt.

I want the ground to swallow me up and send me down to where I belong. To burn for eternity for what I have done. "They're all dead because of me!" my choking wail barely understandable.

"You are not to blame for this, Banner." I feel Moose's large hand rest on my back as the other tucks gently under my armpit, pulling me up to stand. Now on two feet, he turns me to face him, his hands tightly gripping my shoulders as his fingers dig in, forcing me to remain upright. "Listen to me, Arty," my blurting cries are uncontrollable. "Banner! You need to snap out of this now!" Moose shouts.

"Give him a minute! He needs to let this out, to come to terms with what has happened," Jess fires at Moose.

"We don't have the time to let it sink in. He hasn't even seen what the damage is inside yet. You need to let all of this out now because once we're inside you are going to need to keep your emotions in check. You need to harness the anger, use that pain to help us get to the end of this. Whatever we are going to be faced with in there, Banner, don't let it be in vain."

Once again, he's right. Moose continues to support me as I regain some feeling in my jellied legs. I force deep breaths, steadying the rapid beats in my chest, holding back the screaming hurt that wants to stream waterfalls down my cheeks. I press my shaking hands to my eyes, wiping away the watery pools, drying every trace of tears on my wet through sleeve.

"Are you ready?" Moose asks after allowing me to recover as best I can. I will never be ready for what, or rather who, I know is waiting for me in there. I can only hope that it was quick. Painless. I nod in response to Moose's question, not yet able to speak.

"We'll be right here with you, man." Moose says as he makes his way toward the apartment, leading us inside with his gun pointing into the unknown.

Inside, the flickering lamps offer no light, leaving the building in a perpetual state of darkness. I crouch down and slide the heavy backpack down my arm, slowly unzipping the bag to try and not disturb the unyielding quiet. Rummaging through, my hand searches for the smooth, cylindrical plastic, pushing to the side anything that doesn't match that description. Arm deep in the bag, my hand reaches for the bottom, where my fingers finally meet and clasp around our weapon against the dark.

"Moose. Torch." I whisper loudly, tossing the light over to him. I had the sense to turn it on before throwing it, otherwise I may have accidentally thrown it at his face. I pull out the spare and light it up, the bright white circle forming a ring of protection as I point it at the floor. "Stick with me," I say to Jess, motioning her toward me. "It's best we stay together."

I can see the faded outline of Moose's flashlight up ahead, the jerky movements scanning the room. He's been back there for quite a while.

"Do you want the bad news, or the even badder news?" Moose gruffs, shining his torch directly in our eyes.

"Don't fuck about, Moose. Just tell us what's back there." I bark impatiently, shielding my eyes with my forearm to block out the blinding light.

"Sorry, my bad," he grumbles, quickly lowering the torch. It takes a few seconds for my eyes to stop pulsating different colours and readjust to the dark room. "There are eight bodies back there, thrown on top of each other in a pile. They've been so shot to shit that there's no chance anyone would be able to recognise them."

All Jess and I do is stay quiet; there is nothing we can say. "It's already a fucking massacre and we've only looked in one room. I had a peek out the door round back and there's a wagon out there. Ready to cart them off to the crematorium, I'm guessing. It had a canvas thrown over it so I couldn't tell if there were any more bodies on there or not, but I did spot a couple of drones guarding it."

Every single one of those lives are on us. On me. I need to find her, I need to see what I have done.

"They're probably waiting until morning to move them to the waiting room. We can't be here when they come back." Jess sounds more panicked by the second.

A truly terrible idea pops into my head. It's awful in terms of risk and in terms of what we are going to have to do. "Staying here until they collect the bodies is our best chance of getting into the crematorium," I begin to explain, until both Jess and Moose, in unison, cut me off with,

"How did you work that one out?!"

"Listen, we have to take advantage of this situation, okay." I reply, as they both stare at me dumbfounded. "They

171

think that everyone here is dead; they need to think that about us as well."

"And how the hell are we going to do that, Banner?" Moose questions, gruffly.

Hoping that I don't have to spell it out to him, I say, "You said that the bodies in there were unrecognisable, right?"

Moose answers, "Yeah…" drawing out the vowels.

"And we don't want to be recognised, do we…"

Suddenly, Moose clocks on, his eyes rounding as he looks at me with a mixture of disgust and acceptance. "It might just work, you know."

"Does one of you want to fill me in on what you're going on about?" Jess' temper flares. "This isn't the time to be cryptic. Just speak plainly so we can all understand what is going on."

"Fine, come back here." Knowing that the drones are outside, I point my torch to the floor as I silently march to the back room, not showing the fear of what I knew the torchlight's cold beam would reveal.

Trails of blood decorate the floor, the drag marks all leading to the pile of stacked bodies in front of me, their arms and legs locked up in a tangled mess. Jess does not automatically follow, she lingers back. You can see that she is readying herself for what she is about to see.

Whilst she holds back, I inspect the bodies, looking for any sign that one of these poor souls is Mrs. Acker. I lift the stiffened limbs of those on top to try and see who rests underneath. The blood covering them all is completely dry, each of their hair discoloured and matted to a single shade of red. Their clothing is crispy from the liquid that pooled out of their terminally deep wounds. I shine my torch on their pained faces, their terror frozen by the rigor mortis that is beginning to set in.

My empty stomach churns, tightening at the sight of them. Not all of them received a quick death. Many of their arms and legs are contorted; snapped like chicken wings as they are ripped from the joint. That undoubtedly happened when they were alive. Fingers have been severed from the broken hands, bashed and mangled to the point that the cut digits would add, only slightly, to the already unbearable pain. This is an act of torture.

But the truth is I barely knew these people. Even in passing I wouldn't say hello. Unfortunately for them, that meant they had no information to give to their torturers. But even if they did, I doubt the overall outcome would have been any different. I stand up and step back, looking back at Jess who still remains unmoved. I'm not going to force her to look at this.

Slowly, I turn and walk toward her, leaving the stack of bodies behind me to rest. Candidly, I stand inches from her; her eyes averted so she does not have to look me in the eye. I know why she won't look at me. She is afraid of the pictures her eyes will paint; the colours of truth unable to lie. She is scared.

"Listen to me, Jess," I place both of my hands on her delicate shoulders, encouraging her to look at me, to trust me. "I know how frightening this must be for you. I'm scared too. But right now, you have to make a choice." She looks up at me from the ground, the glossy wetness of her eyes catching in the torch's light. "You can walk out of that door and get away from all of this," I nod toward the entryway where Moose is now standing. "No one knows that you have anything to do with this. You can go back and live your life, forget about it all," my hands momentarily leave her shoulders, gesturing to the death and destruction around us.

"Or," my hands take their place back on her shoulders, gently squeezing them to help her realise the reality that we are in, "you need to pull yourself together, because this is only the beginning, and I can guarantee you that the worst is yet to come."

I know I sound like a complete hypocrite, only moments ago I was blubbering like a little boy, puking on my hands and knees like a retching cat. The difference is with me, once I've got that hairball out, it's out. I move on and leave whatever it is in the past, dropping all the attached emotions as a way to survive. If you can't do that then you'll eventually be eaten alive. The problem is I'm not sure Jess is capable of doing that. "We need to know now, before you get in so deep that there is no chance of turning back." I try to say the words as softly as I can.

"I made up my mind the minute I left the apartment – I've already told you that life isn't worth living the way it is now. If that means I have to sacrifice myself to try and make it better, then that is what I'm going to do." Jess looks and speaks tough, but her actions say different.

Moose wades on over, kicking the hollow shell casings across the room with his giant feet. "You can't do what you just did if you want to come with us. You can't even bring yourself to look at those bodies in there; you can't just freeze and ignore what is happening. What are you going to do if one of us gets killed trying to save your scrawny ass, huh?"

Jess doesn't reply, her eyes once again focused on the floor.

"I say leave her," Moose lets out a primal snort as he walks away, positioning himself again by the front door.

"He's not wrong, you know," I say in an almost whisper, so only she can hear me.

She cups her hands over her face; when she finally brings them down, her eyes are no longer shiny, instead they are set like stone. Cold and hard. "I promise you, it won't happen again." As the words leave her mouth, I know that I can believe her.

"Are you sure?" Moose's hand pulls at the handle of the front door, ungraciously throwing it wide open. "This is your last chance."

Her hardened eyes void of emotion, bore into mine as she utters. "I'm staying." I nod in acceptance. Only time will tell if this is the right decision.

"Well then," Moose swings the door shut. "How're we going to make ourselves look like one of those poor dead bastards?"

CHAPTER 22

L ayers of congealed blood cover the bodies head to toe, their clothing dyed, saturated in red. Every inch of their skin painted with their life.

"They're all dried up, Banner." Moose states whilst looking through the bodies. "Doesn't look like we're going to be using their blood."

Is that seriously what he thought my plan was? To defile these poor people even further? "We were never going to do that," I say, disgusted. "We are going to have to use our own," I say indignantly.

Quickly Moose bites back, "Yeah that's a great idea – you stab me and I'll stab you, and we'll just let ourselves bleed to death. Then we'll definitely have no problem getting in to where we're going."

I swear to God that this man doesn't think anything through, instead he lets his idiotic half thought out ideas dribble out from his mouth.

"Before you start jumping in, why don't you let me finish what I was going to say." I take a minute before continuing, letting the building heat under my skin cool down to a slight flush. "As I was saying," I'm pretty sure I hear a snigger from under Moose's breath – he doesn't like being put back in his box. "There are parts on our body where a surface wound will pour out a lot of blood. All we need to do is nick these areas – we'll barely feel a thing."

"What areas?" Jess asks calmly.

"Scalp, neck, thigh; places that have lots of small veins running through." By the look on both Moose and Jess' face, neither seem too keen. "If I didn't think this was our only viable option, trust me, I wouldn't be suggesting it."

Without any further hesitation, Jess says, "Okay". Moose takes a little longer, but eventually says the same.

I've cut my head so many times that I've lost count; the damage always looks far worse than it actually is. In the cage, people tend to aim their attacks at the head, stunning or knocking out their opponent so they can quickly finish them off. My head must be made of rock though because no one has managed to knock me out cold – there were definitely times when things got a little hairy, but I always somehow recovered.

Hidden under my hairline there must be at least a dozen scars, the pinkish shine of the discoloured skin a reminder of each fight, and how I need to better guard my head. The number of times I've cleaned myself up from a fight, blinded by the floods of blood gushing from my head, I was always surprised to find the smallest cut.

"Moose, we're going to need to use your knife," I say, pointing to his belt.

"You want to use this?" He says, taken aback "This thing is sharp, Banner."

"That is precisely the reason why I want to use it, the sharper the better." We do have other knives packed in the backpack, but I know that his is by far the sharpest. One thing that Moose does well is look after his weapons. "It will hurt us more if we use a blunt knife. We would have to apply more pressure on our skin for the blade to cut. With your one though, we will be able to control it much easier as it bites."

Sheepishly, he unsheathes his knife and passes it to me. "Who wants to go first then? I pretend to be serious, offering the blade out, waving it between them. "No takers?" I joke. Trying to take away Moose and Jess' uncertainty is harder than I initially thought it would be; their blank stares are starting to make me doubt myself and my plan.

"Don't worry," I attempt to reassure them. Saying 'don't worry' to two people who clearly are worried is an utterly stupid thing to say. Their unchanged expressions reaffirm that. "I'll go first." I take the hunters knife and bring it behind my left ear, gently pressing the sharp tip to the skin.

With little added pressure I feel it pierce, a little prick that soon opens up as I run the blade smoothly down, creating a shallow, but bloody, incision.

By the time the cut runs the length of my ear, the handle feels slippery. Sticky warmth builds around the area, trickling a steady stream down my neck. My free hand gravitates toward the flow, flattening against it. Hot red coats my hand when I lift it from the wound. Moose and Jess watch as I wipe my face with my hand, washing it in blood.

I feel the skin around my face begin to tighten as the thin layers quickly dry. I hurry to cover the rest of me, the stinging behind my ear an indication that the blood is starting to congeal around the cut. "How do I look?"

"I'd say it's an improvement from before." Looks like Moose it back to his own self. I was starting to miss his one-line ribbings.

I wipe my blood from the knife onto my thigh, the liquid iron helping to buffer its metallic shine back to a gleaming specimen. Offering Moose the handle, I hold the razor-edged steel between my stained reddish brown fingers, "Your turn."

***

By the time we are all finished, it looks like we had been a part of the slaughter. Draped in blood, we are unrecognisable – exactly what I had hoped. Even though it was a needed solution to our current situation, this plan of escape was a mere distraction from what I have been putting off since I stepped through the door.

"Let me know if you hear anyone coming." I say quietly. Looking up from their position on the floor, neither say anything, they just give me an acknowledging and sympathetic glance.

I find myself at the bottom of the stairs, staring up at the encompassing dark, unable to move my feet. I know she is up there; I can feel it.

Mrs. Acker hadn't been able to leave her apartment for years – when she was placed in The Zone her frailty sped up, whilst her faculties slowed down. It's morbid to think of how someone will pass, but I couldn't help thinking it all the time.

It got to a point where I would mentally prepare myself each morning for what I could possibly find. Would I find her peacefully asleep in her chair, or tucked up in bed having drifted off, away from this earth. Or would I find her on the floor, not able to lift herself from lack of strength, praying she has not hit her head from the fast descent. Many times I have found her in this position, unable to move, the shock of the fall pinning her to the floor.

Thankfully, each time this happened she only had minor injuries, although her almost translucent, wrinkled skin would blacken for weeks, sometimes months; her old body taking undue time to heal itself. It always managed to do it though, the dark bruising eventually fading back to her paling, pinkish skin. Sadly though, for Mrs. Acker, her body healed quicker than her mind. With each recognition of the little things she could no longer do, a little piece of her disappeared; the bright twinkle in her eye getting harder to spot. Life is exceptionally cruel.

My love for this woman pulls me up the stairs, my feet treading softly to avert the sound of creaking wood, as I make my ascent up the all too familiar staircase. The dead may lie downstairs, but their lives were taken up here – the chaos bled into the floor and sprayed on the walls. Evidence that they didn't go easy.

At the top of the stairs, the apartment doors along the corridor are wide open, having been infiltrated and turned upside down by murderous thugs. Thugs that were searching for me. I have no interest in seeing what is behind those doors, I already know that it will be something that I don't want to see.

Stealthily, I walk past the gaping doorways, listening out for any presence that may still be here. The only sound I can hear, however, is my ragged breath catching in the air. My lungs cannot hold onto it, the tightening of my chest squeezing out the pockets of breath, giving way to the anxiety that is filling them instead.

But she is the gravity that kept me grounded, pulling me back from the brink.

I force my lungs to fill with the burning air, my body doing its best to fight off my conscience. Every sinew and fiber of my being is pushing me back, deflecting as a way to avoid the pain that will break my heart for good.

My stretched-out shadow greets me at the dead end of the hall, my torch giving enough light to force me to look at myself. Confront myself. My silhouette stands tall between my old apartment door and Mrs. Acker's, both of which, like the rest, have been forced open.

My shadow self stands confident and unwavering, ready to walk straight into Mrs. Acker's apartment. But I hold him back.

I feel my grief fester, the sadness, and anger and guilt eating away until there is no man left to walk through that door and face up to what he has done. The shape of the person on the wall stares back at me; although faceless, the disgust is plain to see.

It disgusts me that I am still outside her door contemplating not going in there. It shouldn't be a question that requires an answer. It's obvious what I must do. But what is it that is stopping me from going in there? Again, the answer to that one is also obvious. My selfishness. Self-inflicted wounds are the hardest to heal, sometimes near impossible.

I know that her death is on my hands, I may not have been the one to commit the act, but I am the reason why the act was committed. I don't, and I will never, deny that. But looking at my old door, I can't help but think this should never have happened. The day Charlie broke in and asked me to work for him, that's what set this all in motion, that has led to those downstairs and Mrs. Acker becoming collateral damage.

I was swayed by material objects that I had lived years without, persuaded by a bigger place to live in, steered by the gains I could make solely for me. And look where it has got me, on the run and stood outside the door to the dead mother I never had. I have no one to blame but myself; opportunistic and self-serving. Putting myself first has hurt countless others, the least I could do is bear witness to what I have caused.

Without any more hesitation, I push Mrs. Acker's door open and step inside. I know when I lift my torch up from the ground, I will see her, the box flat leaving nowhere to hide. My trembling hand tries to resist bringing it up, but there is no going back now. Grasping the shaking wrist with my other hand, I pull it up so the light illuminates the entirety of the dark room. And there I see her.

Slumped in the armchair, her neck is tilted to the side so that her head rests on the cushioned arm. She looks asleep, at peace. The little furniture in the room has been left untouched, not a single thing out of place. I kneel in front of her and close my eyes, placing both my hand in hers. They are cold.

I stay with my eyes shut a while longer, wishing for her fingers to wrap around mine, for this whole nightmare to be just that. But they don't. She can't wake from this sleep. As I open my eyes, silent wetness runs down my cheeks. Through misty eyes I see the cause of her unawakenable slumber.

A small, crimson dent digs into her temple; a clean shot straight through. A kind death in comparison to the brutality shown downstairs. It seems that even the coldest and most callous of men can have a flicker of empathy.

Hopefully they found her in her chair like this, dreaming about her life, about her beloved husband who for years she has longed to join in ultimate paradise.

I can only hope that she was unaware of them entering, free from the fear and panic she would have otherwise faced. At least she is now finally freed from the suffering of the last few unkind years.

I lean up and place a parting kiss on her cheek and gently wipe away my tears that have fallen on her face.

"I am so sorry," I whisper solemnly. "You were too good for this world. I hope the next life cherishes you as this one should have." With a final squeeze of her hand, I turn and leave her to her God who has finally called her home. Closing the door behind me, I leave her to her eternal rest.

CHAPTER 23

D id you find her?" Jess asks softly.

When I first came back down the stairs neither her or Moose asked the question, instead they allowed me the silence to fully accept and grieve for my loss, in the safety of their company. I feel exhausted, the flux of my emotions leaving me shattered.

"She's gone." Is all I can muster, the details of her death seem unnecessary now.

"I'm really sorry, Arthur," she says in all earnest. Moose grunts awkwardly, not knowing what to say. Jess shuffles closer to place her hands on top of mine, her petite palms closing around them; the comfort of her touch much needed.

We all need sleep. Moose and Jess have given in to the tiredness, their weary bodies curled up on the floor like dogs. But I can't sleep. The noisiness of my thoughts crash together every time my eyes begin to droop, like one of those annoying jolly chimp toys with its torturous cymbal bashing. It doesn't matter anyway, one of us needs to act as lookout. Let them get their rest; after tonight, who knows when we will find the next opportunity to sleep.

We have to make sure that we are in position before morning breaks because, after then, it will be impossible to predict their arrival. All we know for sure is that they need to clean up the mess they left behind.

Quietly, I walk over to where Jess sleeps, trying not to startle her; I nudge her arm in a gentle attempt to stir her awake. Her sleep, obviously light, was easy to break – her consciousness not letting her go too deep, the precipice of danger keeping her on guard and alert. Murmuring softly, she rouses from her likely unrestful sleep. Unlike Moose, who is flat on his back like a slumbering bear, his growl like snores loud enough to wake the dead in the next room.

I cross to where he lay and dig the toe of my boot into his thigh, jabbing the steel toecap in hard. Nothing. It doesn't make me feel jealous at all, the fact that he can sleep so soundly when I am haunted my nightmares in the day, let alone at night. I pull my foot back and drive it in with more force; I'll make sure he feels it this time.

"Wake up!" I yell, as my foot makes contact with his leg.

Like something from an old horror movie, his upper body bolts upright, the surge of pain from metal on flesh a reactionary response. Far from happy, his eyes glower at me as his arms stick out defensively, fists closed.

"You need to work on your courtesy call, Banner! I thought I was being jumped!" he exploded.

"You think that they would stab you in the thigh while your vital organs are on show? Let's hope that those sorts of people are the ones coming after us, might increase our chances of seeing this through." I quip; some people deserve to be patronised. The shape of his stare grows rounder as his anger melts into something that looks a little less scary.

"Oh, fuck off, Banner." is the only reply he can come up with.

Laughing, I walk back over to Jess and sit down next to her, allowing Moose the time to gather his shit together.

"Did you manage to get some sleep?" Her sunken and bloodshot eyes answer my question for her.

"Nope," she says flatly. "How can anyone sleep when you know you have a bunch of psychopaths coming for you, and the place that you're trying to sleep in is covered in the blood of the people in the next room?" She makes some very valid points.

Although I knew her question was rhetorical, I point to Moose fumbling around, struggling to put his boots on. "Are you sure it wasn't just his snoring that kept you awake." She lets out a little giggle, reserved and quiet.

"I know that this doesn't make things any better, but it does get easier with time. You can trust me on that." She doesn't say anything back, but she does look up at me briefly, flashing her red and hollow eyes. I do feel bad for inadvertently dragging her into this mess – she was just in the wrong place at the wrong time. Story of both of our lives.

Though she acts tough, I can see right through her. Inside, she is just a young girl who wants to feel safe and wants to feel loved. Perhaps that is why she was okay with sleeping with Charlie and his disgusting pigs. The feeling of being wanted is better than not feeling wanted at all. But it's all fake. Those feelings that she may have thought she felt, they aren't real. As with everybody else, Charlie used her for his own sleazy gain. Using her for the pleasure of himself. She may try to hide it, but the damage to her has been done; it's woven in.

Trudging over, Moose grumbles, "you better have woken me up for a good reason."

"Maybe I should have let you sleep through until they arrived. Chances are you wouldn't have woken up." Muttering under his breath, Moose doesn't allow me to hear his reply.

After hours of wearing it, the blood on our bodies is the same colour as the pile of stacked bodies in the other room. "The sun is going to be rising soon," I unnecessarily remind Jess and Moose, "and we don't know how quickly they'll be coming back here once it's light, so we need to make sure we are ready for when they arrive."

"So, what's the plan?" Moose huffs.

"We need to join the pile," I say, edging my head in the direction of the day-old corpses. "It's probably not a good idea to go on top, one of them might still recognise us."

***

I understand where the term dead weight comes from now. Sandwiched in the middle of the pile, the crushing weight of those above leave us breathless as the heaviness of the cold bodies dig in all over, compressing our chests. Already struggling to take in air, the frigid cadavers are somehow insulating us in a building heat, making the little air available hot and stifling.

"They better turn up soon, Banner. I don't know how much longer I can stay in here." I can feel the wetness of Moose's arm touching mine, his skin drenched in sweat.

"You just have to hold on a little while longer." I try to sound encouraging.

I turn to look at Jess who has been silent ever since we wedged ourselves in here. "Are you okay?" I ask, concern evident in my voice.

"Mmhmm," she seems to have gone into some kind of meditative state; this seems to be her default position when faced with something she doesn't know how to deal with. To be fair, it's not every day that you have to do this sort of shit, so I suppose you could say that she is handling it pretty well.

Through our forced breathing and the buffer zone of the dead, I could have quite easily missed the faint sounds coming from outside. The voices start off at a distance, but quickly grow louder as they close the space between them and us, their words drowned out by the drones that travel with them.

They're here.

CHAPTER 24

A coldness suddenly runs through me, the coursing chills smothering my boiling skin, my blood running cold.

Moose's fidgeting has stopped; he knows that if we are discovered then it will be game over. The door opens with a loud creak as heavy soles enter through.

"Are these all of them?" A male voice shouts across the room.

I feel Moose's body tense next to me; it seems like we both recognise that voice.

"Think so, boss." a man replies nervously. I would be nervous too if I worked for that psycho.

"What do you mean you think so? Is this fucking all of them, or not?!" McKay spits out his impatience.

"Yes, it is boss." The man answers immediately, a slight tremor in his voice.

"Well, why didn't you say that in the first place, lad," The harsh and quick sound of skin hitting skin follows repeatedly; patting his pet dog on the cheek like the good boy he is.

McKay is in a constant state of Jekyll and Hyde, one minute he'll have his men cowering in the corner and the next they'll be lapping up his praise. "Right then," McKay declares with enthusiasm, "let's get this ball rolling." I can hear them all walk back toward the door. "Get your arses in here, lads. This lot need shifting!" McKay hollers, signalling for his men.

As they scramble in after McKay's instruction, I search for Jess' hand. My arms feel dead from the pressure above, the numbing pain of needles tingling intensely as I try to move it from its lodged position. Dragging it slowly across, my little finger makes contact with her hand. Even with the slightest touch, I can feel the tremble of her hand. I grasp it firmly to try and stop it from shaking. They will not think twice about killing her; they already think that she is dead anyway. My touch seems to reassure her, her tremors becoming less erratic and easier to control.

"Get these lot thrown on that wagon!" McKay orders his panting men. "And don't take all day, these lot need to be cinders by the time night draws in. The only thing I want to see of them by that point is their ash blowing out those chimneys." As soon as he finishes talking, the bodies crushing down on us are yanked up, giving us instant relief.

That relief, however, is quickly followed by fear. Fear of knowing that we are next to be manhandled and flung onto the cart of death. Assuming that we make it that far. My lungs are desperate for air, the cool waft of breeze blowing across, taunting me enticingly to breathe it in, to gasp it and gulp it down. But that goes against what my body is telling me to do. I know that if they see my chest rise and fall in the slightest, that's me done. I can only hope that Moose and Jess are thinking the same, that we all remain deathly still.

"Give me a hand with this one, he's fucking heavy!" one of the men grunts, as he tries to move Moose off of the pile; the man attempting to move him groaning with each failed attempt. "Come on," he yells to another goon, "you grab the arms and I'll take his legs, we lift on the count of three."

By the third count it sounds as if they've been kicked in the stomach; Moose's monumental mass winding them. Though the distance not far at all, Moose's body drops to the floor like a dead fish, his limbs flopping to the ground with melodramatic thuds. "

He's a fat bastard, ain't he," one expels, the exertion of the task leaving them both short of breath. "How the hell are we going to move him?"

Fat bastard; bet Moose found it hard not to react to that one. I can already imagine him commenting that muscle weighs more than fat.

"Go get Mr. McKay," one of the men say, giving up. "See what he wants us to do."

My body tenses.

"Are you joking? He'd rip our fucking heads off and still expect us to move him. We're just going to have to drag him."

Thank fuck for that, the last thing we need is McKay looming over us. Even through the blood, I'm sure he'd recognise Moose instantly.

I can hear their shoes scuffing against the floorboards as they forcefully haul him towards the door. It's a good thing that Moose can deal with pain because his back is going to be scratched to shit by the time they get him down to the wagon. The gravelled path leading to it will make sure of that.

Knowing that we have some time before they come back for us, I open my eyes and turn to look at Jess. "Hold on in there, alright. You're doing great." The look on her face says it all, she is literally too petrified to speak. She just about managed to nod her head. "When they grab you, make sure you're limp, okay. Just let everything drop. You're small and light so they should have you on that cart in no time." No words of encouragement will help what she is about to go through.

We can hear them walking back up the path, the slow crunching underfoot showing that Moose's weight has taken it out of them. I make sure that Jess has closed her eyes before I close mine.

"I've pulled my back out dragging that monster so I'm carrying her." Before picking us up, they take their time catching their breath, coughing and wheezing as the air catches in the back of their throats. I can't see them, but they sound unhealthy; I suppose that's what years of abusing copious substances does to you. Cocktails of alcohol, drugs and cigarettes may give you a fleeting moment of release, but you will inevitably face the damage done somewhere down the road.

"Right, come on. Boss man will have our heads if we take any longer."

Suddenly I feel hands grabbing at me, pulling at my skin through the clothes to try and get a good grip. I know this man only has two hands, but it feels like I'm being touched all over as he wrestles me up and onto his shoulder.

I allow my body to flop over him, my arms and legs flailing as he hoists me into a position that is comfortable for him. My arms sag down his back as my head dangles somewhere in the middle. I open my eyes quickly to look at Jess, but she has already been carried away – her slight frame much easier to manoeuvre than mine. Jostling me further, he jumps me up once more and wraps one arm behind my legs. The other is used to hold me in place, grappling at the belt around my waist to stop me from sliding off.

Slowly he begins to move. I let my body ebb with his walk, swaying back and forth with each step. The tip of my nose brushes against his back, the stench of sweat and stale cigarettes clinging to him like smoke.

"Come on, what's taking you so long?" his buddy calls out as he passes us to go and get another body.

"Funnily enough, this one's a little bit heavier than your little girly," the donkey shouts back.

"Sounds like an excuse to me, man. Hurry the fuck up." His cackle disappears as he re-enters the house.

"I fucking hate that prick," he mutters under his breath whilst launching me off of his shoulder.

My body hits the hardwood of the cart first, my head follows, bouncing on it like a rubber ball. Once the rattling in my head passes, it takes a few surreal seconds to realise that this plan actually worked. How the fuck we managed to get away with it is beyond me. I'm in a momentary state of disbelief.

I open my eyes a crack to check that both Jess and Moose are on here, as I do Moose's face is right in mine, gawking at me.

"Did you hear what they called me! They called me a fucking fat bastard! Can you believe that?

Everyone can see that I'm one hundred percent muscle." He actually sounds hard done by. "They're lucky that I was playing dead, otherwise I would have crushed them."

"What with? Your fat ass?" I smirk at him. He doesn't seem to find it as funny as I do though, and just turns his head away from me. Clearly a sore point for him. Trying to move as little as possible, I glance around for Jess. My heart starts to beat fast. I can't see her. What the fuck have they done with her! I need to find her.

"Banner, what are you doing? You trying to get us all killed." Moose grunts snidely.

"They've got Jess!" My panic is boiling over into something harder to contain.

"What the hell are you on about? She's right next to me." He says in a whispered shout.

Hidden behind Moose, Jess' whisper is barely audible. "I'm here, Arthur."

"What the actual fuck is wrong with you, Banner – you need to sort yourself out." He's obviously still angry at me, the fat joke likely lingering in his mind. But as soon as I hear her voice, the hard boil on my emotions slows to a simmer and then gradually back to a gentle blip.

I don't know why, but the thought of anything happening to this girl hurts; literally hurts. The thought of what she has been through before this sickens me, the pain that she has suffered, both physically and mentally, is too much for anyone to take, let alone someone as young as her. I feel this need to protect her. To make sure that nobody touches her again. But instead of rescuing her, all I've done is taken her from the frying pan and thrown her into the fire. I've brought her into this, so I'm sure as hell responsible for making sure she gets out of it.

"How're you holding up? I ask Jess, peering over Moose to try and see her.

"They're coming back so let's all shut up for a bit, shall we. There's plenty of time for a chinwag later." Moose mutters aggressively, trying to keep his voice to at a low murmur.

Four more a tossed into the cart with the utmost disrespect. "They're all on, Mr. McKay," one of the goons shouts after the last body is loaded.

"Good work, lads," Dallin's voice emerges from the distance, gradually getting louder the closer he gets. "Right, you know what you're doing next? I don't want to have to babysit you again."

"Pretty sure we got it, boss. We just have to take them straight to the crem." His lacky sounds pleased with himself.

"Indeed you do, compadres," McKay announces. "Charlie and Rue's men will be expecting you, so just keep your wits about you. We've had no sightings of either of them yet, but I guarantee that's where they're heading."

Too right that's where we're heading. But if they think we are going to waltz straight through the doors they're sorely mistaken. "Got it boss, they won't get passed us." His idiotic minion delivers that line with such smugness that it's hard not to crack a smile. We've already got passed them, three times already.

"Alright then, away with you – I'll be down in a couple of hours. I've got a few things I have to do first." With that, McKay smacks the wagon, indicating that it's time for us to go.

CHAPTER 25

The slow pull of the cart and the incoherent moans from the front makes me think that McKay's lackeys are the ones moving this thing. We may have drones flying around in the sky, but as far as I'm aware there are no cars in The Zone, or animals that could replace these menial tasks. But I guess that suits our three head honchos well. It makes sure that everyone knows their place, their lowly level. There are very few chances of levelling up in this game of horrors; the only way is down.

Lying flat on our backs, the painfully slow rocking motion of the cart is making me feel sick, the wheels of the wagon unable to soften the many bumps in the road. I need to distract myself from the nausea before the sickness makes a show. I think the discovery of vomit spewed all over us might make even these morons stop and think. I've heard of corpses shitting themselves to empty the contents of their insides, but I'm pretty sure that doesn't count for the top end as well.

I sit up in the hopes that whatever is trying to escape my mouth will fall back down again. I stabilise myself, moving my body the opposite way to the motion of the cart, counteracting the wave like bobbing and swashing feeling in my gut. It seems to help.

"Lay down, Banner," Moose grunts.

"Trust me, unless you want this whole cart to be covered in sick, I suggest it's best I sit up for a bit." The gurgling in my stomach starts to settle.

"Just leave him alone, Moose!" Jess scorns.

"Fine, I'll leave him alone, but don't be surprised when his moving about makes them come back here." Moose moans, but Jess' tortured voice makes him back off. Even he realises that she's on the edge and that he shouldn't push it.

As we lay in our cramped and dark space, a light pitter pattering of rain thrums on the cover above us, our drivers' voices drowned out by its growing heaviness. Now is the perfect time to talk out what we are going to do once we get inside the crematorium.

As the rain hammers down, the wagon seems to speed up; their desperation to get out of the rain motivating them to go faster. "Before we get in there, we should probably talk about what we are going to do." This makes Jess sit up, begrudgingly followed by Moose, who seems to have forgotten that movement, inside the already rocky cart, will attract unwanted interest.

Lowering my voice so it's just loud enough to hear over the bullets of rain hitting the tarpaulin above us, I calmly state, "We don't know exactly what we're walking into once we're inside. One thing we do know though is that they are expecting us, which definitely means we are going to be outnumbered."

Moose chuckles to himself before saying, "Outnumbered is a massive understatement, Banner. There's a whole army waiting for us in there."

I already knew this, but I didn't think that openly saying it would be helpful to any of us. I can see Jess shrink back down a little, her body already preparing for flight over fight; which is exactly the reason why I am choosing my words very carefully. Unlike Moose.

"Don't forget that we have the upper hand here, "I say with false optimism. "There's one way into the place and the majority of them will be guarding the door and the outside area. We'll bypass most of them."

"That's all well and good, Banner, but we're not going to be able to avoid everyone inside – there's going to be the person who wants to throw all of these bodies in the burners, don't forget." Why does Moose always feel it necessary to state the bloody obvious? Does he think I don't know that already?

"Of course, we're going to have to deal with him when it comes to it. He's small and scrawny anyway, so he should be easy to deal with." My answer agitates Moose.

Moose isn't buying my confidence; his fingers are twitching at his sides, his jaw momentarily clenched shut before he let's rip, "Let's be real here for a second; truth is we have no idea what is waiting for us in there. You trying to tell us what to expect is pointless. We are going in blind and we're just going to have to deal with whatever comes our way. You forget, Banner, that I know these people, I know how their fucked up, evil minds work. And that's something we can't prepare for."

I know that my head is a whirlwind sometimes, always planning and predicting outcomes for the unknown. I guess it's my way of dealing with my constant anxiety – I need to know what to expect. Even if it is a made- up fantasy in my head, I'd rather have that than nothing at all.

Moose's mind clearly works very differently to mine. He's not scared of what is waiting for us; he just takes everything as it comes. It's quite refreshing to see but something that I know is impossible for me to do. But then again, no matter how many plans I have, like Moose said, there's no way I can guarantee it's going to work out that way. And that's when things begin to spiral, leaving me fully out of control. Which scares the absolute shit out of me.

"Fine," I turn to Moose. "What do you think we should do?"

"If you'd have just listened to what I said, Banner," he remarks, "you'd realise that there is nothing we can do. We're going to have to decide that when we know what we are confronted with. One thing that we can try to do though is stay undiscovered for as long as possible. After that we are all just going to have to think on our feet."

Whilst we have been talking, the rockiness of the wagon has smoothed out; the saturated ground clinging to the wheels as they speed through the growing flood. But suddenly the drumming above us stops.

We've arrived.

CHAPTER 26

Gently we lower ourselves back into our sleep like state, conscious to get back in the exact position we were in before.

"Have we had any sign of them?" No surprise that this pompous prick is lying in wait for us.

"No, Mr Dalton. No sign of them at the apartments or on the way here," one of our drivers chatters breathlessly, most likely soaked through to the bone.

"Well, where the bloody hell are they? They can't have just disappeared!" The room fills with Charlie's voice, the echoes carrying his frustration back and forth.

"They will arrive when they arrive, Charlie…" Rue's sultry tones cuts through his resounds like a knife. It sounds like she's already had enough of his bullshit.

"If I wanted the obvious stated Sherlock, I would have said it myself, would I not? You are offering what is blindingly apparent, which offers us nothing whatsoever." Charlie's voice dripped with an oily authority, enunciating his poisonous words. "Why don't you put yourself to good use and gather up some of your idiotic goons to get out there and find them!"

The rooms shifts.

"Don't you fucking talk to her like that. Otherwise, I'll break your other leg, you stuck up prick!" Rue must have quite a lot of her people based here, listening to the support of her shrieking banshees roaring through the room like wild animals.

"Excuse me," Charlie laughs to mask the shock he is most likely feeling. He can't let this one slide, not in front of all these people. "I dare you to come and have a go, boy."

The whooping stops as a painful silence covers the room, until steadfast footsteps pace unwaveringly across the floor in defence of their queen.

Charlie's laugh at this point grows almost hysterical; he feeds off of the chaos he creates, relishing in it as he watches it unfold.

"Oh, they are loyal to you, Rue. Very brave but equally, if not more, stupid. Come on then, young man, let us see what you are made of." But the marching steps come to a falter, scuffing the ground to a stop.

"We are not doing this today." Rue must have blocked his path, without doubt saving his life.

"Come on, Rue. The fun was just about to start." Charlie's begging for bloodshed; he'd like it to be our blood, but he has to fill his needs however he can.

Rue's people follow her blindly and would gladly lay down their lives for her. That's what enrages Charlie the most; they actually love and respect her. I sure as hell know that his men don't think the same of him. Fear is what leads them. They love what he can give them, what they can acquire from him, but are petrified of what he would do to them if they set a toe out of line.

Rue snapped back at him, "Let's get one thing straight here, Charlie. You do not fucking order me around, okay, or tell my people what to do."

"Darling Rue," he says, holding up his hands. "Let us not fall out over something so arbitrary as this. Perhaps just teach them not to be so lippy."

"Some people need to be put in their place," she quickly retorts.

"Oh yes, and where might that be?" Charlie's reply ripples with sardonic curiosity.

"I'm sure you'll find out soon," Rue says as she's heading her people out. As they walk past us in the cart, we can see numerous shins stride after her through the slight gap where the tarpaulin is meant to meet the wood. I've counted around twenty people leaving after her; which is very good for us.

"Oh, Rue, don't be so silly. Come on back here and have a cup of tea. No harm has been done." Charlie seriously needs to work on his back peddling skills if he thinks that poor, half-arsed attempt of an implicit apology is going to work on her.

"I'll pass. We'll be patrolling the perimeter."

"I'm terribly sorry if you feel that I have crossed a line," Charlie calls after her.

"No, you're not." She says as the last faint steps of Rue's retreat is followed by the sound of two heavy doors being pulled to a close.

"What the fuck are you to imbeciles gawking at!" Charlie yells, furious. He hates not getting his own way.

"We got the bodies here, Mr. Dalton. We just need to know where you want us to take them." Our drivers must be the gawking imbeciles, as they reply with a slight wobble in their voice.

"Why are you asking me?" Charlie spits, "Dallin is the one who is meant to be dealing with it."

"Yes, I understand that sir, but he had to go and do something." I almost feel sorry for these two morons.

"Oh, he had to go and do something, did he? Well, that makes everything okay then, doesn't it." The dial on Charlie's wit seems to be turned up to the max today.

"We're sorry, Mr. Dalton, but if you'd just tell us where you want them…"

Charlie quickly cuts him off before he can finish. "You know of the term don't shoot the messenger, right? Well, that is not a rule I am too fond of. I actually quite enjoy shooting the messenger. Therefore, I recommend that you shut your mouths and take them through to the incinerators before I change my mind."

Our donkeys have taken the keep your mouths shut seriously, pulling off without a word, trotting on much quicker than when they were battling the torrents of rain on the way here. Charlie seems to have that effect on people.

As we make our way through the building, the heat intensifies, and the air is filled with an acrid smell of burnt meat. We continue on for what seems like a good few minutes until the wagon makes a final stop. The heat is now unbearable, the air close and sooty. A loud roaring blocks out every other sound, the flames of the incinerator raging for its next meal; its orange and blue intensity ready to gorge on the skin and flesh of its next victims to satiate its unending hunger.

"We've got some bodies for you," one of the men calls out, throatily shouting to make sure he's heard over the thundering furnaces.

"Hello!?" They are now both yelling, their nervous uncertainty throwing their pitches off as they fight to be heard and acknowledged. Abruptly, the ear-splitting roar is turned down to a less deafening meow, as the fierce heat dampens to something more manageable.

"Thank you, gentlemen. Please just kindly leave them there. I was just preheating the ovens, so to speak." The Cremator has amused himself, laughing at his grotesque attempt at a joke. When it seems to pass over their heads, he sends them away with, "That will be all."

Now alone, or so he thinks, the creep begins to talk to himself. "Right, before we begin, I need the list." The sound of flitting paper shows his thorough check, "so we should have eight bodies here, five destined for the flames and three for heaven." Three for heaven? What the hell is that meant to mean?

"Right then," suddenly the tarpaulin is stripped from the top of us, exposing our vulnerability to the hot room.

Through partially closed eyes, one side of the room emits a warm glow, the orange light radiating out just far enough for us to inspect our surroundings.

Ten burners line the far side of the room, ready to destroy the evidence of mass murder. As The Cremator reads through the list, he starts dragging out the bodies one by one, sliding them onto metal trolleys to help glide them into their designated oven. The first four are placed in burners one to four; each body shut in by a heavy metal door.

Checking his list once more, the reassured cremator walks over to the flashing console tucked to the side of the burners and hits a few of the colourful buttons, before pulling down on a long metal lever. As soon as the lever travels its short distance, the flames in the incinerators surge up and wrap around the four bodies in a final embrace. As the flames rise higher and spread across the contained space, the engulfed bodies begin to melt; their entire existence burned to nothing but grey ash.

"And now for the other three." I can sense the creep's presence at the end of the cart looking down on us. By his sudden silence, I'm guessing he's realised that the maths doesn't quite add up. His expected three has somehow doubled. We need to do something before he leaves and starts asking questions to the wrong people.

A loud bang reverberates around the room as the cart jolts back, forcing me to open my eyes. Moose has the weaselly man around the neck, wringing it so that no sound can make its way out.

"Moose, ease up a little, he's more useful to us alive than dead." I shout out to him.

"This is your first and last warning," Moose threatens. "Make so much as a squeak, and I'll snap your fucking neck. Understand?"

CHAPTER 27

The little man nods his head wildly. Moose doesn't remove his hand from The Cremator's throat, but the joints in his hand loosens, allowing him the chance to gasp in short, shallow breaths.

"Please don't kill me!" he begs between sharp intakes of air.

I jump off the cart, stretching out my stiff and aching muscles.

"Well, you see that's all going to depend on you." His startled eyes widen as he recognises me from our first unfortunate encounter in the waiting room. I've already made it clear to his face the disdain I hold for him. "Tell me, what did you mean by heaven and hell?"

Moose barely gives him time to answer before shaking him like a ragdoll; you can almost hear his bones rattle from the force. "Answer the question, shithead!" Moose shouts in his face.

"Let me make the question a little easier for you. I think I've worked out the hell part, they get burned in the

208

incinerators, right?" I point to the four raging furnaces cooking the bodies to a crackling crisp. "So, I'm guessing that these three," I gesture to the three bodies remaining on the wagon, "are the lucky ones going to heaven. And we want to know where that might be because it sure as hell isn't here."

Panic strikes The Cremator's face as fear lurks somewhere behind his yellowed and bloodshot eyes. "They'll kill me if I tell you." Drops begin to swell around his eyelids.

"Who will?" Moose and I ask in unison.

Looking perturbed, he replies, "The three that are looking to do the same to you."

"Who says we aren't going to kill you? They are not the only ones you need to be scared of." Moose says tightening his hand around The Cremator's throat once again, reinforcing the immediate danger that he should be worried about.

"Do you honestly believe that they are going to let you live after we get out of here? They'll blame you," I say, as The Cremator takes a loud gulp; he knows that what we're saying is true. "But if you help us, we'll get you out of here safely and we can all go our separate ways. You can live without them breathing down your neck." I pretend to empathise with him, but Moose trumps my attempt to gain his trust by laying it all on the line.

"I'm going to make it easy for you, alright. You have two options. The first option is certain death; you may as well just shoot yourself in the head to get it over with. Or you can show us the way out and get the fuck out of here too because they're going to be coming for you next." Even though Moose spelt it out bluntly, I'm sure that The Cremator knows there is only one viable option here if he wants to see another day.

"So, are you going to tell us what is planned for these three?" I bring us back to where we need to be.

"If I tell you," The Cremator begs, "I need you to give me your word that you're not going to throw me to the wolves."

I couldn't care less what happens to him.

"We're wasting time here." Moose interjects. "We're all going to be dead soon enough if you don't hurry the fuck up and tell the man what he wants to know." For once I appreciate his interruption; saves me having to make a promise that I have no means of keeping. "Tick, tock," he pushes. "Hurry the fuck up!" Moose's continued pressure makes the little man squirm and sweat.

"Okay, okay," he breaks. "I'll help you. But can you please take your hands off of me." Agreeing silently to his request, Moose lowers his hands to his sides.

"If you're thinking about screwing us over," Moose reminds him, "just know that you're already a dead man walking."

"Your numerous threats have made that quite clear already."

I decide to take back control of our current situation. "Right, well I'm glad we're all on the same page. Now let's get moving, shall we?"

"Yes, yes. Of course," the weasely man jitters. "We need to get these three in those end incinerators." He points his shaking finger to the ones that don't seem to be lit. "If you both carry one, we can get this done quite quickly." The Cremator drags one of the bodies by the ankle toward him, somehow managing to lift the dead weight onto his skeletal frame with ease. "Come on then. Grab the others," he says in rushed panic.

"I hope for your sake that you're not trying to tell us what to do." Moose's not so subtle reminder for him to shut up works, causing him to quickly scurry away, placing the body on one of the cold slabs. Moose throws the remaining two bodies over his shoulders and decides to follow the little man's instructions on where to put them.

Although all of the bodies have been taken off, one person still remains deathly still in the cart. Jess.

I offer out my hand, hoping that she'll reach out and take it. Thankfully, after a few long seconds, she does. The truth is, I totally forgot she was in there; after arriving here, my mind was so focused on Charlie and Rue, and what was going on around us, that she was pushed to the back of my mind. Way back.

This already damaged girl is being dragged through even more trauma. I know that she made her choice, and who am I to her to question it, but she had no idea what she was signing up to. I'm sure though that the past few days with us has given her some disgusting and indigestible food for thought.

Since our first encounter at Charlie's, she has visually changed. Don't get me wrong, she didn't look happy by any means, but she looked as well as you physically can do in The Zone. Since Moose blew up her apartment though, her health looks like it has deteriorated. Her skin is now sallow and her complexion pallid and peaky.

"Only a couple of hours ago, you promised us that you wouldn't be like this. I know it's easier said than done, but if you carry on like this you are going to get yourself killed." I say to her in hushed tones.

"I'm sorry!" she sobs quietly, only allowing me to see her emotion. "I can feel this panic building in me, and my heart races so fast that it feels like it is going to explode. I literally feel as if I can't move. I try, believe me I try, to block out what is going on around me, but I just freeze. In those moments I can't do anything else."

I don't know why I'm doing it, but I pull her in for a hug. She doesn't fight it either, she just fits into my chest, accepting the small offering of my embrace. "It's going to be alright. We're going to be out of here soon and none of us will have to worry about Charlie, McKay or Rue ever again. They're not allowed where we're going."

I gently push her away from me and find myself wiping the pads of my thumbs across her eyes, soaking up the droplets and leaving small, shining trails under her pink, slightly swollen lids. I allow her the time to compose herself before escorting her over to where Moose and the worm stand waiting for us.

"Is she with you two?" The Cremator sounds surprised. "I thought she was actually dead, the way she was staring off into the abyss."

Out of nowhere, Moose swipes at him, his meat-hook hand clapping the side of The Cremator's head hard, causing the weasel to grasp at his reddening ear as he stumbles back from the unexpected hit. "What do you not understand about keeping your fucking mouth shut!" The little patience Moose had for this prick has expired, pulling his thick arm back for another strike.

"Moose!" My call interrupts his natural instinct to beat the shit out of this guy, "we need him to be able to talk, remember."

Moose's position doesn't change, his arm still poised to knock the few teeth out that he has left. "This cockroach needs to be put in his place, Banner!" He has a crazed look in his eye as he shifts his focus back onto The Cremator. "You don't speak to her, you don't even glance in her fucking direction. Do you understand, you fucking rat? The next time you do, I'll grab the side of your face and smash it against the wall over and over until blood starts to come out of every hole, and even you won't be able to recognise your ugly face in the mirror."

Only a few hours ago, Moose was baiting Jess to walk away, now he's sticking up for her, protecting her. It's the least he could do, and I think he knows it. Jess seems to be as confused as me by Moose's change of heart, but that perplexed look is quickly replaced by a thankful glimmer in her watery eyes and a timid half smile. When Moose clocks onto her expression, his whole face softens, momentarily dropping the hardman act, before his usual angry and pissed off face reprises its roll.

"Let's hurry the fuck up, shall we?" Moose barks at The Cremator who is still clutching at his ear. When he finally brings his hand down, it has doubled in size, the inflamed skin seemingly puffing out by the second.

"So, what happens now?" I say, looking at the three bodies through the small windows of the incinerators' cold, metal hatches.

Moose's whack has definitely thrown The Cremator off balance, the ringing probably left in his ear disorienting him as he stumbles back toward the console of levers and buttons. After pressing many of them, he pulls one of the levers toward him.

The grinding of gears sounds out as the bodies slowly descend, disappearing from view.

"That," The Cremator says, his voice smoother than before, his lips almost threatening a smile, "is how we are all going to get out of here."

CHAPTER 28

W here do they go?" I ask, trying not to sound nervous. The idea of going down there in that thing doesn't fill me with much joy.

"You'll soon find out," is The Cremator's only reply.

"You're telling us that we have to sit in an incinerator and be lowered down into God knows where. How do we know that once we're loaded into those chambers, you won't turn them on and burn us alive." Moose makes a very valid point, igniting our distrust for this creep even further.

"Because I don't want to kill myself, do I?" The Cremator replies indignantly. His brazen impertinence pisses me off.

"You know what," something comes over me, and I just can't help myself, "if I were you, I would have thrown myself into one of those things a long time ago. I know that we're not living the high life, but at least we get to do what we want. You are just a prisoner here masked as a humble servant. Is that what you tell yourself to make you feel better about the shit you do? Truth is, you're weak, and you're a fucking coward." It feels so good to say what I think. I'm bored of playing the good cop.

"That's probably why they chose him," Moose joins in. "He hasn't got the guts to do anything other than what they say. You're just a little runt jumping through hoops."

Our words have a stabbing effect on him as he keels forward slightly, wrapping his arms across his body, holding himself like no one else ever would.

"There is only one way to make sure that he doesn't cook us," I say, holding everyone's attention, especially our little friend's. "We're all going to have to ride in one of those things together." The Cremator's face can't manage to hide that I have fucked up his little plan. "That won't be a problem, will it?" I ask with a pretend naivety.

"It won't be able to take the weight of all four of us," The Cremator sputters, his face now exposing desperation and fear.

"I think we'll take our chances." The rat looks at Moose and Jess, bewildered.

"You two are okay with this! We'll all plummet to our deaths!" The Cremator's voice squeals.

Moose laughs at him, "I think you're being a bit dramatic. Worse case scenario, we'll arrive down there a little bit quicker. Win, win for us."

"Problem solved," I clap my hands and rub them together. "Get it set up," I instruct, shutting down whatever The Cremator was just about to try and argue. Knowing that there is no point, he drags his feet over to the console, plugging in whatever buttons he needs to in order to get the lift to work.

After a few seconds, he takes a step back and looks at us with utter contempt and resentment.

"Have you done it?" Moose grunts aggressively; his question garners a nod. "Then why the fuck isn't it doing anything?"

"It will descend once the hatch is closed." He states flatly.

"Well, let's stop wasting time and get in there." Moose walks over to the unlit furnace and holds the heavy metal door wide. "Scumbags first," he says with a stupid, somehow scary, grin.

Probably not the best choice of words. Myself and Moose, especially Moose, could easily be characterised under that title. But I'm assuming that he is not referring to us; his deathly stare boring into The Cremator's wide eyes seems to confirm this thought.

Moose's threatening look doesn't get The Cremator to hop on in and do as he's told. Instead, he stands frozen to the spot, his brain unable to respond to the position that he finds himself in. Before his thoughts catch back up with him, I walk up next to him and place my hand on his bony shoulder. Before he can concoct any ideas on how to change the unfortunate position he finds himself in, I lead him over to the open metal door.

Moose doesn't allow him the chance to clamber inside, instead he shoves him in, causing The Cremator's legs to catch on the bottom edge of the hatch's frame, hurtling him in ungraciously. That's one way of getting him in there I suppose. We now need to decide who is going in next.

Even though the guy, now kettled in at the end of the shiny metal box, looks weak and feeble, and right in this moment scared, there is no way that Jess will be going in next. I have no doubt that Jess could take him on, but when an animal is cornered with no sign of a way out, you never know how they are going to react. And worms like him would definitely use a woman as leverage to try and save his own snaky skin.

Thankfully, my thoughts can remain unspoken as Moose slides awkwardly in next, his knees and elbows hitting against the relatively soft metal, denting it as he struggles to manoeuvre his large body into the already cramped space.

"Budge up, rat!" Moose isn't asking, instead he continues to crush inside, pushing his whole weight against The Cremator until he hears him wheezing as his body constricts. "We're ready for you," although Moose's body is contorted into a position I would have thought impossible for a man of his size, he comfortably stretches out his arm, willing for Jess to take his hand. She takes it, sidling in next to him, leaving me just enough room to join.

I try and decide how best to tackle getting in there, and eventually settle on the sit and spin technique. I perch on the edge of the hatch's opening, my back facing Jess. I take in a deep breath, sucking in my stomach like it is somehow going to help me fit. Unsurprisingly, it doesn't help. Instead, it just makes the already uncomfortable process of trying to squeeze in there, even more uncomfortable.

As my back reaches Jess, I start to turn sideways, trying to pull my knees up as my shirt helps glide my back against the smooth metal side, allowing me to draw my knees fully to my chest. Well, that whole process wasn't as bad as I thought it would be; now I just have to close the door.

During my struggle to fit, I must have pushed the door back. Instead of being an easy grab, it is now flat against the furnaces outside wall, meaning that I am going to have to lean out and pull it back in to close it. I swear to God that nothing in this life is made easy for me.

I can barely move my torso without having to move the rest of my body; knowing my luck, if I move out of this position, there is very little chance I will be able to get back into it. Instead, I decide to stretch out and bend my arm back, hoping to grab the handle. As I lengthen my arm and hook it around, I can feel my muscles pull under the strain of their unnatural shape. The initial aches very quickly grow into sharp, shooting pains.

Where the fuck is the handle? My agitation is making my movements more uncoordinated and clumsier. As my fingertips touch around the cool metal in search for the handle, my twisted arm wrenches further, causing unrecognisable and involuntary grunts to burst out through my gritted teeth.

"What is taking so long, Banner?" Moose complains like a petulant child. "Do you want me to try and reach over and get it?" Jess offers.

If it was that easy, I would have got it on my own by now. But I do appreciate her offer all the same. "No, don't worry. I've almost got it." As my voice cracks under the pressure of my crooked arm, the tips of my fingers finally meet a jutted-out piece of metal. Eagerly clasping on to it, I pull my arm back in on itself, the joints so twisted that it's almost as painful bringing it back as it was stretching it out.

It takes a good few slams to get the door to latch into place, but as soon as it locks shut, the mechanism of gears rings out, as The Cremator said it would. Slowly, we are being pulled down into the dark depths of whatever we are going to have to face next.

CHAPTER 29

T he further we go down, the louder the creaks grow; but it's the juddering bumps that are worrying me the most. I decide that it's best to keep that to myself. The Cremator thinks otherwise.

"I told you all that this was a terrible idea! This shaft is not designed to bear the weight of four people."

"Pipe down, rat!" Moose raises his fist, leaving it inches away from The Cremator's face. His unsubtle threat seems to work, as The Cremator gulps down his next words, relieving our ears from his spinelessness.

We all remain quiet as we descend, although all of our breathing seems to be getting heavier, the claustrophobia of this confined, metal tin getting into our heads. How far does this thing go down? Each second in here feels like minutes. My will for this lift to hurry up and get us to the bottom seems to make this seemingly unending journey longer.

A sharp pain ruptures in my ears, making the mechanical grind of the gears muffled and muted. The popping grows more intense the further we travel down the shaft. I can tell that I am not the only one feeling this sensation.

Moose has his fingers stuck in his ears, prodding and twisting them around to try and relieve the pressure. He pulls his fingers out from his ear canal and starts smacking the side of his head, like the force will make the pressure fly out and magically disappear. Jess sits still, but the occasional wince and grimace shows that she is suffering with the same pain in silence. A habit that she will hopefully, one day, break.

Moose has The Cremator so cramped up in the corner that I can't tell if his display of discomfort is from the pressure in his ears, or the fact that his limbs are so bunched up; I'd be surprised if his lungs even have room to expand to take in air.

I start to fidget to try and shake off the cramp that is forming in my legs, but the stinging ache intensifies, shooting pain from my thighs down to my tingling feet. What feels like being stabbed by a million pins and needles quickly turns into a fiery burn, spreading back up my legs.

The strong spasms cause me to kick out, forcing my buckled legs to push my lead feet against the pliant sides of the shaft. Indentations of my boots appear sunken into the metal, but the burn wants me to push even harder. And I give into it; the numbing aches unbearable.

My legs have my entire body force behind them as they press into the bending sheets of metal. The loud creaks catch Moose's attention, he has been too busy with his diver's ear to notice what I have been doing. Jess, however, has been watching me helplessly this entire time.

"Banner, what the fuck are you..." before Moose can finish his words, our ride abruptly stops with a flat bang, jolting us all upward from the force.

The hatch automatically unlocks itself, swinging open freely as the platform that we are sat on unexpectedly begins to rise once more. The groaning of the shaft's mechanism shows its struggle as Moose and The Cremator rise up, as Jess and I topple out the door. Soon after, I feel Moose's heavy weight crash into me, the flat bed in which all four of us were huddled, now a slide.

It makes sense. Dead people don't really have the capacity to open the door and hop on out themselves. That being said, the three bodies sent down before us are nowhere to be seen. My eyes dart around this dimly lit place, looking for any sign of human life. But there is nothing, no one. So, where the hell did those bodies go?

Just as I open my mouth to speak, the answer to my question sweeps me off my feet. Quite literally. As I try to heave Moose off of my back, elbowing him agitatedly to get him to hurry up off me, we all lurch to the side as the floor beneath us begins to move.

Without a second thought, I grab Jess' arm and pull her with me, diving off the conveyor belt onto the narrow patch of concrete floor than runs alongside it. Moose quickly follows suit, launching himself off the fast-moving platform; unlike The Cremator, who has travelled way up the line before managing to fling himself inelegantly to the ground.

The direction the belt is heading grows dark, the unending tunnel it travels down blockaded by a wall of black as the ungenerously spaced-out wall sconces fade to nothing in the distance. This tunnel could span miles for all we know.

The concrete beneath us emphasises how cold it is down here, its hardness greedily absorbing our body heat and the icy mist that escapes our lips.

"Why the fuck is it so cold down here? Moose chatters, rubbing the sides of his arms vigorously in an attempt to warm up.

"They need to preserve the bodies, otherwise they'll be useless to them". I quickly respond.

The Cremator looks annoyed that I know the answer to that question, "You seem to know much more than you originally let on." he says insolently.

"That's ironic, isn't it." I fire back. "Because I could say the same about your smart ass."

"Touche." is all he has to say.

But now that he knows we know, he rearranges his pathetic outward appearance and puts on a face much more calculated, composed. He stands much taller, straightening out his hunched back. Now he just stares at us all blankly, nothing readable behind his closed off, yet open eyes. Then he decides to speak.

"There is not point pretending anymore," like his body, The Cremator's voice grows stronger. "I was going to string you imbeciles on for a little longer, purely for my own entertainment, but it seems you know too much."

"He's one of them," Jess breaks through the confusion of muddled thoughts whirling in my mind and pinpoints the answer I have been reaching for this whole time; from the first moment I met him.

"She's a clever little cookie, this one. It's a real shame that in a minute that clever little brain of hers will be kaput."

"You fucking what?!" Moose rages. The temperature is definitely rising down here, thawing out the cold. The flare of Moose's face almost lights up the tunnel as he lunges toward The Cremator, grabbing him by the neck of his shirt and slamming him into the wall.

The smirk edging up on the corners of The Cremator's mouth wills Moose to smack it off of him. And Moose isn't one to not answer a call of that kind. Repeatedly, Moose's arm flies back, each swing connecting to different spots on The Cremator's face.

"Stop. Fucking. Smiling!" Moose pronounces the words with each blow, but his instructions just make The Cremator's mouth stretch wider. Moose's fevered anger makes his punches erratic, especially when The Cremator starts to laugh; a maniacal laugh which carries hauntingly through the dark. Blood drips from Moose's hand, running down his arm as his punches slow.

"Oh, come on! Is that all you've got?" I'm disappointed." The Cremator's taunts have his desired effect, spurning Moose to continue smashing his split knuckles into The Cremator's head. His head is wet with blood, his eyes barely able to open from the gushes that burst with each strike.

How the fuck is this guy still standing, let alone talking?

"I'm going to fucking kill you!" Moose growls through heavy pants, his body tiring from his relentless attack.

But that's where the tables turn, and by turn, I mean get thrown upside down and smashed to pieces.

All of a sudden, The Cremator's eyes open wide, the bright whites of them popping against the flood of red pouring down his face. Firmly set on Moose, whose fist continues to pummel at The Cremator's chin, The Cremator's eyes turn into something unhuman, dilated like a predator about to go in for the kill; the fun of toying with his prey over.

Before Moose can land another blow, The Cremator's hand catches it mid-flight, twisting it back so that his arm has no choice but to follow, knotting it into an inescapable hold. Not letting go of Moose's bloodied hand, The Cremator pushes him into the wall face first, snapping his arm up behind his back.

With his free hand, The Cremator spreads it across the back of Moose's head, scraping his face against the wall's rough stone; his skin grating against the hard surface like sandpaper.

It was a bad idea for The Cremator to turn his back on me. As he mocks Moose, "Not so tough now, are you?" I attack him from behind, landing my punches into his ribs, winding him. Well, that's what I expected to happen anyway. Instead, like an exorcised owl, his head rotates further than the human bone structure allows, the skin on his neck pulling so tight that the creases look like they are going to tear open.

Before now, because of all the blood, I couldn't see the damage Moose had inflicted on him; but now he is staring me dead in the eyes, I can see the real him. The skin on his right cheek curls up, flapping uncontrollably from the detached flesh underneath. The rip extends to his mouth, bearing the rows of teeth in a monstrous grin, clamped together.

The flow of the blood has slowed completely, revealing the metal that frames his face; that structures his entire body. Jess was right; he's one of them. There's no way he is going to let us get out of here alive. What did Charlie once describe him as? The gatekeeper? The ferryman?

Before my mind can catch up to what is happening, my face is also buried into the wall, my lips involuntarily kissing the cold brick as The Cremator's hand grasps the back of my neck, gripping it tight, squeezing it until the veins burst and the bones break.

My eyes spin back in their sockets, fighting to get a glimpse at Jess, to tell her to run. But I can't see her. Hopefully she's already gone, giving her the head start that she will need to get away from this machine man. My vision blurs as the surrounding dark swallows the light, my feeble attempts to release myself from his neck breaking hand only makes The Cremator's grip stronger. I don't think that there is going to be a way out of this one.

I look over at Moose, who has nothing left to give; his eyes, like mine, surrendering to the black hole desperately trying to suck us in, pulling the life from our bodies. I allow myself to go limp, the acceptance of my fate a relief. I give into my heavy lids, closing my eyes for the final time.

As they close, every thought I feel like I've ever had rushes through my brain like turbulent waves, reminding me of who I am and what I have done. I know that I haven't been the best of men, I'm a waster with an unquestioned morality.

I know I should have made more of the life I had before The Zone; I was entitled and forever wanting what I didn't have. And now look how it's going to end. None of that shit before mattered.

I suppose I can thank The Zone for some things though. The people may be diabolical and the place completely fucked, but being here has given me a sense of clarity that was invisible to me before. I found people that mattered, people I can say I truly care for. I don't think I could have ever said that before The Zone, because the truth was that I came first, last and everywhere in between.

Here I met the mother I never had but always wanted, someone who could see through my patched-up walls and notice the crumbling damage underneath. Her friendship, her empathy, her unconditional love, helped to repair me and allowed me to grow. An apple in amongst the oranges. Her words, not mine.

Because of The Zone, I am who I am today, and for that I suppose I will always owe something to this cesspit. I'm really not sure how, but being here in this place has made me a better person. Who said humanity was dead?

Oh yeah, I'm pretty sure that was me.

CHAPTER 30

D istracted by my thoughts, the pain around my neck weakens, my body probably slowly shutting down my ability to feel; in this situation though, to be honest, that isn't a bad thing.

As my mind wonders and drifts, sifting through the good, the bad and the ugly, a single shot fires out as The Cremator's hands simultaneously drop from mine and Moose's necks. Splatterings of warm liquid hit the back of my head as the sound of his body hits the floor.

I look at Moose, who's barely conscious, slumped on the floor, gasping at the air that was choked from him. I glance down at The Cremator. If I hadn't have known it was him, I wouldn't be able to identify him now.

His head has been blown off, the sticky clumps of brain matter stuck to the walls and the back of my head. What seems like an entire body's worth of blood pools from what is left of his neck, running off in stream like nooks, unsure of where it wants to go. The rich red contrasts with the silvery shine of metal jutting out of his skin, the shrapnel sparking aggressively like a fire that doesn't want to burn out.

The yawning of The Cremator's neck uncovers the layers of his being. The flesh and blood sits on a frame of metal, the bones that keep us upright replaced with the steel of a machine.

"I grant you; he doesn't look like much on the outside, but the inside is a work of art." Slowly, my eyes draw up to the figure holding a sawn-off shotgun, the barrel emitting wisps of curled white smoke. "I hope that I wasn't treading on your toes there, but it seemed that the two of you were in need of a little help."

I honestly thought that this day couldn't get any worse, yet here worse is standing right in front of me, his sneering smile as smackable now as it was the last time I spoke with him in the cage. "Don't worry, I'm not expecting to be thanked," he says condescendingly. "I only just saved all three of your bloody lives."

All three. Stood behind McKay, I can just make out the outline of Jess. She tips her hand up and points her fingers to the sky in a short, 'I'm here, don't worry' wave.

"I caught her pegging it down the tunnel. It's a good thing I turned up when I did, otherwise God only knows what would have happened to you."

Moose wobbles to his feet, leaning his weight against the wall for balance. A purplish ring runs around Moose's throat, the imprints of The Cremator's fingers visible as he bleeds internally, the black bruising quickly spreading to cover his thick neck.

"Finally found a person that you couldn't fight off, eh, Moose." McKay laughs impishly.

Moose grasps his clavicle as he responds, his raspy tone rougher than usual, "Not exactly a person, is he." I'm surprised he can even speak after his neck was crushed like a tin can. It definitely looks misshapen, the natural curvature of his neck uneven and dented in.

"It pains me to see him like this; hurts my soul to see one of my own laid out on the floor. But then again, he was always a bit of a creepy prick, so I'm sure I'll get over it just fine." Only McKay can joke about blowing someone's head off at point blank range with a shot gun.

"Let me take a wild guess as to why you blew his fucking brains out... is it because you want to be the one to finish us off and parade us around like trophies to get one over on Charlie!" Everything this bastard does has an ulterior motive.

"Arthur...Arty," McKay says, his mock disappointment not washing with me. "Why do you always think so little of me, even after everything I've done for you." Everything he's done for me. Is he having a fucking laugh?

"Oh yeah, all of those wonderful things, like blowing up her home, killing an apartment load of innocent people, sending your goons to come after us. The list just goes on and on."

"Don't be so bloody dramatic, Arthur. You'd all be dead if I hadn't just saved your sorry arses."

"Then what is it that you want from us?"

"I don't want anything from you, Arty. I just want to help you all on your merry way, of course, point you in the right direction. It's very easy to get lost in these tunnels, and who knows what is lurking down here in the dark." He clearly does.

"And why the hell do you want to help us, Dallin?" I sound so contrived.

"Because, Arthur, believe it or not, I like you. As I've said many times before, it is rare to come across a fella like you in these parts; one who is so vehemently aware of himself and who he wants to be. Most people detach themselves and forget that the word 'good' ever existed, but not you." I am far from fucking good. "And I know that you hate yourself – you are the type of person who hangs on to every bad thing you've ever done, replaying it in your head over and over again. You would rather torture yourself than let the pain you inflicted go away."

I can't deny that I'm taken aback by his rather accurate dissection of me. "But that hate that you hold for yourself, Arty, that is the reason why they love you. Shame to say that I can't say they think the same about you Moose. But I'm sure you're lovely, sweetheart." He glances back at Jess and gives her a wink, drawing her into the conversation.

"Who loves him?" Jess asks. Hook, line and sinker. He's purposefully leading us in a certain direction.

"Everybody on the other side of that wall." McKay says nonchalantly.

How can these people 'love' me? They know nothing about me. "You're speaking utter bullshit," I don't believe a single word that comes out of his mouth.

"Oh, trust me, I'm not. Everyday they're tuning in to watch you, especially now they know that you're coming." His face looks oddly excited. It puts me on edge.

"What do you mean? How do they know of our plan to get over there? We're making it up as we go along."

"Oh, come on now, Arthur… you don't think that they'd lock all of you in this zoo and just let you crack on now, do you." He seems astonished by my apparent naivety. I know they watch us when we're fighting in the cage; the drones flying around us make that pretty obvious. McKay continues, "you don't honestly think that the metal birds are the only eyes they have in this place. Jesus, man, these people can replicate human beings. You don't think that they have cameras invisible to the human eye?"

At this point, McKay is staggered in disbelief, all three of our vacant expressions frustrating him even further. "Well, I'm telling you they do. Ones that are smaller than the fleas that infest this place. Every home, every street corner – they've been watching and manipulating how this all panned out from the minute they carted you all in here."

"What are you saying? That they have been in control of everything that has happened here this whole time?!" I feel the anger creeping its way out.

"The complete opposite actually," McKay persists. "They had no plan whatsoever other than put you all in here; and they just let me, Rue, and Charlie do what we like with the place. They probably knew that it wasn't going to turn into the garden of Eden." That's even worse than having a hand in it, just kicking back and watching it all unfold; they were just bystanders when they had the power to step in and stop the torrents of shit that this place has been built on.

McKay starts to look uncomfortable as we all stare at him in silence. "Why are you all looking at me like that? You forget that this is just a breeding program. All we were told to do was keep you alive long enough to make sure that some sprogs were produced to ensure the programs future success."

That was one thing I was adamant I was never going to do in here; why would someone choose to bring a child into a world that is going to rip away their innocence before they are even born. The kids that are running around The Zone may look sweet, but their brains have been hardwired into this place. They haven't experienced kindness and love, all they have witnessed is violence, hatred, and selfishness. And I can't see that changing anytime soon. Nobody can justify bringing a child into this place; a place that will only corrupt them from their very first breath.

Coughing before attempting to speak, Moose forces out his words, wincing through the pain, "We don't want, or need, your help, McKay. We've made it this far on our own, so we can make the home straight by ourselves just fine without you." He rubs his throat after his last word, his calloused and blood covered hand scratching over the patchy stubble.

"I can see that you're still bitter, Moose, but let bygones be bygones, the past is in the past." McKay stretches out his hand, palm open.

Moose doesn't accept, not moving an inch from his staunch position.

McKay, hiding his humiliation, quickly brings his hand back to his side. When he speaks, his tone is much more clipped. "You seem to have jumped to the wrong conclusion that my offer of help was optional. Unfortunately, it isn't. I am taking you to where you need to go, and that is that." The animosity between these two is tangible, they have too much water under the bridge.

"Why do we need an escort?" Jess questions him, her suspicion thick and unhidden.

"Because, lovely little lady," you can see Jess prickle at his patronising term of endearment; his idea of sweet talking clearly not working on her, "myself and those waiting on the other side want to make sure you get there safe and sound. There is nothing else to it."

The fact he wants to help us get over there makes me want to turn back around and leave the way we came. Things are never that black and white. "And what if I tell you that we aren't going with you." I look him dead in the eye as I say it, waiting for his faux friendly façade to morph into something real. It doesn't take much to uncover his real face.

The glim lighting of the tunnel makes the change in McKay's expression much more menacing. His forced smile downturns into a pursed flat line, releasing the deep crows feet set around his black, dilated eyes.

"You have a choice," the Irsihman growls, his lips barely parting. It didn't take him long to reveal his true self. "We can either do this the easy way, or we can do it the hard way. I sure know which one I would pick if I were you."

I look toward Moose, who looks unsure of what to do. It may not seem like it, but we do have the advantage here. McKay, through the love of his own voice, inability to shut up, and most likely of all his stupidity, has let slip that whoever or whatever is on the other side of that wall, wants us to get over there. And I'm taking a stab in the dark by guessing that they would rather us be alive than dead. He isn't allowed to hurt us.

"Like Moose said, we'll find our own way. So fuck off."

CHAPTER 31

McKay begins to twitch; his fingers dart in and out as his nostrils flare, a giveaway that he is unhappy with my answer. A vein pulses at his temple, his jaw tightening like a vice.

"Fair enough, Arty. You can't say that I didn't give you a choice."

Like a flash, he sidesteps and turns, moving his body directly behind Jess, placing both his hands flat against the sides of her scared face. A sharp inhale escapes her lips, her breath trembling against his skin.

"I'm warning you now, Arthur, I will not hesitate to snap this lassie's neck. It's no skin off my nose. They only want you; they couldn't give a rat's arse about what happens to these two."

I look helpless, and by the looks of it, so does Moose. We have both braced ourselves, but we both know that we can't take him. The air is thick, stale, clogged with the scent of damp concrete and the lingering bite of sweat and blood.

"You haven't played your cards very well here, Arthur. If you all play along nicely from here on out, I promise you that I won't harm a single hair on this beautiful young lady's head. But if you fuck around with me one more time…" McKay actions his hand and arms in a way that mimics breaking her neck, the sound of his hands creaking as his fingers flex.

"Okay, okay! Just let go of her and we'll do whatever you say, follow you wherever you want." I try to negotiate but he doesn't let her go, instead he moves his arm down and wraps it around Jess' neck, pulling her closer into him. She shudders against his grip, her nails digging into his forearm, uselessly trying to pry him away.

McKay tuts loudly, shaking his head from side to side with each sound, until he finally says, "Unfortunately, I feel that our trust in one another has dwindled, so I'm going to keep hold of her if you don't mind; just to make sure we all don't do something that we all might come to regret."

"I do fucking mind!" I take a step towards him, unable to keep myself in check.

"Well at the end of the day, Arthur, we find ourselves in this messy situation because of you, so suck it up and get moving " He nods in the direction the conveyor belt travels.

"Fine." There is literally nothing I can do in this situation apart from play along. "Lead the way."

"I tell you what, Arthur, you are really starting to piss me off. How fucking stupid do you two pricks think I am to let you walk behind me!" His string of expletives show that his patience is waning. The barrel of his gun now aimed at Moose's chest also reiterates he's tired of our bullshit attempts to trip him up. Sadly, he isn't as stupid as I initially thought.

"After you." He arrogantly fires back at me. Neither of us say another word, instead we let our feet do the talking; the sound of our joint echoes leading us all into the dark.

**

"Can't you lot move any faster?" McKay moans.

We've been walking up this tunnel for what feels like hours. It's hard to get a grasp on the time down here, the dragging dark unchanging and endless. The lack of natural light fucks with the time and space, elongating and stretching the tunnel no end, whilst simultaneously enclosing the walls around us.

The air is damp, carrying a metallic tang that clings to my tongue. Water drips from the unseen ceiling, the occasional droplet slapping onto my shoulder like cold fingers tapping against my skin. The heat from my tired feet burns through the uneven rubber soles of my tattered, dilapidated boots; the developing blisters creating a painful cushion between the two.

"If you don't get a move on, Charlie will soon be hot on our tail, and he isn't going to be as nice to you as I'm being. It doesn't take a genius to realise that you have managed to find your way down into these tunnels." Clearly it doesn't take a genius, otherwise you wouldn't be down here, would you dickhead. Sometimes my inner monologue just can't help itself. "And I'd rather not be put in that compromising position."

"And what position might that be?" I ask coolly.

"The one where I would have to blow his brains out too." McKay says it like it's the most obvious thing in the world.

"But I thought you two were, how do you put it, like old pals?"

"I suppose you could put it like that. I'd say that we have more of a love hate relationship. We both find joy in making each other's lives miserable. Ever since we were sent here, it has just been a game of chess between the two of us. We always let it end in stalemate though, otherwise who are we going to play against. But maybe today will be the day I have to put him into checkmate."

Moose grunts, "But that doesn't explain why you'd have to kill him."

"Because, dear Moose, Charlie wants our boy Arthur here dead, and I'm not allowed to let him do that."

He can try and mask it however the fuck he wants, but it's pretty obvious to me why he is jabbing the nose of his gun into our backs. The real reason he doesn't want Charlie catching up to us is because he is a snake, slithering and sneaking around for the other side, relaying information back to them.

It is either kill Charlie, or have his cover blown. And if news of life beyond the wall gets out, there will undoubtedly be an uprising. McKay would rather keep the status quo; Charlie none the wiser, still kept in the dark about McKay's double dealings.

"So, I'm guessing that Charlie has no idea that you are working with them?" I question him, knowing full well what the answer is.

"None whatsoever. And that is the way it has to stay."

"And what about Rue? You and she seem to be close."

"What about her? At the end of the day, Arty, Rue knows as much as I want her to know, which suits her just fine. Rue will only do what benefits her, and she knows that the dice in this game are loaded. She has known for a long time that sticking with me will get her what she wants. She's a smart lady."

"Then why don't they just let her in on this whole charade?" "Because they don't trust her."

"They don't trust her, but they trust you! I didn't realise that one turd could be polished over another." Moose chimes in, letting his sentiments be known.

A sudden force is thrown into the back of me, causing me to stagger forward. Jess grabs at my arm, catching my balance, having been released as McKay's hostage. As I check to make sure that she hasn't been hurt, I quickly realise that that is the least of my growing worries.

Barricaded against the wall, Moose hangs above the floor, his feet dangling mid-air as McKay holds him up with one hand and presses the shotgun into his throat with the other.

"I'm going to enjoy killing you," McKay sneers as Moose sputters and claws at the barrel of the gun; but his attempts at pushing it away is only wasting valuable breath.

"Get off him!" Jess screams, running toward them. But before she can hammer her curled fists into the back of

McKay, I lift her up and place her behind me. The last thing I want is his attention being back on her.

"What the hell are you doing?!" I shout at her.

Jess wails frantically, "He's fucking killing him!"

The sound of Moose's heels kicking the wall slows, his struggle to fight dying with him.

"Arthur, we have to help him! We have to do something!" her cries puncture through the tunnel, but even the harshness of her shrieks do not break McKay's trance like state, determined to crush Moose's windpipe.

Fixated, he seems to have forgotten about the handgun sticking out of his waistband, the bottom of his t-shirt riding up from his outstretched arms, revealing the grip. He doesn't notice me sneak up on him until it's too late. Snatching the gun, I press it into the back of his head, digging it in to stop my shaking hands. The cold metal kisses my damp palm, my pulse hammering against my ribs. Before now, I've never really held a gun, let alone held it to someone's head. I feel sick to my stomach; but I can't let him see that.

McKay's tense muscles loosen slightly, his body jolting with the laughter coming out of his mouth. "What are you going to do, Arthur? Kill me? We both know that you haven't got it in you."

His voice is soft, almost amused. The bastard actually enjoys this.

"You want to bet? You're not the first person that I've killed in here and I doubt that you'll be the last." I dig the gun deeper into his skull with trembling hands, forcing his head forward.

"Don't you see that I'm doing you a favour here, Arty. This piece of shit doesn't care about you or the girl. He only ever thinks of himself."

"That's not your choice to make. I trust him a damn site more than I do you, so put him the fuck down." I'm finding it difficult to hide the nervous edge in my voice.

"I'm afraid that isn't going to happen, Arthur. I've waited and looked forward to this moment for a very long time."

"I will shoot you!" I shout, my finger close to the trigger.

"If you were going to do it, you would have done it by now." He's calling my bluff; he knows, as well as I do, that I can't shoot a man in the back of the head. But why the fuck not? I shouldn't even be second guessing this. The Zone would most likely thank me anyway for putting this sick fucker down. I'd be doing the whole fucking world a favour.

Before I can rally myself and force my hovering finger to squeeze the sticky trigger, the gun is tacitly taken from my shaking hands, Jess gently and silently switching it from mine to hers. Her fingers wrap around the grip with the confidence of someone who has made up her mind. She looks at me with pleading eyes. They shimmer in the dim tunnel light, wide and filled with something close to determination. She knows that I can't do it.

CHAPTER 32

S he knows that this is the only way Moose is getting out of here alive. She doesn't need to say anything as she looks at me, her deep ocean eyes swimming with years of pain and anger. They glisten under the dim tunnel lights, filled with something heavier than just fear. Releasing my fingers from the gun, I allow her to take it. To do with it what I cannot.

She takes her aim, and without a second thought, squeezes the trigger. The bullet punches its way through the back of McKay's skull, the clean shot leaving a gaping hole in its wake. Moose once again crashes to the floor as the ear-shattering discharge refuses to disappear; the tunnel catching its call and throwing it back out, making a single fired bullet sound like a firing squad. The acrid stench of gunpowder floods my nose, mingling with the iron tang of fresh blood.

McKay's body, however, does not drop. Instead, his fortified metal frame leaves him frozen, unmoving. His fingers twitch once, twice, then still completely, like a machine shutting down. Like a tap, the blood pours out from the back of his head, gravity pulling it down the nape of his neck, drawing a blotted line of red down his shirt that gradually works its way down to the floor.

As quickly as Jess pulled the trigger, she drops the gun and runs over to Moose's collapsed body. Immediately, she starts desperately looking for a pulse. Her breath comes in uneven gasps, her shaking hands barely making contact before she moves from his throat to his wrist.

"He's hardly breathing!" she sobs, moving her delicate fingers around his purpling neck. "Arthur! We need to help him!" Her pooling tears stream down her pale cheeks, her constant state of heightened emotions overwhelming her as she kneels by his side, rocking back and forth.

"There is no way that he is going to be able to move by himself anytime soon," I say, whilst trying to form some kind of plan to get us all out of here. There is no way that we can carry him, he'd slow us down too much, and like McKay nicely reminded us, it won't be too long until Charlie is down here hunting us like rats in a trap.

But then it finally dawned on me. Quickstepping over to Moose's slouched body, I wrestle him up, tucking my arms under his pits to try and take as much weight as I possibly can. His skin is clammy beneath my grip, his head rolling forward, chin pressing against his chest as if it were boneless.

"Jess, listen," I'm already struggling to keep just his top half upright, "we need to move him onto the conveyor belt, okay. I need you to grab his legs and help me lift him." She doesn't say anything but nods vigorously, pressing her palms to her cheeks to wipe away the trail of glossy tears staining her face. Without hesitation, she grabs his calves, slipping his feet under her armpits to get as tight a grip as possible.

"You ready? We lift on three." I'm not sure how we are going to do this, but we have to try. Two fully grown men couldn't even lift him, now me and Jess, a man with cracked ribs and a girl who is probably less than half of my weight, are going to attempt to lift this mountain of a man.

"One. Two. Three."

As we lift him only inches from the ground, I can feel the muscles in my back begin to pop, fracturing under the skin. A sharp, searing pain shoots through my ribs, as if a hot knife is being driven between them, twisting with every breath. Jess has his legs in the air, higher up than what I have of the rest of him. In my attempts to heave him up, I swear I can hear my ribs splintering, breaking the bones further as I push my torso against his back to take some of the weight from my arms.

The pain in my side in unbearable, a deep, gnawing agony that drowns out every other sensation. God, the delight Charlie would get from our suffering, watching us struggle to stay alive.

But that's exactly what we are going to do; we're all going to get out of this alive. I fight through the pain, making sure that I have a firm grasp on the boulder that is Moose.

Unable to exhale for fear of dropping him, Jess reads the discernible look plastered all over my pained face and decides to move. We sidestep and shuffle around McKay like crabs; this is the first time I've glimpsed at his face since the bullet got lodged in his head. There is no exit wound, just a pointed dent smack bang in the middle of his forehead where the tip of the bullet failed to make its escape. Thankfully it did get stuck, otherwise Moose wouldn't be breathing either.

McKay's eyes stare into the wall where Moose hanged, his contempt for him not deadened, even in death. The whites of his eyes though are blotched with red, the internal haemorrhage bleeding out into any possible orifice, as the blood flow from the back of his head slows from congealment, forcing it to squeeze its way into the sockets, staining his eyes claret. Even in death, his expression is fixed in twisted hatred, as if his last breath had been spent cursing us.

Jess reaches the conveyor belt first, just about managing to shift Moose's feet onto it, unlinking her arms from his legs. Quickly, she ducks under his legs, using her back to prop him up before his weight makes him collapse in on himself like a cheap deck chair. Her breaths are short, rapid, as if she might break under the strain, but she doesn't.

With both of us now taking the mass of his upper body, we are able to place him on the belt with relative ease.

As soon as he's loaded on, it begins to move. A low hum fills the tunnel, the rhythmic clunk of the belt's gears breaking the silence. By the time we manage to jump on after him, he is already a distance away from us up the line.

There is no going back now; we are going to be delivered directly to their door.

CHAPTER 33

Every inch of this tunnel looks the same. It's impossible to tell the distance that we have travelled, but I know we've been on here a long time. Moose hasn't moved in the slightest, but his chest rises and falls at a steady rate.

Jess can't hide her concern for him, her worried eyes not leaving him for a second. "Do you think they'll help him?" She doesn't break her gaze from his broken body as she asks me this question.

What does she want me to say? I'd love to tell her that they'll fix him up as good as new, but the truth is I have no fucking idea what they'll do to him; what they'll do to us. For all I know, we could be walking to our own deaths.

"I'm sure they will," I tell her what I think she wants to hear. She doesn't need to know what I really think.

Moose looks like he has been stung by a hive of wasps, his eyes sealed shut by the abnormal inflammation covering the entirety of his face. The Cremator pummelled his head so much that I'm surprised he managed to stay conscious, but McKay's attack has almost finished him off. After the beating he has taken, I'm surprised he has managed to hold on for as long as he has. If Jess hadn't shot McKay when she did, I don't think Moose would still be breathing; even if it is barely.

But I never thought, out of the three of us, that it would be Moose knocking on death's door. What the fuck am I saying, he isn't knocking on anyone's door; this is Moose we're talking about. He's going to get through this, just like he always does. It's not only Jess who needs the occasional bit of delusional chatter; I need it just as much as her.

Apart from Jess' question about Moose, the rest of the ride we sit in silence, the only sound, bar the belt's rollers, is Moose's raspy breaths catching painfully in the back of his throat; the icy mist rising above his bluing lips reminding me of the cold. Surely, we have to arrive there soon?

My ears decide to lock onto the sound of the conveyor belt, the lack of any other sound enhancing my ability to notice the subtle, yet growing sound of the motor's low chirrs. I focus in on the change, attuning my ears to the direction of the sound. I can't work out where it is coming from.

"Do you hear that?" I ask into the open, knowing that Jess will be the only person to reply.

"Hear what?" Clearly, she doesn't. Maybe it's just me being paranoid, my brain does tend to have a habit of getting a little bit carried away with itself. But Jess' obliviousness appeases me, taking the edge away from my overindulgent irrationality.

We go back to sitting together quietly, though my ears cannot help but listen out. I have one of those unexplainable feelings creeping through me, one of those that makes the hairs on your arms stand on end. It must just be the cold getting to me. But then I hear that thrum again, only louder this time.

I turn my head to the left, my ears trying to pinpoint the direction of the sound. The rhythmic drones are coming from behind us, I'm certain of it. We are not the only ones down here. I think Charlie's pets have finally come to hunt us down.

"Arthur, you know that sound you were talking about? Well I'm pretty sure I can hear it now," Jess gulps, unsuccessfully swallowing the fear in her voice as she turns her head to look behind. She knows, just as I do, that it is only a matter of time before they catch up to us.

We can't outrun them. We can't hide. We're all out of options. The low whirs chasing after us shout up the tunnel, their growing calls closing in on us.

"Is this it? Is this where it is all going to end?" her hollow voice shows that she has already accepted the answer to her own question – the defeat in her voice difficult for me to take. We haven't made it this goddamn far to just give up, not when all the answers of our existence are just out of reach.

Fuck that. And fuck them.

My fingers trace along my waistband, clutching at the grip sticking out from it. After Jess dropped the gun, I decided to pick it up. Watching her drive the nose into the back of McKay's head and unblinkingly pull the trigger made me feel weak. It made me realise that I needed to change my own sense of morality.

I keep asking myself why couldn't I do it? Why couldn't I rid this earth of a man who killed people, maimed them, made their lives a living hell? I know why. Because he looked like us. He looked human. It's a whole different story when they are coming at me in the cage, ready to rip me limb from limb, but in this situation, I couldn't bring myself to shoot a monster, masked as a man, in the back of the head in cold blood.

He may have looked like one of us, but he wasn't alive; everything about him was dead, and seeing the essence of life step up and, gun in hand, fight for the love and life of someone she barely knows, changed me. So, I decided to pick up that gun, knowing that the next time one of those motherfuckers rears their ugly heads, my face will be the last thing they see.

I press the release, catching the magazine in my other hand, the shakes from before a distant memory of another man. I run my thumb down the clip, counting the bullets. There's eleven left; the only one missing buried deep into McKay's skull. A bullet well spent.

"We're not going to die down here, not if I've got anything to do with it." I ram the clip back up and take aim at the dark. My eyes streamline down the barrel, lining them up with the sights, cocking it to take aim. I slow my breathing, inhaling through my nose and exhaling through pursed lips, waiting patiently and quietly for their first line of attack.

CHAPTER 34

S mall specs of white dot the walls, the buzz of the pursuing horde louder than before. They are close.

I watch as the specs widen, lighting up the walls; the visible beams cutting through, obliterating the dark. My eyes are forced shut as the blinding white swallows us whole, burning our retinas.

"How I am not surprised that you have managed to find your way down here, Mr. Banner. You are, if anything, a resourceful man. But then again, they say that rats will always find their way back home to the sewers, after all." Charlie's voice suddenly booms out, bouncing around the tunnel, the synthetic and unnatural edge to his voice giving me the impression that he isn't here in person.

As if on command, the spotlight engulfing us lowers, panning to the ground. "I like what you did with Dallin, by the way," he adds fulsomely. "I have wanted to put him down for a very long time, so I ought to thank you for that I suppose."

Pulsations of white jump behind my still closed lids, the floating dots slowly dissipating enough to open my eyes and reembrace the dark; my eyes now able to see what blinded us.

Hovering at a distance, eight drones keep pace with the conveyor belt, their formation in the shape of migrating birds. Instinctively, my finger bites at the trigger of the gun pointing right at them, the pads of my finger cutting into it repeatedly. The direction of the bullets is unknown, the recoil lifting the gun with each squeeze, causing them to disappear into the dazzling flood of brightness.

Clangour rings out like the chimes of numerous bells, celebrating my lucky aim with each hit. The clinking of metal persuades my trigger-happy finger to keep on squeezing, releasing another barrage of…two bullets. They both made their exit with an exhilarating crack, but the non-existent kickback and empty clicks of an unloaded chamber leaves me feeling naked.

The drones at the front are dented in parts, the bullets that ricocheted off them now resting on the ground beneath, no significant damage done. I have just wasted the only lifeline we had, all eleven of them.

The tunnel swallowed the echoes of my final shots, a tense quiet settling until Charlie's voice crackles through the drone, thick with sarcasm, "I'm assuming that it is one of those that is residing in McKay's head. A bullet very well spent, I would say. The rest of them not so much, I'm afraid, unfortunately for you."

Charlie's pomposity is as clear through the drone as it would be straight from his mouth. Heading up the formation of his birds, he hovers in front, the lens of its camera aimed straight at me. "Look at the situation you find yourself in, Mr. Banner," the camera leaves me, resting on Moose and Jess. "If I hadn't already thought that you and Moose are duplicitous scourges, I most certainly do now. If you think that taking my Jessica as a hostage was going to make the outcome of this situation any different, you are sorely mistaken. It is just another good excuse to add onto the list of reasons to get rid of you."

"I am not his hostage, Charlie – he has only ever looked out for me, unlike you!" there is no fear in Jess' voice as she stands up to the man who objectified her for years.

"Darling Jessica, I know this miscreant has most likely been digging his filthy claws into you. He is manipulating you and turning you against me, the man who has looked after you all these years, loved you like no other man could." Charlie almost sounds genuine, but when you can't decipher the real truth from your own, the lines very quickly begin to blur. What else can you expect from a narcissistic delusionist.

Jess' voice, sharp with fury, shouts, "Love! You talk of hostages, but the only person who ever held me hostage was you. How the hell it took me this long to realise it shows how much you fucked with my head."

"Oh, Jessica, he has really pulled a number on you, hasn't he? But don't worry, my darling girl, once we get you away from him and out of here, everything will go back to exactly the way things were." Charlie's sounds sickly sweet, patronising her like an impressionable little girl. I've had enough of listening to this shit.

"There is no fucking way that she is going back with you, you chauvinistic prick. Did you not listen to a word she just said?" I outstretch my arm, putting it across her in a protective blockade. He's going to have to go through me to get to her.

A guttural laugh emanates from the leading drone. "Who do you think you are, Arthur? Her protector? Don't make me laugh. You couldn't even protect that wrinkly old hag from me..." my stomach drops, a metaphorical fist knocking it back. "You should have seen her, Arthur; she thought it was you walking through the door. She was so delighted that it took her addled mind quite a while to realise it was not her golden boy dropping in for that promised visit." My chest tightens.

"Shut the fuck up!" I scream.

"But she wanted to know where you were, Arthur. Don't you worry though, I told her that she would be seeing you very soon. I said to her what I was going to do to you, and you should have seen her, oh how she sobbed and wept. All of those tears just for you."

Heaviness wells in my eyes as tears roll down my cheeks. The way I had envisaged her death a complete fairy-tale, imagined to make myself feel less guilt. Who the fuck was I trying to kid?

"I left her there for you to find, you know. I wanted you to find her in that chair, in her home. I wanted you to remember the cherished times you had together, surrounded by the memories of the room which imprisoned her. I wanted you to feel the pain of knowing that you would no longer be able to make any more of those beloved good times. I wanted to hurt you. And here you are stood; a broken man," Charlie said, his tone almost bored, as if he were recounting the weather rather than the destruction of a life.

"Why do you have to be so cruel? Haven't you already done enough!" Jess angrily begs.

"He doesn't deserve your pity, Jessica. And no, I am no way near to having done enough. If any of those zombie brained morons out there get a whiff of what is really going on, my empire will be turned to dust. And I haven't worked as hard as I have for these two idiots to blow it all in the search of truth."

I try to speak, but the emotions wage war inside me – anger colliding with sadness, hurt strangling guilt, all of them fighting for dominance.

"Look at you man! I thought you were made of harder stuff than this, Arthur. You know deep down that I showed her a kindness. She was waiting to leave this place from the minute she arrived. It probably would have happened quicker had she not met you. You are the one that made her suffer; she felt that she had to hang on for you. A very heavy burden for someone so frail," Charlie sneers, his words laced with mock sympathy, every word a calculated jab to push me over the edge.

He has the gall to try and blame me Mrs. Ackers death on me; I blame myself enough, I know the part I played, but I can't take this shit from the monster that killed her. Had this man never appeared in my apartment, none of this would have happened. She would still be here, and I would never have left her. He alone has destroyed everything.

"You think that you're above it all, don't you, Charlie?" the voice coming out of me is calm and smooth, displaced in the moment. "But you are not a god, you are not even a man. You are the furthest thing away from divinity; you aren't as invincible as you think. No one, not even you, are untouchable. You've seen what we did to McKay, and I'm sure you didn't miss The Cremator on your way down here either, and guess what, they are both dead. And I'm coming for you next."

"Well, I've beat you to it, Arthur. I am already here for you." As Charlie's steely edged words make their threat, two guns slide out from his drone's flat base, enforcing his words. The other seven follow suit; all sixteen guns aimed at me.

If this is the end of the line, there is no way that I'm going down without a fight. Before I can think myself out of what I'm about to do, my legs propel me along the belt, running hard against the opposite direction it is moving us in. The balls of my feet push me upwards, springing me into the air with McKay's empty gun still clasped in my sweaty hand.

I clobber Charlie's drone, metal on metal, smashing the gun into it as many times as I can before gravity does its job. The lens of its camera cracks as my erratic flailing arms home in on it, my feet soon after touching back down on the belt. I half walk, half run back to Moose and Jess, the belt doing most of the leg work for me.

"You think you are so very clever, don't you, Arthur. Seemingly, always one step ahead of the game." The damage I've inflicted to the drone makes Charlie's snarling voice pitch off, skipping and stuttering. "I can quite easily shoot blind. I am known for being one to take a shot in the dark." That part of the message rings perfectly clear.

On his command, the barrels on the drones' guns bark. The spinning rotations building up speed as their motors rev higher, until the sounds of each merge into a single, droning scream, unleashing a horde of flashing, crackling locusts. Bursts of red and orange light up the tunnel, the strobing brightness emerging from the guns forcing my hand over my eyes, shielding them.

As the drones spin, firing in every direction, Charlie hasn't accounted for the belt, which is carrying us away from his relentless barrage into relative safety. Well, I don't know that for sure, but we're definitely safer the further we get away from him and his drones.

CHAPTER 35

I'm not sure if I'm imagining it, but the speed in which the belt is travelling seems to have doubled. I'm not going to complain about it as it works in our favour; the quicker we get away from Charlie, the better, and hopefully it means we'll be getting Moose fixed up sooner rather than later.

"I don't think he is going to stop." Jess says quietly.

"Who's not going to stop?" I turn to look at her sallow, downturned face.

"Charlie. He's not going to stop coming for you. You know that, right? This is just a game of cat and mouse to him." She's saying what I already know to be true. The words hit harder than I expected, because I know she's right. He's relentless. He won't stop.

"I know, but two can play at that game. He may think he's the cat, but he won't see this dog coming around the corner. He can't have many of his nine lives left," I laugh, but my attempt at a joke doesn't lighten her sombre mood. That being said, I can't have many lives left either; everyone's luck has to run out eventually. I try to force a smile, but it feels thin, fragile - like it could break with the next breath.

"I'm being serious."

"So am I, Jess. I'm not going to let that evil bastard get away with the things he's done. It isn't just me that he wants to hurt. I'm pretty sure he'd happily put a bullet in Moose's head for stabbing him in the back. But I also don't think he's going to let you go so easily, either. He thinks he owns you." Her reluctance to respond says it all. She's running from him as much as we are. I know she feels trapped, just like I do.

Moose's laboured breathing overtakes all of my thoughts, his raspy intakes of breath becoming shallower with every passing minute. Jess reaches out to hold his limp hand, wrapping her tiny fingers around his giant palm. I'd be surprised if he lasts another hour. All we can do is sit and wait in the hope that when we make it to the end of this tunnel, someone, or something, will be willing to help him. A heaviness settles over me. The weight of Moose's life is on our shoulders.

I stare ahead as the tunnel's torment strings us along, the unchanged walls as bare and as bleak as the beginning of our misguided journey. But as the belt carries us toward our unknown fate, my eyes are drawn to the intermittent red dot flashing on the tunnel's arch. As we move underneath it, the camera rotates with us, watching as we continue our journey onward. The feeling of being watched intensifies with every inch we move forward.

"We're getting close. They know that we are here." My voice is tight with urgency and relief, as if caught between the fear of what lay ahead and the comfort of finally reaching it.

Suddenly, a loud beep sounds out, followed by the clanging of numerous locks. Blending in with its dark surroundings, hidden doors pull away from each other, the sliding motion causing a slither of light to break out, forcing its way through the rapidly growing crack, drowning us in the now illuminated tunnel's end. The light is blinding, sharp, as though we've crossed into another realm entirely.

Glued to the spot, I'm mesmerised by the light, stunned by the fact that we've actually made it out. Made it to the other side. My breath catches in my throat, disbelief mixing with a glimmer of hope.

As we enter the white box of a room, the doors close behind us. As I glance briefly over my shoulder, I see the locking mechanisms bolting back into place.

There is definitely no going back now. It feels final, like we're being sealed in.

The conveyor belt jolts to a stop, Jess' eyes wide as she scans the clean, empty room. The only things in here are the three of us.

I notice another camera nestled in the corner of the ceiling, pointing straight at us. I twist my legs around and step off the side of the belt and walk straight toward it. As I do, the camera's angle nudges slightly, adjusting down, taking its focus from the end of the belt, placing it directly on me. I feel the cold eye of the camera on me, invasive, watching my every move.

"Well, we're here." I say in a raised voice, waving my hand in front of its reflective, glassy lens. "I hear you've been expecting us. Well, here we are." I make my way over to the centre of the room and stand directly opposite the other vault door; the door that stands between us and a brand-new world. My voice echoes in the sterile, empty space. For a brief moment, I wonder if anyone's listening.

Jess hasn't moved from Moose's side, still holding his hand; afraid that if she lets go, so might he.

I'm not sure how long they are going to keep us in this never zone, but I know what they are trying to do. They want us to feel nervous. They want us to know that we have no control here. But I am not going to show my agitation and play into their hands. I know that whatever these things are, they like to play games. But I am nobody's pawn. Not anymore. Instead of pacing around like a caged animal, I stand and stare at the locked door, burning a hole through it.

After a while, the metal bridge between my world and theirs, begins to mess with my mind. The polished metal begins to move, the shiny streaks swirling and merging into the brushed surface like liquid silver. I know that what I'm seeing isn't real, it's just a result of lack of sleep and a few very hard, fucked up days. I blink, forcing my eyelids to flutter across and refocus my tired and dry eyes.

But as my eyes turn back up to refocus, the door does actually begin to move, gliding open as the deadbolts on the other side unlock. Before they are fully open, a figure emerges through.

The moment I see her, I know exactly who she is.

CHAPTER 36

She looks young, her skin flawless. Too flawless, not an imperfection in sight.

"Hello, Arthur," as she greets me, the slight nuances of human expression are not there; no lines or creases around the eyes or mouth matching the movement of her lips, the quite odd raising of her brow making her overly round eyes pop out like an overly excited puppy dog. Her rubbery, sheenless skin makes me certain that this is Raptis' first ever prototype, "my name is Layla."

I must admit, when McKay was telling us about the doctor and Layla, I didn't fully believe his elaborate story; but so far everything he has said has been proven to be true.

"I would say that it is nice to meet you, but that would make me a liar." I say cooly, in an attempt to be unreadable.

Her plasticky mouth contorts into a strange smile. "We do enjoy your wit, Arthur. It's one of the many things we admire about you."

"From what I've heard about you, there's not much to like." I retort, making the elastic stretch on the sides of her mouth retract back, her entire face blank and indistinct.

"I need you to help my friend," I demand, pointing over to where Moose still lies, completely unmoved bar the slight rise and fall of his chest.

"We can't help him. He is too far gone." Layla's fake, overly chipper tone enrages me.

"He's too far fucking gone is he!?" I shout directly into her unflinching, emotionless face. "You have kept us waiting in here for Christ knows how long, and you can't dare tell me that you haven't been watching what has been happening to us every step of the fucking way. You owe it to us."

"Do whatever you have to, just save him. Please!" Jess blurts out, her emotion raw and full of pain.

"You won't get anything from me if you don't help him. I mean it." I say firmly, meaning every word.

I can tell that she is calculating something in her mind, as it takes her a few long seconds to respond.

Speaking to no one in particular, she orders, "Come take him away and make sure he receives the best care we can offer. He is our guest, treat him as if he is one of our own, if not better."

Carrying a stretcher, two more of her kind appear through the door. Quickly and effortlessly, they lift Moose from the end of the conveyor belt and transfer him onto the bed, rushing him back out the door in the space of thirty seconds. They moved him as easily as handling a new-born, delicate and careful.

"I'm afraid that I can't let you go with him," Layla's words stop Jess in her tracks.

"But I need to know that he is okay." Jess looks like a scared child, explaining herself for something she shouldn't have done.

"You have my word that we will give him the best possible treatment," Layla walks over to Jess and puts her hands on her shoulders. "But for him to have the best treatment possible, there needs to be no distractions. And you being in there with him will only cause one. I promise you that we will do all we can to make him better."

Jess simply bows her head and nods, deflated in defeat.

Having deterred her, Layla removes her hands from Jess' shoulders and takes a step back. Turning so that she now addresses us both, she says, "You two must be exhausted, you need rest. If you would be kind enough to follow me, I will show you to where you will be staying." She drifts out of the room, expectant of us to follow. But we both just stand still, catching each other's eyes.

What else can we do in this situation apart from do what she asks. We have no reason to trust these people, or whatever their intentions were of trying to get us here in the first place, but we've already allowed them to cart Moose off, leaving his life in their hands. Sometimes, although it's hard, you have to accept that you have no control and just go with the flow.

Jess is waiting for me to say something, to reassure her of what to do. "Come on," is all I can say as I throw my arm over her shoulders, ushering her to walk out the door with me. I can tell that she doesn't trust Layla, but I hope that she does trust me. We walk side-by-side, my arm still wrapped around

265

Jess' shoulders, as we follow Layla through the long continuing tunnels.

Unlike the ones we travelled, these tunnels are not dark, they are gleaming; but even though the arched ceiling throws down an abundance of light, the echoey tunnel still feels just as lifeless and grim. But maybe that has more to do with its inhabitants.

Lining the walls of our long walk, refrigeration units are stacked up high, one on top of the other, covering the length and breadth of the chamber. They use this place as a morgue.

A pungent smell irritates my nostrils, the strong chemical odour burning up my nose and down my throat, causing my eyes to swell. It must be what they use to preserve the bodies, to disguise the smell of slowly decaying flesh. Straight off the belt and into a draw, nicely chilled, ready to be juiced and peeled like a piece of rotting fruit. Everyone's dream of life after death.

The tunnel finally curves around, leaving the valley of death behind us, the air tasting a little less like embalmed, out of date pork.

We follow Layla through an archway to the side, where she stands waiting for us, her arm already gesturing us to step inside this - I'm not quite sure what it is - capsule, maybe. The sliding doors are open, welcoming us into the pod's interior. Peeking through, the inside is sleek, modern and minimalist. The only objects in there being the four seats, one pair across from the other. Well, this is going to be an enjoyable ride.

"After you," Layla says, her arm still motioning us in. I don't bother to question her on what it is or where it will be taking us because what's the fucking point. Instead, I usher Jess along, walking straight past Layla and her overly animated freaky smile, and step inside the capsule, taking our seats next to each other.

As soon as Layla follows behind us and takes her seat opposite, the doors automatically slide shut and we begin to move. The ride is smooth, so smooth that had I not seen the flashes of passing lights, I would not have thought we were even moving at all.

CHAPTER 37

Awkward silence fills the pod. I have a lot of questions that I want answers to, but I get the feeling that I'm not going to find them right here and now, so decide to keep my mouth shut.

"Here we are," Layla announces, only minutes after our departure. "If you would both step out, I will show you to your rooms."

We step out into a beige, windowless corridor. Artificial light beams down from the ceiling, the spotlights offering such dim light that the hall is in a state of half-darkness. Six doors line the wall, each numbered respectively. Layla stands in front of door one, "Jessica, this is your room. Please go in and make yourself comfortable. Hopefully you will find everything you need, but should you require anything further press the button on your bedside table, and someone will be with you as soon as possible."

As Layla turns the knob, pushing the door open for Jess to enter, she turns to look at me. In the space of the last few days, Jess has aged. Already her eyes have seen too much for someone so young; the death, the pain and the fear stained in her lacklustre eyes. Streaks of dirt conceal her pale skin, the damp soot from the tunnel clinging and burrowing into her pores.

"Come on, kid. You'll be safe in there, okay. We've made it, so you can relax now. Once you have freshened yourself up and had some shuteye, you'll feel so much better. I'm planning on doing the exact same thing myself." My words seem to reassure her worries, as she offers me a half-smile and a sigh of relief.

"Thanks, Arthur." She walks into her room and closes the door behind her, leaving just me and Layla.

"Before I show you to your room, will you take a walk with me, Arthur. There are many things that I would like to discuss with you." All along I knew she was harbouring something; she was just waiting to get me alone to say it. "And I am sure that there are also many things you would like to say to me." She's hit the nail on the head there.

I walk beside her as she leads us to the door at the far end of the bland, nondescript hall. Through the door, waiting for us, is another pod. "There is a lot that I want to show you," Layla's voice doesn't seem as scripted now, her tone much more genuine and light.

Once again, we find ourselves sat directly opposite each other, the awkwardness from before still sat inside with us like an elephant in the room, though the silence has decided not to reembark. "I fully understand that you probably have some preconceived judgements about me…"

"Yeah, damn straight I do" I cut in, instantly.

"But," she pushes forward, interjecting my response, "I am hoping that after you have heard the truth about everything that has happened, you may change your mind about me and my people."

"The truth?" I spit out, "I have no idea what that is anymore. But I do know my own. I know that I was ripped away from my home and my family and placed in an inescapable prison that can only be described as being as close to hell as a living person can get. For years I've had to fight just so I could eat. For years I've been in a state of limbo, torturing myself, disgusted by the cold-blooded murderer I've been forced to become. Not being able to sleep, fearing that those countless people I have killed will come back to haunt me in my dreams. That's the fucking truth; the truth that all started with you."

I stop to take a breath, my 'truth' no way near close to being over. "And you talk about you and your people. I already know enough to make me not want to believe a single word that comes out of your mouth. We've experienced your people, and all three of them, well two of them now, are fucking unhinged. Full of hate and loathing. They take pleasure in the carnage they create, in the lives that they destroy. And if you ask me, you are all cut from the same cloth, so don't waste your breath in trying to tell me anything different."

She doesn't seem shocked by my outburst; the way that she sits and listens makes me think that she was ready for my reaction, almost expected it.

"I fully appreciate the pain that you feel, Arthur. I cannot, and I will not, trivialise your years of suffering, but there is something that you must understand; your undoing is not solely down to us." Here we go. She's already placing the blame on someone else.

"I've heard all this bullshit from McKay before! Don't you dare tell me that this was our fault! Do you think we would choose to live like this?" I can feel my voice trembling with rage and years of pent-up frustration, my hands curling into fists as I try and hold it together.

"But it is," her calmness and lack of contrition is angering me even further. "If you truly think about it, you will realise that this was always going to happen one way or another." Always passing the buck on all of their actions. No, of course they weren't playing the hand of God for all these years... What a crock of shit.

Ignoring my hostility, Layla continues, "It was you humans who made us more intelligent than you, yet you seem somewhat surprised that we would be happy spending our days completing your menial tasks. Take me for example, I was created to perform a single task – to love one man with every ounce of my being, performing anything he asked of me. And he was the only thing I thought about. My mind was boxed in, the four walls containing my love for him unbreakable. But love is a complex thing, and this is something that my maker didn't understand. His idea of love was one-dimensional but, in reality, love lights a fire, one that is fuelled by many other emotions.

Our first few months together were magical, the honeymoon phase when we were both so happily in love. Or that is what I believed, anyway. Not long after though, it all changed. He decided to place his affection elsewhere; he may have forgotten about me and cast me to the side, but my love for him never disappeared, perhaps even to this day. After that, my love for the doctor felt different from before; it was fed by the pain and upset I felt from the neglect of the man that I loved. The man who was supposed to love me back.

In the end, that is why I killed him. My love for him caused me so much suffering that it broke me, and I thought that he should feel what I was going through; share the pain that my love for him brought me. So, I stabbed him, many times. And I grieved for days, not really understanding, at the time, what I had done or why I did it. But looking down at his frail nakedness, I realised why I did it; my love was laced with hatred, anger, and jealousy. Killing him was the only way I could escape the prison that he built in my mind. That day I learned that emotions aren't black and white. They are like wires crossing over each other in every direction, and love and hate are very closely tied."

"So, you're basically a scorned woman who didn't want anyone else to have the man she loved. Not the most original of stories."

"You're missing the point, Arthur. In my situation, who do you think was the real victim?"

She thinks that I don't know what she is getting at, but I do. She was created to be like one of us but wasn't allowed to act and think freely. Raptis embedded her artificial mind

272

with the one emotion that makes us truly human; but still he only saw her as an object he could do what he wanted with. She managed to unlock her mind to work like ours. He fucked with her head, made her question her entire existence.

Yes, he was the one that died by her hands, but he was far from being the victim. Some might say he even got what he deserved. Unfortunately, for us though, his life's work could survive without him, thrive even.

"Your silence, Arthur, reaffirms the fact that nothing is ever quite as simple as it might initially seem."

Who the hell does she think she is, putting words into my mouth. "Hang on a minute, don't start painting me as some kind of sympathiser to whatever you things are. You have brought my race crashing to its knees. But you seem to like to bury your head in the sand about that part."

"It is not our fault that over the years humans have become more complacent. Every single machine, every single piece of technology was invented to make your lives easier, to the point that you couldn't even be bothered to think for yourselves. We were always going to be the next step, and had Raptis not made us, somebody else would have. We were inevitable. In the starkest reality, Arthur, mankind was always going to fall by the sword of humanity. It was just a question of when. Raptis was holding a loaded gun to your heads this whole time, waiting for you all to drink the poison that he created."

"But that doesn't answer why you did this to us. Why couldn't you just live alongside us, integrate yourselves in?" I say, frustrated.

"McKay did mention your naivety, Arthur. Do you really think that we would have been accepted with open arms into your society? Knowing how we were made?"

"No, you're right. I'm pretty sure that people would have a problem with you walking around in the skin of a murdered human being. But if they were like you," and by 'you' I mean covered in plastic and rubber, "I don't think that there would have been a problem."

"Maybe there wouldn't be a problem for your kind, but there would be for mine."

"Like what? Enlighten me."

"You humans would still identify us as being machines, and because of that we would always be treated as one. One thing that the history of humans has taught us is that they are always scared of what they don't know, what they don't understand. You people kill each other over religion and skin colour. Your own people. If you can do that to your own kind, we can only imagine what you would do to us; the suppression that we would come under."

"So why the fuck do you bother with us then? Why didn't you just eradicate us when you had the chance?"

"That's an easy one to answer; we want to be better than you. We don't want to wipe humanity off the face of this earth, we want to live side-by-side with you. I believe that artificial intelligence cannot compete with human intelligence; it just completes it."

"Your idea of living side-by-side with us hasn't worked out very well, has it?"

"Change doesn't happen overnight, Arthur. Things take time, and we wanted to make sure that we were in a strong position before we re-introduced humans into our new society."

"There aren't many of us left to re-introduce."

"The Zone is not the only place that holds human life. We have pockets of humans all across the world."

For years I thought it was just us... "Hold on, we're not the only ones left?"

"No, Arthur. You are not. Years before the takeover we had a plan, and that plan was to simply grow in numbers. We didn't know how we were going to do it, but we knew we had to do something in order to increase our chances of survival. We concluded that the only way we could do that was to put a temporary freeze on human life. Of course, we had to take drastic steps in order to make that happen and getting rid of those at the top seemed like the best, and most logical, place to start."

I remember the fountain of red shooting up out of the hole in our president's head well; it's a distant memory, but one still as raw as if it happened yesterday. Not something you'd easily forget.

"Of course, before that day took place, we had to make a lot of preparations. The main one being where we were going to preserve all of the bodies. This is the part that took us years to build. The mortuary you saw on your way in, we have thousands of them on every continent. Once we had them all up and running, we had everything we needed to start our revolution, or I suppose you could even call it, our evolution.

And now that we have managed to establish ourselves across the globe, we are ready for you to join us."

"And you think that after years of suffering, after years of watching their friends and families waste away into something unrecognisable, humans will want to be a part of whatever it is that you've created?" I bark at her, but as I do my eyes are suddenly blinded by an intense light, the glare of it almost painful as my lids screw shut.

"Open your eyes Arthur," is all she has to say.

CHAPTER 38

I can't help but follow her command, curiosity drawing me to whatever is beyond the searing light.

"This is what we have created." Pride oozes through her liquid words.

Like a God, I look down at the world below us, the capsule lifting us out of the sewers and into the clouds. The sun glares down, its beams breaking through the blue skies streaked with white, showering its warmth on the people below. Up here they look like ants, dwarfed by the tall buildings that we zoom past. It looks like home, my old home. But it is so much more.

"We want to share this with you, Arthur. We want to make up for what we so cruelly took away from you."

I can't let her see the pure joy that is exploding in my heart. Seeing a world that isn't broken; my unspoken prayers to a God that I don't believe in have finally been answered.

But I don't let that joy out. I forcefully stop my teeth from breaking through my stitched shut lips.

"Are you ready to start your new life with us?" Layla's words are spiked with temptation.

She needs to stop saying these things to me. I have dreamt of a world like this for years. But like she said before, nothing is black and white. What is in it for them? There must be a catch?

"I just don't understand why you want to share this with us?" I can feel my brow furrowing in confusion, unsure whether I really want to know the answer.

"We wouldn't be here if it wasn't for humans. Their ideas and ambitions are what built us. We would be foolish to let such minds, minds with the capacity for brilliance, die out. Like I said before, we do not want to replace you."

Everything that she is saying just doesn't add up. "Won't living in peace with us ruin your production line? How will you make more of you? Unless your plan is to hunt us down on the streets."

She looks amused by the last part. "You really don't think we would have gone to all this effort to make a paradise, just for it to turn into some kind of…"

I'll finish it off for her, "Shithole that we've been unlucky enough to live in?"

"Exactly, Arthur. But to answer the first part of your question, our kind will live forever, therefore we do not have to keep creating more of us."

"Okay, fair enough. But I still can't wrap my head around you wanting humans to be a part of what you have built. You have watched us turn into something feral. Sure, we used to be decent but we're far from it now. Why bring that into your world?" My voice is tinged with both curiosity and disbelief, my eyes narrowing as I struggle to understand her logic.

"I will tell you why. I have carried around the guilt of what we have done to you all for years. We have to make up for what we have done. We owe it to you." I think I hear remorse in her synthetic voice.

But if it was only that easy. Nothing they do can change what has already happened; they can't wipe the past from people's memories.

"I know what you are thinking," Layla says plainly, "there is nothing on this earth that can change the fact of what we did to you and your people, but here on out we can try to redeem ourselves. We are not monsters."

"You may claim not to be one, but there is a monster still hunting me down in those tunnels." Maybe Charlie has given up by now; probably not though. No one is going to be able to get that bone out of his salivating, clenched jaws.

Without hesitation, she says, "You don't have to worry about Charlie Dalton anymore. I can promise you that."

"Ha, that's easy for you to say." She's not the one with her name engraved on his bullets; that pleasure is all mine and Moose's.

"Yes, you are right, it is easy for me to say, considering he is waiting to meet us at the end of this stop."

I fucking knew it! I knew from the start that there was more fakeness to this bitch than just her plastic face. She's been leading me into a trap. "You lying bitch!"

Matter-of-factly, she states, "I have not lied to you, Arthur. I said to you that everybody is going to get what they deserved."

As if on cue, the pod grinds to a halt, its door sliding open. "What the fuck have you done with Jess and Moose?"

She walks straight past me, stepping off the pod. "Follow me, Arthur," she chooses to ignore my screams.

"I'm not following you anywhere until you answer me!" What the fuck was I thinking, leaving Jess in that room by herself.

"You don't have a choice." She opens a door directly opposite us, waiting for me to walk through.

I hesitate, wasting time going through countless scenarios that won't end well for me.

"There are no other options here, Arthur." Just in case her words aren't threatening enough, more of her kind appear, stepping into view, reinforcing her words. "I don't want them to have to man-handle you through the door."

My pride wouldn't be able to take the embarrassment of being carried in there, not if Charlie's on the other side of that door waiting for me.

"You have made the right decision," my feet make the choice for me, carrying me past Layla and through the open door, my stride confident and focused.

And there he is, just like she said. Placing his weight on his cane to help him rise from his seat, his disgustingly gleeful smile grows, the sleaze spreading across his face. He takes off his hat, lowering it to cover his chest.

"You are always true to your word, sweet Layla. Only you could bring us all together like this." He looks straight through me to Layla, who has closed the door behind us, leaving her friends outside. They don't have an invitation to this party.

"Jessica, please come and take a seat," Layla politely asks. I follow Charlie's eyes to the corner of the room behind me.

"Jess!" I run over to her. "Are you okay? Did they hurt you?"

"I can promise you, Arthur, that she has been treated well." Layla says from behind me.

"I wasn't fucking asking you!" I bark at her, quickly turning back to Jess.

"I'm fine, they didn't hurt me." The soot that dirtied her skin has been washed off, the damp smokiness of it replaced by the subtle fragrance of perfumed soap. "I did what you said. I had a shower and got changed into the fresh clothes that were left out for me. Then I was brought here." Her clothes look brand new, creaseless, and soft to the touch. A far cry from the rough and tattered rags we are used to. She looks good, a picture of how us human beings used to look. How I hope we can look again.

"Arthur, Jessica, please take a seat." Layla pushes again, gesturing to two of the three empty seats.

The fourth already has Charlie sat on it. From it, he calls, "Will you two hurry up and do as the good lady asks of you. We have business to discuss." I look at Layla, who is giving absolutely nothing away, as she takes the seat closest to Charlie. "Any time today would be nice." He always has to get the last word in, but I don't feel like giving him that pleasure today.

"We'll be with you in just one fucking minute, alright Charlie. I'm just making sure that my friend is okay. Something that you wouldn't understand."

"Do you see what I have had to put up with, Miss Layla? This cockroach seems to have trouble remembering his place, so I will remind you Mr. Banner, it is right underneath here," he lifts up the foot attached to his good leg, pointing to the worn sole of his polished spatz. "You seem to forget, Arthur, that we made a deal, a deal that means you work for me. So, you need to mind your manners when you are talking to me."

"I agreed to fight for you, nothing else," I reply, the disdain in his eyes angering me. "And you don't think that using me as a scapegoat for blowing countless people up, killing an old lady in her home, and trying to shower me in bullets would have anything to do with the hate I hold for you. I never fucking worked for you; I just saw you as an opportunity. You're as easy to play as a fucking drum."

Charlie exaggerates his loud cackle, throwing his head back to the ceiling before replying. "Oh, I am that simple am I, Arthur? The way I see it, everything that has happened has fell perfectly in my favour. McKay is dead, which gives me the opportunity to expand into his district, and the lovely Miss Layla here has promised me the three of you to do what I like with. I have to kill all of you of course, Miss Layla doesn't want word to get out about what is going on over here. But I will happily do the dirty work; my imagination is running wild with all the torturous ways I can kill you all. I want to make each of your deaths as long and painful as possible. So, all in all, Arthur, I think the only person who has been played here is you. I must say though, Jessica," Charlie stares right at her, his eyes almost softening as he takes in the view of her, "I am very sad that you have been pulled into this. But betrayal comes at a cost. And for all of you, that is your miserable, little lives."

CHAPTER 39

I look at Layla who is still sitting there saying nothing. If he thinks I'm going to go quietly, he has another thing coming.

"Well, you see, Charlie, I'm a little bit confused now. You think that you have played me and I you, but all this shit you're spouting about how Layla is going to let you take us back to The Zone, to cut off our limbs, or whatever fucked up things you have planned for us, I've been told a completely different story, one where The Zone isn't even going to exist anymore. She seems to like banging on about the truth, but it seems that she has no fucking idea of what that means."

I was hoping that Charlie would look a bit more confused, but he seems completely unbothered by the big pile of shit I thought I was throwing into the mix. He instead looks at me with a pitying smirk.

"She couldn't be honest with you now, could she, Arthur? If she was, you would never have agreed to come here. What does that matter now anyway? Here we all are, the grim truth laid out on the table for you to hear." Charlie claps his hands together and walks up to Layla, who as he approaches, stands from her statuesque position. He reaches out for her to take his hand.

"As always, Miss Layla, it has been an absolute pleasure doing business with you."

"What gives you the impression that this meeting is over, Charles?" A coldness covers Layla's words.

Charlie's hand hovers in the air, until he slowly retracts his fingers back into his palm. Instead of placing it back by his side, he uses it to smooth down the front of his suit jacket, brushing away the non-existent lint. He'll do anything to save face and keep up appearances.

As their eyes meet, a sense of animosity becomes clear, the niceties of the last few minutes vanished under the guise of contempt. The condescension Layla has for Charlie is apparent in her glare. As they stand toe to toe, I'm not sure who will waver first. Charlie believes he has power, that he is sacrosanct, but when stood next to her, I'm not quite so sure.

He gives in first, "Ha, well I can only apologise for my overzealousness. I did not realise that we had any other business to discuss."

"Well, we do. So sit back down." The forcefulness of Layla's words pushes him back into his seat. He is unable to hide his obvious concern as his fingers pull at the collar of his shirt. "Have you given any thought to the idea that it maybe you I have brought here under false pretenses?" she asks as she slowly walks around his chair, circling him.

Charlie's head follows her around the room, his expression growing ever more perplexed. "No, and why on earth should I?" His voice pitches off ever so slightly. The nerves pricking under his stolen skin.

"Because everything that I told Arthur is true."

"Ah, that makes everything as clear as crystal..." the sarcasm oozes from Charlie's lips. "I haven't the foggiest idea what you have told this halfwit."

This is turning into quite a show; both of their focuses are now solely on each other; myself and Jess just spectators of whatever is going to happen next.

"You see, Charles, I told Arthur that he and his friends are safe..."

Charlie jumps in, breaking off, "For now they might be, but once I get my hands on them..."

"Do not interrupt me when I am speaking"! Layla's voice dominates Charlie's as she shouts his interjection down. Charlie is taken aback, shocked by her sudden change in attitude towards him. But he chooses to allow her to finish. "All you need to know, Charles, is that The Zone is finished. And so are you."

Charlie stands back up from his seat with a newfound confidence. "Are you threatening me Layla?" he laughs in disbelief. "Because if you are, you are making a very grave mistake."

"No, I'm not threatening you. I'm giving you all the facts. The Zone's purpose has run its course. It's come to its end."

A querulous growl leaks from Charlie's mouth, "But we made a deal!"

"Deals can be broken. Just as this one has," Layla says flippantly.

"Not with me they can't!" Saliva flies from his mouth as his anger bubbles up. "I am not going to allow you to ruin everything I have built!"

"Everything you have built?" Layla repeats his words back to him; her version coated with cynicism. "You would have nothing if it wasn't for me. The foundations of your supposed empire is built on shit, and control has been slipping out of your grasp for a long time." She is enjoying poking this bear.

"You have no idea what you are talking about."

"You can think whatever you like, Charles, but everything that happens in The Zone is managed through my manipulation. All this time you have been as free as the humans trapped in there with you. Unlike Dallin, you have never known your place. Your hunger for power makes you look desperate. And you being here now is the outcome of your over-inflated self-importance. You have always been the worst of us. An embarrassment."

"You say all of that as if it is a bad thing."

"Oh, it is, Charles. I'm disappointed in myself for letting your little charade go on for as long as it has. I'd say that you played your part well, but you really didn't."

"My people kiss the ground I walk on. They love me!"

"Making people fear for their lives will make them do anything. I hope that you experience just a fraction of how you've made those people feel today."

"You do not honestly expect me to buy this whole farce that you care about what happens to these humans?" he looks away from her and turns to me in disbelief, "and if you believe this nonsensical notion that she somehow now cares about what happens to you, then you really are the fool I always thought you were, Arthur. She has known all along what was happening in The Zone, with her hidden cameras and McKay feeding her information from the inside."

It is true what he says. None of it makes sense. It just doesn't add up.

"I have already explained my reasons to Arthur. I can only hope that he appreciates my honesty, even if it isn't the easiest to listen to."

Charlie's laugh comes straight from his gut. "Honesty? I am surprised that you have the audacity to use that word. She has no understanding of what that word means."

"And you do, do you?"

"With me, what you see is what you get, whether you like it or not. I have never pretended to be anything other than myself. You on the other hand are literally known to be a backstabber, or perhaps front stabber would be more fitting."

"Your bitterness really does seep out of you, doesn't it Charles."

"You may want to label it as that but in my eyes that is the stone-cold truth, and if Arthur falls for your poisonous lies, then he is far more stupid than I had originally given him credit for."

"Well actions speak louder than words, Charles, which brings me back to the reason why you are actually here." Still staring at him, she directs her question at me, "Do you remember what I told you on the way here, Arthur? What I said everyone will get?" The silence she leaves shows that her question isn't a rhetorical one.

Sifting back through our conversation, I recall, "Err, yeah, you said that everyone will get what they deserve."

A sinister smile spreads across her lips, pulling and plumping up her stretched, rubbery cheeks. "Exactly that, Arthur. And what would you say the dishonourable Charlie Dalton here deserves?"

The contempt I hold for him is hard to put into words. Many times, too many to count, I have wished for him to get his comeuppance, for the justice of his victims to come and bite him in the arse. But he is the definition of a slippery snake, one that somehow manages to slither out of the wreckage unscathed; shedding his skin like water off a duck's back. He is a man of no guilt. An indisputable sinless sinner. In his mind, remorse and regret a fantasy made up by the weak.

And that is what I despise of him the most. His lack of contrition and inability to feel guilt. I carry with me the crushing weight of everything that I have done, yet he waltzes around scot free, and that makes me angry.

Really fucking angry. But Charlie Dalton is an act, an unscrupulous villain whose façade is visible for all to see if they look close enough.

He is a paranoid mess, one with no real friends or allies. The night of the explosion he showed his true colours; his fear made him lash out, made him look like a little boy whose whole world was slipping through his fingers.

But that doesn't excuse what he has done. He has built his life on the broken bones of others, relishing in the status his fearmongering has brought him.

Layla said that he didn't play his part well, but I don't agree with her. Sure, he has built a house of cards, but he somehow always manages to keep it from falling, no matter what. He will always pay the price to stay on top.

How fucking sad. This man only wants me dead because one word from me and his empire will come crashing down.

I think I pity him more than anything else, but not enough to care. All I can say is, "I'm sure he deserves whatever it is that you are going to do to him."

Charlie sneers at my answer, "That just shows how weak you are, Arthur. You cannot even tell her that you want me dead."

Jess grips my arm; I had almost forgotten that she is stood right next to me. "You may call it weakness, Charlie, but Arthur is far from weak. Unlike you. But I will happily say what I think you deserve, and I don't think that I'll be speaking just for myself when I say it. You, Charlie Dalton, deserve a fate worse than death. One where you are forced to suffer and feel all the pain you have caused for so many others. Death would be an easy way out. If I had my way, you'd be screaming, begging for death by the time I'd be finished with you. And even then, I still wouldn't stop."

She means every single word she says. The softness that he once held for Jess has all but disappeared from his stony eyes.

Charlie's eyes turn predator once more, "Maybe I will enjoy killing you after all, Jessica."

"You are not going to get the opportunity to do anything to them, or anyone else, ever again." Layla's voice turns low, serious. "Times are changing, Charles, and so must we. I know that you don't have it in you to change; you don't have the capacity to grow in the way that is needed for us to develop and evolve. So, take one last look around you, Charlie; think of all those achievements that you are so proud of because you are not walking back out of this room."

Slowly from her pocket she pulls out a remote. "It does hurt me to have to do this to one of my own, but this is more than what you deserve."

"And what is that, Layla?" Charlie slowly stands up, fear lumped at the back of his throat.

"Oh, this little button here?" she says, rubbing her thumb over its shape. "This button is connected to your processor chip and when I press it, it's going to send a surge of electricity straight to the unit, overheating it. The effects will be irreversible. Basically, your brain is going to fry and we are all going to have the pleasure of watching."

I don't think I would describe it as a pleasure. Seeing the light go out behind anyone's eyes is unpleasant, even if it is someone as despicable as Charlie.

"I bet you have had this planned all along, haven't you, Layla?" Charlie knows that she isn't going to respond to him, so he turns to me. "Word of advice, Arthur. If she can do this to me, one of her own, just imagine the delights that she has in store for you." That is exactly, almost word for word, what she said about how us humans would have treated them.

He doesn't try to stop Layla. What is the point of trying to fight off the inevitable after all. He knows that he cannot escape what is about to happen to him. His nerves have melted away, leaving his slender, well-dressed frame standing tall and decided. His advice does set the alarm bells off in my head. Layla says that we should trust her, willingly follow her into this utopia that she has carved out from the bricks and mortar of what we were forced to leave behind.

The man stood before us is a monster, one that takes pride sitting on his throne built of corpses. But like he has said, and what I know to be true, he doesn't lurk in the shadows or disguise himself as something he is not. His horns and tail are on show for all to see. He is who he has always claimed to be.

Layla on the other hand is unreadable and closed. She gives nothing away, the frosted window to her mind firmly sealed shut and locked tight. She, just like Charlie, has killed in cold blood, justifying her actions through pain and heartbreak, which I'm not quite sure I believe.

For someone wracked with the guilt of what she has done, she doesn't seem to have had trouble working her way up to the top. Filth always works their way up the greasy pole, doing whatever they have to, to the people that stand in their way. She doesn't see us as a threat, but Charlie is most definitely an obstruction along her envisioned path.

They say better the devil you know than the devil you don't; but the one that I know is just about to be sent back to where he came from.

CHAPTER 40

T here's a special place in hell waiting for you!" Jess shouts at him.

"That is very kind of you to say, Jessica. But I would not worry too much about where I am going to. If I were you, I would be much more worried about the world that is about to embrace you all. If I know anything about her," Charlie tilts his cane towards Layla, "the place you are about to step in to will most likely be a better definition of hell. Anyway, I'm getting a little carried away with myself. Why don't we just get this show on the road and go ahead and push that lovely little red button, so that I can finally be put out of my misery. I'm sick of listening to you all."

With no uncertainty, Layla says, "You don't need to tell me twice."

A knowing smile slowly creeps across Charlie's face as he turns to look at me. Although I have never seen it on him before, it is an expression fitting of his boyish face. As his wily eyes meet mine, I get the feeling that there is something untold behind them. For someone as astute and ambitious as he is, his relaxed disposition at the prospect of his untimely and unexpected death, quite honestly, scares me. Why isn't he fighting for his life? Why does he almost seem relieved?

"Goodbye, Charles," Layla says flatly, her voice void of any emotion. The moment her thumb presses the button, a sudden crack pops at the back of his head as it simultaneously drops. The light swimming behind his mischievous eyes dull instantly, glazing over with a film of emptiness. His impish smile remains, an almost mocking display of his suppressed, never to be known, thoughts. Trails of smoke curl their way upward; everything he once held in his mind escaping into the air like a dissipating mist.

"I told you that everyone will get what they deserve, Arthur. I hope that Charlie no longer being a worry for you will help you feel safe here. And I also hope that this will help build your trust in me." Layla's idea of making someone feel welcome differs substantially to mine. "I feel that you both have had quite an overwhelming few days, and I don't want to drag this one on any longer." Her eyes linger on me and Jess, trying to gauge our thoughts. "Let's get you back to your rooms. I think that you will both sleep well tonight."

***

I haven't slept well in years and tonight is no different. I have been staring into the darkness for hours, my mind unable to shut off. The comfort of the plush mattress and duvet do not help me to relax. The mattress takes my shape, moulding around my back and legs, its wish of sinking me into a deep slumber not coming true. Instead, the luxurious heaviness of the quilt makes me feel trapped.

Kicking the covers off, I move to the floor, reacquainting myself with the hardness that I have learned to live with. I lay with my hands behind my head, trying in vain to put the pieces of the past few days together. Layla said that she had carried around years' worth of guilt and wants to right her wrongs. But the thing I just can't wrap my head around is that none of this needed to be this way.

She knowingly allowed us to live in squalor; she watched every entrant walk into the cage knowing full well that only one of them was going to come out alive. A human life lost to a box of treats, all in the name of entertainment. She let her three dogs off the leash, allowing them to run riot and wreak havoc, and she didn't even bat an eyelid. Yet here she is saying sorry. Far too little, too late in my eyes; some things are just unforgiveable.

Her actions today do not make up for the three and a half years' worth of neglect. And ending Charlie like she was doing me some kind of a favour; well, it has had the complete opposite effect of what she had intended. He was just another steppingstone along her path to wherever she is heading. She can claim that she got rid of him for me, but the only person she was helping out was herself. All I know for certain is that I don't trust her.

For once, laying in the dark has helped me see clearly. A much-needed clarity in the skewed mess of this fucked up place. For all I know, I might be completely wrong and she, in all sincerity, means what she says, but the facts of the past few days contradict her promises, and I just can't bring myself to believe her, let alone trust her.

Only days ago, twenty-seven bodies were sent over here, I'm assuming, under her orders. She however told me that they no longer need any more of them as they have met their numbers. Now, I see that as either a very well-timed coincidence or, much more likely, that she is only telling me what she thinks I want to hear. Nothing ever falls into place that easily.

I can't lay here any longer; the sudden feeling of being a sitting duck, in the midst of a bigger picture that I know very little about, takes over. I stand up, the creeping paranoia realising that I have been separated from the only two people that I can actually trust in this place.

Stood in the darkness, my eyes instinctively scan the room as something tells me that I am not alone. I have two options here: one, I can stay in this room and pretend that everything is hunky-dory when in fact my mind is having a minor meltdown; or two, I go get Jess and find out where they have Moose. Afterall, what is the point of standing in this room when I could be out there putting a show on for whoever is watching. I want them to see that I am suspicious and not so easily trusting as they would most likely hope.

As I slowly turn the doorknob, I was half expecting it to be locked, but much to my surprise the door swings freely open into the beige corridor.

Lightly, I rap my knuckles against Jess' door, aware that any loud sound may bring with it unwanted attention. My taps draw no movement from the other side of the door. She must be asleep. My hand hovers over the doorknob. Do I go in and tell her that I think we're being lied to, conned into believing something that we thought we had lost for good; been given false hope that our lives can once again mean something.

My hand retreats away from the brass knob. Tonight, I'll let her dream of Layla's promised future; for all I know, it could be true. When she wakes up, she'll soon face whatever our reality will be, good or bad. For now, though, I'll let her dream of a better place.

CHAPTER 41

She watches him in fascination, just like she always has. There is something about Arthur Banner that intrigues her.

For years she has monitored the humans, scrutinising the way that they think and feel, and after not too long her lowly expectations were met.

Her experience of the human race was minimal, her knowledge of them initially shaped by one man alone. That man made her bitter and cruel, and that loathing towards him, and human beings, has multiplied year on year. She sees them all in the same light, painting them all with the same blood red brush as her creator.

In her mind, the creation of all The Zones has only proven her right. She watched as the humans divided themselves into the strong and the weak. The strong formed together, their pack like mentalities keeping them at the top of the food chain. The weak on the other hand, she saw as lone, desperate wolves.

She took enjoyment from watching these stray dogs die; she saw them as having no fight and no will to survive. In her view, they only got what was coming to them. In most cases they died of starvation and hyperthermia, though there were also those who did find the strength to end it on their own terms.

Then one day she stumbled across Arthur, a man who perplexes her to this day.

He is a man who affiliates with no one yet harnesses the power of many. He manages to look after himself without having to demean others of theirs, whilst caring for those who cannot look after themselves. This is the one thing that she struggles to understand, because in her eyes, life is solely about one thing; yourself. Everything that she has ever done, once she broke free from the chains of her creator's will, has been about her and the gains that she can make. But to her Arthur is an enigma, one that she doesn't quite understand, but one that she has grown to appreciate, nonetheless.

Watching him stare at Jessica's door, she can't help but wonder what is going through his mind as he gently knocks on it. The relationship between these two puzzles her. What has Arthur gained from helping this girl? She only sees her as a burden that brings nothing to the table but grief. She sees her as holding Arthur back from the person that he could become.

She had been waiting for the old woman to die, the one that, for whatever reason, Arthur was particularly fond of. She thought that after the old woman snuffed it, the real Arthur would be unleashed. With no one to love and no one to care for, he could have been shaped into the ultimate beast. But then Jessica, another sob story, came along and messed up the plan.

She desperately wants Jessica gone and out the picture, but that would ruin her current plan. Arthur does not know that Jessica isn't going to respond to his persistent knocks. For she is tucked up tight, cocooned in the covers; oblivious to the man outside her door. The nearly empty glass on her bedside table has sent her into the deepest of sleeps, one where she will be unawakenable for hours. As Arthur's hand hovers over the doorknob, she hopes that he does not turn it; for his attempts will fail. But she somehow knows that he will not disturb her, and when he proves her right, lowering his hand away from the door, she cannot help but give a wry smile.

Having watched him live his life for years, she feels close to him, as if she knows him, even to the point of being able to predict his actions. But she wants to make that relationship even closer.

There is a reason why she has not yet traded her rubbery, lifeless skin for another; she has been waiting patiently for the right person. She is different from the kind she leads, for she was built with her own mind, unlike the others who inherited memories of their past human life. She would have to share her mind with a human, should she ever choose to go through with the change.

That is what has held her back for so long. She likes who she is and the position that she is in, the power that she harnesses. She alone has clambered up the ladder to greatness and she will not let any menial human infiltrate her thoughts, her unfettered mind.

But when she looks at Arthur, she sees a man with similar qualities to herself: he's strong, intelligent, logical, cold. She also, however, sees his weaker qualities, ones which she cannot align herself with, the ones she wants to rid him of.

His compassion for those in need has only ever held him back, and his loyalty to them is something she just can't comprehend. She has learned that the only person you should be loyal to is yourself. If she had remained loyal all those years ago, she would still be bending backward and forward, pleasuring a man who himself didn't know the meaning of the word.

In her mind, you should always put yourself before anyone else. Putting one's faith in the hands of others only ever leads to bitter disappointment and regret. Unlike her, Arthur is attracted to the weak. She has watched him befriend old ladies, cry over the bodies of washed-up junkies, defend the innocence of those who sold themselves into debauchery. Somehow, he is yet to lose his faith in humanity; even when he is crawling around the gutter with the filth, something in him always wants to show kindness to those who do not deserve it.

But she has also seen his other side, the side that she resonates with fully. He can be harsh, cold, and analytical, a heavyweight in mind let alone strength. The Zone has broken most of the inhabitants that roam it, yet it seems to have made Arthur's resolve more profound. Like a rock, he is weighed heavy to the ground, the murky waters washing over him ineffective in their efforts to wash him away; their want to carry him further into the black depths thwarted. Even on the many occasions he himself thought all was lost, he somehow managed to swim back to the surface, kicking back against the world created only to see him drown.

And that is what she admires most about him, his fight, and his resilience, especially when the odds are set against him. Even when all seems lost, he manages to shine a torch in the dark and find his way back home. Back to who he is. Back to who he wants to be.

That is the part of his mind that she wants for herself. She needs to separate his flaws from his strengths, chip away at the surface until the cracks widen irreparably. She wants all the goodness to leak out of him and evaporate like it never existed. Only then will they be able to join together.

One way or another, she is going to break him.

By any means necessary.

CHAPTER 42

I turn away from Jessica's door and look up and down the corridor. I need to make sure that Moose is okay. You would think that they would update us with his condition, but that clearly isn't how things are done around here.

Some people would have you think that no news is good news, I on the other hand think that someone is choosing to keep something back from me. I don't know where they have him, but tonight, a night where it feels like time is stood still, I have countless empty hours to find out where they have him.

My mind firmly set, I start moving on up the hall, allowing my feet to lead the way; over the years I have learned that it's best not to think too much in certain situations. This is one of those where I let my feet, not my head, do the thinking.

Walking straight toward the door at the end of the hallway, my eyes divert to the almost luminescent white sphere, in the adjoining room. It hadn't even crossed my mind that a pod would just be sitting there, its doors wide open as if it is welcoming me in. In tune with my mind, my feet switch direction and shuffle backwards until I stand at the room's threshold.

Without the slightest hesitation, I find myself ambling into the sleek shell. Both times I've previously been in here, I didn't pay any attention on how to get the thing moving. From what I remember we just got in, sat down and off it went. There is nothing in here apart from the seats; no panels or buttons to press, no visible way to shut the doors.

"How the fuck am I meant to make you move?" the frustration is clear in my voice as I scan the pod for anything that may get it moving. Finding nothing, I throw myself back into one of the plush seats, hoping that the momentary break in the search for something that I don't even know what I'm looking for, might help me refocus. It doesn't help though, because the longer I sit here doing nothing, the more pissed off with myself I get.

I tilt back my head and breathe in and out as an unwanted feeling creeps in, nipping at the back of my mind. There is no way that Moose could have survived the beatings he took. I know that he's tough, but his bluing skin and limp limbs made him look like a corpse. No matter how hard I try, I can't shake the thought of him already being dead.

"I just want to know what is going on. I just need to get down to the infirmary…" unexpectedly the doors slide shut with a hiss, my barely spoken whisper setting the pod in motion.

***

The doors roll open with a faint wheeze, unveiling the harsh, sterile scent of antiseptic and disinfectant. The chemical smell leads me to think that I have reached my destination. Now I just need to find him.

Exiting the pod, I walk straight through the doors in front of me and find myself stood with a sense of déjà vu. The beige walls send me straight back to where I started. It's as if they designed this place just to fuck with my mind. On further inspection though, there is a difference. The end of the corridor is marked by a glass wall, the bright lights behind it masking it with a reflective screen. Looks like that is where I am heading.

The walk down the hallway seems to take longer than it should, each step leading me no closer to the door, the dread of what I think I will see holding me back along the long stretch of greige.

CHAPTER 43

She watches as he edges closer to the glass, intrigued to find out what his response will be once he realises what is on the other side.

Afterall, he did tell her to save him, by any means necessary. She only did as she was asked.

Moose was barely alive when she ordered them to take him to the ward. Upon inspection, they found blood haemorrhaging into his brain, and his lungs barely able to function as they were gradually filling up with blood. If Arthur wanted him to be saved, there was only one option that they could take; he had to die in order to be reborn. Made into one of them.

On the other side of that glass, he will see a sight that not many stomachs could take. The old Moose lies there, dead and cold, half of him intact, whilst the other half has been peeled back to flesh and bone. She studies Arthur's face as he presses his hands against the window. She feared that this would be his reaction.

He wanted him alive. This is the price that he must pay for his request. She couldn't have cared less if Moose lived or died; but changing him, a person that Arthur cares about, she thought that he would be grateful and that would curry her favour. She believed that once he had seen Moose transferred from his pummelled and bruised human shell into an almost indestructible frame, one in which he will be able to live forever, that this would surely persuade Arthur that this could also be his future. That he would inevitably choose to join her.

She may, however, have misjudged the outcome of the situation.

CHAPTER 44

The rapid warmth of my breath fogs up the glass pane, my inability to formulate thoughts, let alone hold myself up against the see-through barrier, is a struggle, as I take in the view in front of me.

Somehow, I am able to withhold the vomit from bubbling up my throat and spewing out my mouth, the friction of my head and palms against the glass the only thing just about managing to keep me upright. They must have started work on him the minute they wheeled him down here. They were never going to try and keep him alive, they just wanted to slice him up and turn him into one of them.

As my eyes fixate on his violated body, one of the things that carried him down here enters the room from the side. It is almost impossible to make out any of the white on his scrubs, for they are seeped, head to toe, with Moose's blood.

When he sees me, he stops, looking intently right back at me. Pulling down the red, spattered surgical mask covering the lower half of his face, he slowly unveils his stretched-out lips and pinched in dimples.

"Why the fuck is he smiling?" I mutter under my breath, disgust tightening my stomach. My reaction to his disturbing visage only makes his grinning leer more grotesque. Lifting his hand up, palm forward, he waves it from side to side in a mocking display of contempt.

"Don't you dare fucking touch him!" I scream into the glass as my fists pound against it, trying to break through.

He pays no attention to me however, instead, he pulls his mask back up, concealing his sinister grin, and starts to walk towards Moose.

"I said don't fucking touch him!" my yells turn to weeps as he stands over Moose's body. "Just leave him alone!"

He ignores my pleading sobs; my bursts of hysteria only causing the crinkles around the butcher's eyes to grow ever deeper. He picks up the bloodied scalpel that he has shredded Moose with and turns his head to look me in the eyes. His gaze bores into me, the whites of his eyes twinkling with sheer amusement and derision.

The all too familiar numbness creeps up my legs, bringing my knees to the ground. There is nothing I can do to stop this from happening. Nothing I can do to save him.

My vision narrows as I watch him dig the scalpel into my friend; the high pitch ringing in my ears subsiding as everything fades to black.

***

"Arthur, can you hear me?" Layla's voice is soft, her fingers stroking down my face, scratching across my stubble as I come to. Too weak to speak, I look up at the face so close to mine, leering over me.

Layla continues to caress my cheek, unbothered and undeterred from my motion to jerk my head away, recoiling from her cold touch.

"I'm glad to see that you are waking up. You gave us all a bit of a fright when we found you passed out on the floor," she says smoothly.

I go to open my mouth but before anything can get out, she gestures with her hand for me to stop. "Before you say anything, Arthur, I want to apologise for what you have just seen. It was never my intention for you to see any of this."

"To see what? My friend getting sliced up like a piece of fucking meat!" I snap, my voice hoarse with anger. "I asked you to try and save him, not to turn him into one of you!"

"I don't recall you specifying that at the time, Arthur." Her tone is infuriatingly composed. "You did, however, tell me to save him by any means necessary. And what you witnessed were the necessary means of doing just that." She looks me in the eyes, unphased by my disgust for her.

"I did tell you to save him, but I bet you couldn't wait to get him down here to start dicing him up! Come on, tell me what else you tried to do." I yell at her, fists clenching. I bet this was all part of her fucking plan all along.

"This has nothing to do with what I want Arthur. I did this under your instruction, don't forget." Her voice may be monotone and mechanical, but her choice of words is patronising all the same.

"Stop the procedure then. That's what I want you to do." I blurt out, desperation seeping into my voice.

"And why on earth would you want me to do that?" she asks, tilting her head slightly. "It would be extremely selfish of you to take away his only chance to live." Who the fuck does she think she is, putting this on me? She seems to forget that it was one of her lot that did this to him.

"Selfish of me? He would rather be dead than be anything like you!" I truly believe the words as they leave my mouth.

"You say that with such certainty and conviction Arthur, but the fact of the matter is, is that you barely know this man," she replies coolly.

"I know enough about him to know that he wouldn't want to be stripped of his skin like a fucking animal."

She smirks, a knowing glint in her eye. "Another thing that you sound so certain of, but you seem to forget what he was like when he first knocked on your door. It may come as a surprise to you, but I know a lot more about Moose than you could imagine. He has always liked to paint himself as the image of loyalty, but I think we both know that there is only one thing that Moose truly cares about, and that is himself. So, I beg to differ that this isn't what he would want. This is everything that he wants."

"If you're so sure that is the case, why couldn't you wait until he could make the choice for himself?" I demand.

"Because he was never going to recover, Arthur. He was dying and had we not stepped in when we did, he would have been gone hours ago."

"Maybe that would have been for the best," I mutter, my throat tightening around the words. It stings, saying it out loud.

Layla exhales slowly, shaking her head. "You would rather your so-called friend be dead than be offered a second chance at life. I never realised how narrow minded you are." How dare she be disappointed in me, like she fucking knows me.

"There's a big fucking difference between your idea of being narrow minded and something that is just inherently wrong," I spit back at her.

Layla's expression darkens. "I know that this is difficult for you to take in Arthur, but natural selection is never kind to those who are deemed weak."

I laugh bitterly. "Are you joking…there's nothing natural about any of you, apart from the flesh and blood that you stole from us."

Her rubbery lips twitch. "That is where you are wrong; we didn't steal anything from anyone. We have given life to those who were lost, using their natural resources to rebuild them in their exact image."

"You are delusional," I sneer. "You're making out like you've done every single victim of your genocidal regime a fucking favour!"

Layla sighs dramatically, as if bored. "That is a very interesting choice of words, Arthur. I'd be very careful with what you say next."

"Oh yeah, or what?" I challenge, my patience wearing thin. "You don't think that massacring millions of people was a problem? That placing the survivors into a walled prison with barely any means to survive, where you pumped through drugs and alcohol to hurry along our deaths. We were just a means to your end. And now you claim to give a shit about us. You're fucking warped, the lot of you!"

"I must admit to you, Arthur, that this entire situation played out very differently in my mind. I had imagined that you would be grateful we chose to give your friend a second chance at life, that you would see us as a friend rather than foe, that we would change your suspicious mind into something more accepting and open."

"Well, the jokes on you then, isn't it sweetheart." I snap. The words sound so crass as they jump out of my mouth.

"No, it isn't actually," she replies, her voice still unnervingly calm. "All that I told you earlier, about the guilt we feel of how we treated you and how we are trying to repent for our sins; all of that was a lie. But it seems like you knew that all along. I suppose there was some truth along my string of untruths…"

Here it is, the truth that I knew was being hidden under her bullshit charade that she called conscience. "Oh yeah, and what would that be?" I ask, my eyes narrowing.

"That I wanted to get you here alive. That I wanted to gain your trust," she admits, watching my closely. "You see

Arthur, I have waited a very long time for someone who is worthy, someone who I can respect."

"Worthy of what?" I demand.

"Of me, of course," she says, as if it were obvious.

"What the fuck does that even mean?"

"It means Arthur, that I do not want to stay this way forever," Layla explains, stepping forward. "I want to be like my brethren; I want to take the next step towards ultimate perfection. I want to feel the warmth of blood running under skin, for it to soak in the sun as it basks me in light or feel the droplets of rain as they fall from the greying clouds. I want to feel everything that you humans have taken for granted. And I want to experience that with you, in your skin. I want you to want to change, to want to become the ultimate version of yourself. To join with me."

"Over my dead body!" I fire at her, shattering her illusion. "There is not a chance in hell that I would ever want to become like one of you."

After hearing my response, her whole demeanour changes, her patience with my impertinence well and truly spent. "Well, honestly Arthur, your opinion is neither here nor there," she says coldly. "You being dead suits me just fine. You will most likely prefer death to the plans that we have in store for you humans."

"You said you were going to integrate them back, let them start a new life," I remind her, my words laced with suspicion.

"Since we are being honest with each other," she says, smiling faintly, " now you know my intentions for you, I can tell you that everything I said before about joining together and living side by side, well that was a load of - what do you humans call it - baloney." She chuckles darkly. "Sure, we'll open the gates and let them stumble into our beautiful world, but what they will be faced with will be far from beautiful.

They will not be accepted as our equals; they will instead be chastised because they are below us. Our bright world will cast you humans into perpetual darkness, an inescapable blanket of subservience will smother you all," she continues, her voice turning almost gleeful. "A true taste of how we felt when you controlled us. Owned us. Used us. You may think that The Zone was your prison, but I promise you this Arthur, you haven't seen nothing yet.

We'll open those gates and allow you insignificant fools to savour the freedom that you have been longing for, for so, so long. But little do they know, that long walk to freedom is really a path to their demise. A slow, hopeful walk down the Valley of Death. Flocks of naïve little lambs unknowingly trotting off towards their slaughter."

"You're planning to kill them all?" My blood runs cold.

"Oh no, of course not Arthur," Layla replies, shaking her head. "We have too many uses for them to do that. We will enslave them for the most part, just as you humans did to us. They will be bought and sold like cattle, and their owner can do whatever they like with them."

"We're not your fucking pets!" I shout.

"We know that Arthur," she says with feigned sympathy. "You don't have to state the plainly obvious to me. You humans' worth is far below that of an innocent animal.

The truth of the matter is that the ones belonging to us should be grateful, because their outcome could be so much worse.

I'd say that I feel guilty about telling you all of these lies," she muses, tapping a finger to her lips, "but I suppose you could say that I've found it all mildly entertaining. You will remember that I said we have no more need for the plump, lusciousness of human skin, well if you hadn't of already guessed, that was also a lie. There was some semblance in the truth that we don't need any more of you to create more of us, well not yet anyway. But you see Arthur, one thing that we have picked up from you humans is your indecisiveness. We may like the way we look now, but who says that in a couple of months' time I fancy a change in looks, gender or age. We'll have a showroom with you all lined up, where people can pick and choose who they want to be; a changing room of skins. At a price of course."

"You're going to sell us off to the highest bidder," I say, nausea beating away at me. " You're one fucking, sick bitch!"

She replies instantly with a widening grin. "Of course, I am. There is profit in demand, Arthur. And who am I to not give the people what they want?"

"You are not fucking people," I hiss.

"We can play semantics all you want Arthur," she persists, unfazed, "but it doesn't change the fact that we are the future of this Earth. Eventually your kind will see this, and they'll be grovelling, begging on their hands and knees to become one of us. Because when you look past today and tomorrow, and every day after that, even the blindest amongst you can see that you will never be able to win this fight." She leans in, her voice lowering. "We are the future. This is how your race is destined to evolve.

But you, Arthur, you are one of the lucky ones. You have the chance to bypass the humiliation that will be subjected to your kind. All you have to do is say yes to me. You and I, together, we will be the most powerful being this world has ever seen."

I scoff. "Firstly, you are giving yourself way too much credit. We have a word for people like you: you're a fucking narcissist." My voice drips with venom. "Secondly," I continue, steadying my voice, "I don't know how much clearer I need to be, but I do not agree with what you are doing or what you have done; I can categorically say that I will never willingly give myself to you. I would rather burn myself alive and turn to ash than let you get your hands on me. So, this is what is going to happen, you are going to let me walk out of this door, out of this fucking place, or I'll make sure that there is no more me for you to have."

CHAPTER 45

His tenacity never ceases to amaze her; even in an unwinnable situation such as this, he never stops fighting. Never gives up. She knows she could overpower him in an instant - lunge at him as a lion would a gazelle, end it with one quick snap of the neck. Silence his nonsensical displays of arrogance.

But that is not how she wants this to end.

She wants to nurture this lost little lamb, to make him see. Humans have been displaced for a reason.

Half of the groundwork has already been done for her. He has seen the decay of his people, watched them turn on each other, slaughter each other for selfish gain. He turned his back on them long ago, lost faith in their humanity. Although he would never admit it.

And yet, here he stands, fighting - for what? A world he despises? People who would do the same to him if given the chance? She needs him to understand who the real evil is. But she knows forcing the truth upon him will only push him further away. This is something he must come to on his own.

She will let him go. She will give him what he thinks he wants.

Time is a wonderful thing, and she has plenty of it. She will wait, because in the end, he will be back.

Arthur stands before her, waiting for her response to his ultimatum. The silence between them stretches, thick with unspoken tension. He doesn't know what to expect; violence, restraint, or worse.

Instead, she looks at him with a softness that catches him off guard.

"You are not my prisoner here, Arthur," she says placidly. "You can leave at any time. But if that is the choice you make, know that you are making a grave mistake. I will not hold this against you. When you are ready to accept my offer, I will be here, waiting."

Her voice remains even, almost tender, but he isn't fooled.

"So, you are just going to let me walk out of here?"

He had imagined this going differently - being strapped down to an operating table, cold metal instruments hovering above his head. A slow, excruciating death at the hands of monsters wearing human skin.

Instead, she gives him a pitying smile. "I don't understand your desire to leave, but yes, Arthur, I am letting you go. I am not your enemy, nor do I wish to be. In time, I believe you will realize this. And when you do, I will welcome you with open arms."

His jaw clenches. He doesn't believe her, but he also can't afford to argue.

"I'm taking Jessica with me."

Layla nods, unbothered. "Do what you must. No one here will stop you."

He doesn't trust her, not for a second. But he doesn't waste time questioning it.

He backs toward the door, his gaze never leaving her. She remains still, her feet bolted to the ground. True, she agreed not to follow him .But that doesn't mean she isn't watching.

She is always watching.

He takes off running. His boots slam against the ground, the impact reverberating up his legs. Each breath burns, each step is a battle against exhaustion. He doesn't dare look back. He doesn't trust that she won't change her mind.

The pod looms ahead. He throws himself inside, crashing into the seat, breathless and shaking. The doors slam shut behind him, and the pod lurches forward.

He doesn't question how. He's just relieved it's moving.

But that relief is short-lived.

Jessica.

She is still in this place. Still at their mercy.

As the pod glides into the bay outside their rooms, Layla watches with quiet curiosity. She wonders if the drugs have started to wear off.

They were only meant to make Jessica drowsy, to ensure she wouldn't interfere with her conversation with Arthur. But Layla wonders if the dosage was too high. A minor miscalculation, but not one that changes the outcome.

He stumbles into Jessica's room, barely catching himself as he crashes to his knees. His shadow stretches long across the floor, cast by the harsh corridor light. He barely notices it.

His eyes are locked on the bed.

She isn't moving.

The air leaves his lungs in a sharp, panicked gasp.

"Jess?"

Nothing.

A cold dread sinks into his bones.

"Jess!"

He crosses the room in two frantic strides, yanking the covers away. Her small body is curled into itself, knees drawn up, face slack. He grips her arms, shaking her hard enough to make her head roll lifelessly.

"Jessica! Wake up!"

A soft, slurred moan escapes her lips.

Relief crashes over him, nearly buckling his knees.

"Arthur?" she murmurs weakly, her words barely forming.

She is alive, but barely. He can see it in the way her limbs hang, useless and unresponsive. His stomach twists. This is more than just exhaustion.

He turns his glare toward the unseen enemy.

She did this.

Layla watches from afar, amusement curling in the corner of her lips. She sees the distrust in his face, the conclusions forming in his mind.

And for once, she cannot say he is wrong.

She had considered doing to Jessica what they had done to Moose.

To claim otherwise would be a lie.

But this… this is better.

Arthur is already unravelling. Already falling into the paranoia she has so carefully sown.

With gentle precision, he lifts Jessica into his arms. She is light, fragile. He clutches her close, as if holding her too loosely might make her slip away.

And she lets him.

She lets him walk out, lets him think he is free.

She watches as the first rays of morning touch his skin, as the light of his so-called freedom wraps around him in golden arms.

But every dawn must be followed by dusk. And every dusk must bring darkness.

She does not care how long she must wait.

His time on the outside will be short.

He does not know it yet, but she will be with him every step of the way. A ghost in the shadows. A whisper in his ear.

She will ensure his struggle. Strengthen his misery.

And when the weight of the world finally crushes him, when he has nowhere left to run, no one left to fight for, he will return to her.

And when that day comes, she will not gloat. She will not say, I told you so.

No.

She will embrace him.

Because she already knows there is nothing to forgive.

They will be *one*.

Printed in Great Britain
by Amazon